CRABBE H. APPLETON
At Your Service

WILSON JACKSON

CRABBE H. APPLETON
Copyright © 2024 by Wilson Jackson

ISBN: 979-8894790602 (sc)
ISBN: 979-8894790619 (e)

The Reading Glass
BOOKS

The Reading Glass Books
1-888-420-3050
www.readingglassbooks.com
fulfillment@readingglassbooks.com

Table of Contents

INTRODUCTION v

CHAPTER 1...1

CHAPTER 2...6

CHAPTER 3...12

CHAPTER 4...18

CHAPTER 5...24

CHAPTER 6...35

CHAPTER 7...46

CHAPTER 8...55

CHAPTER 9...61

CHAPTER 10...69

CHAPTER 11...79

CHAPTER 12...88

CHAPTER 13...94

CHAPTER 14...101

CHAPTER 15...108

CHAPTER 16...115

CHAPTER 17...124

CHAPTER 18 132

CHAPTER 19...140

CHAPTER 20...148

CHAPTER 21...154

CHAPTER 22...163

CHAPTER 23...170

CHAPTER 24...185

CHAPTER 25..192

CHAPTER 26..200

CHAPTER 27..207

CHAPTER 28..214

CHAPTER 29..223

CHAPTER 30..236

CHAPTER 31..247

CHAPTER 32..258

CHAPTER 33..269

CHAPTER 34..280

CHAPTER 35..291

CHAPTER 36..299

INTRODUCTION

This story begins 162 years ago on a cotton farm in Littlestown, Georgia.

But this is not a story about slavery, far from it; it's the story of a trade between a disillusioned slave named Appleton and the devil.

One night as Appleton lay writhing in pain on his ragged cot of hay and straw, his back bleeding from the supervisors' scathing whips, only one thought ran through his mind over and over.

"I can't die like this; I gotta be free."

He had no wife or children, but he liked Bernie, the milkmaid from the house, and from the way she always turned away with a smile, he hoped she liked him too.

Sometimes, he would imagine what freedom would feel like. To walk anywhere he chose to, with Bernie in his arms, without a care in the world. Yes, he would like that very much.

As the pain wracked his frame that night, he tried to picture Bernie's face and imagine again what freedom would look like, but when that failed, he angrily thrust the image from his mind.

Where would a man like him go?

How far would he run before their dogs and bullets found him?

The rest is an Appleton family legend with varying details depending on who you ask, but everyone agrees on one point: Appleton found a way to sell his freedom......... Permanently.

Was it madness that drove him to such a bargain?

Perhaps the answer could be found in the rumors that Bernie was to be sold to a family who needed a wet nurse.

The night before Bernie would be gone, there was a hideous howling from the barn Appleton and a dozen slaves slept in. A howling that seemed to reach into your soul and awaken your deepest fears.

That night, the fierce dogs that feared no man lay whimpering in their kennel, and when morning came, Appleton was nowhere to be found.

He was not particularly a hardworking fellow in the fields, and his master was loath to chase him, trusting the bounty hunter to find and bring back the errant slave who would be taught the lesson of his life, but when Bernie's bed was found empty, Appleton's master flew into a rage and sent four men on horseback and all seven dogs to search all the way to the shores of the white waters, but for all their troubles, men and beast alike, not a trace was found of the man known as Appleton nor the maid known as Bernie.

Appleton turned up several years after the 13th Amendment with no explanation and a heavily pregnant Bernie, and they set up shop in Creektown.

People who met him often mentioned that he was always looking over his shoulder.

10 years later, he dropped dead while saddling his horse, his face twisted in agony. The coroner ruled the cause of death as an exceptionally violent heart attack "It's as if his heart burst wide open."

Now our story picks up speed as we travel several generations down the Appleton family tree to Obadiah J. Appleton, a salesman who made a tidy sum traversing towns selling whatever his words could sell. Obadiah scoffed at talks of the supernatural. He believed only in himself and his ability to talk about money. Out of the pockets of people who listened to him.

This would change 13 days after his thirty-seventh birthday when the devil visited him.

It started as a freak thunderstorm that shook his little cottage to its foundation, but Obadiah was content to let the storm run its course while he smoked a cigar. In the next room, he could hear his wife singing to the children to soothe them.

Then the howling started. A blood-curdling brashness that seemed to be coming from the outhouse.

His wife walked into the living room, "Honey, what is that god awful sound? The children are trembling. My song's no good; would you please have a look at it?"

Obadiah frowned, "let me be, woman! It's just some noise. It'll be over soon. Just sing louder or sommin'."

"Please Dear, the children are scared!"

"Fine, I'll check it. I'm sure it's nothing" he said, putting out his cigar rising with a grunt.

He picked up his torch and on second thought, his rifle too. He was not a man that scared easily, but he liked to be prepared.

Obadiah found himself shuddering the closer he got to the howling. By the time he pushed open the rickety doors, he was sweating and covered in goosebumps.

A figure of a man leaning against the wall just beyond the reach of the torch's glare.

"Who the fuck are you?!" Obadiah roared and swung his gun to bear on the figure.

"I have been called a thousand names by a thousand men. Your kind call me the devil," the man said, but his voice reverberated everywhere and nowhere.

Obadiah felt a chill run down his spine at those words, but his aim never wavered.

"I don't care what they call you. What are you doing on my property?"

"I'm here to collect a debt owed to me." The devil stepped into the light and looked straight into Obadiah's eyes, and for the first time in his life, Obadiah felt a knee-buckling fear that set his teeth on edge with a dread that rooted him to the spot. His mind powerless against the assault of a mind so complex that it raged at the seams of what made Obadiah human, his mortality examined and cast aside and his soul sent spinning through eons of terror and horrors beyond what any human consciousness could bear to fathom.

When he came to, only a minute had passed, and the only word he could utter as he lay crumpled at the devil's feet was "please."

"Why do you beg me? Your ancestor promised me a life if I set him free, a fair deal."

Obadiah struggled to raise himself into a sitting position, "Surely, that's an old wives' tale. Everyone knows that."

The man who called himself the devil smiled, but there was no humor in it.

"I do not expect humans with such fickle memories as yours to comprehend the binding force in fair trade, nor do I have the patience to explain. By the powers that be, I claim you as...

"Wait!" Obadiah spat, mustering the strength to rise to his feet even though they felt like jelly.

"You dare interrupt me!" The rage in the devil's voice assaulted Obadiah's mind like a battering ram against rotten plywood, but Obadiah whispered through gritted teeth.

"I can make you a better deal, worth more than the life of one pitiful human," the man said, and the pressure building against his mind vanished.

"I'm listening." the devil's voice, a hiss.

Obadiah, a seasoned salesman, knew the scent of a sale, and even if his prospect was the devil himself, Obadiah was now in his element and quickly found his voice and his feet.

"Your debt is the 13th blood descendant of Appleton. What if you could have every Appleton?"

The devil's lips curled in a smile, "You would indebt your bloodline to save yourself," he admired the human will to live.

"Eh, we've been through worse. We'll be fine, plus I'll be dead by then. What do I care?" His voice trembled imperceptibly. He was determined not to die tonight.

The devil nodded. "Very well, Appleton, I accept." The last word fell like a thunderclap, sealing the deal in all planes and dimensions of the universe. "This bond requires a blood seal. On a day of my choosing. I'll present you with a chalice of my own blood, and you must drink it to seal this bond."

Then it was just Obadiah in an empty house in the middle of a thunderstorm.

That night, when Obadiah traded his family away for his life, there was another witness; Sara, tired of waiting for her husband, had seized a lamp and gone out to see what was holding him up. She arrived at the door just as the devil revealed himself. There she stood and listened.

By the time Obadiah returned to the house, she was in bed, but she was not sleeping. She was plotting. Her children would not be beholden to the Prince of darkness.

At this point, the story gets muddy with a thousand retellings, but again, everyone agrees that Sara hatched a plan to save her children by mixing some holy water into the vial of the devil's blood.

She had found it in the heavy wooden box under the floorboards where her husband stored items of great value to him. That night, at the stroke of midnight, he crept across the floor, lifted the floorboards to reach into the box, and raised the vial to his lips, gasping as the unholy mixture of the devil's blood and holy water burned the back of his throat like boiling alcohol. Suddenly he was seized by a fit that convulsed him violently across the room until he lay still at the door where his wife found him in the morning, an empty vial clutched in his fist.

Sara had tried to protect her children, but she had created a supernatural mutation, a bond that would give her lineage an advantage against the dark forces forever, but these demons would be able to sniff out Appleton blood like a bloodhound.

As you would expect, the devil was not too pleased to find out, and he exerted his vengeance on Obadiah swiftly and suddenly, incinerating him in his car as he drove home a week later.

Eyewitnesses say Obadiah's car burned with white hot flames, so hot they could be felt from a mile away. It would be a long time before Sara could tell her two children of the trade their father had made and her part in thwarting it.

The devil's blood would run silent for years until the birth of the Appleton boy, Crabbe H. Appleton, on whom this story focuses. The boy that would grow up to be a fearless terror against all that go bump in the dark and forever a thorn in the side of the one they call the devil.

CHAPTER 1

"You, Mr. Crabbe?" the tallest among the two asked. She was a tall drink of water taking a step off a beauty magazine, clad in a silk top and silver bell-bottom pants that hid perfectly pedicured feet in brown sequin platform sandals that twinkled in the streetlight.

"Office is closed. Come back tomorrow, ladies." For a second, he wondered why two beautiful women were in his driveway at midnight, but he had seen worse. He made to sidestep them as best as he could, but the other woman stepped into his path. She was darker and wore a black dress molded to her frame. Her hair was dyed in different hues of the rainbow.

"Tomorrow is a little too late. We need you now," she said, a tinge of promise thick in her syrupy voice, but Crabbe was not deceived; he had fought demons long enough to know that the two women in front of him were anything but women.

"Look, I don't have time for this. Can we wrap it up?" He flexed his shoulders, arms, and wrists in one fluid motion.

"Feisty!" The tall woman hissed and lunged at him. Halfway through the strike, she transformed into her true form. Her feet burst through the straps on her feet.

Covered in fur, and her clothes tore around her frame as she grew seven feet with arms the size of stout branches.

Her hair went from an electric blue afro to blue-tipped razor-sharp quills dripping with poison, and her haughty eyes widened until they were the size of golf balls.

In the place of a woman stood a beast the size of a bear on steroids but twice as dangerous.

Her lunge caught Crabbe in her impossibly long arms and crushed him in a bear hug Crabbe struggled to breathe as the demon's breath dazzled his senses, a stench so repulsive that any other man would weep in nasal agony as his lungs burned, but Crabbe was not any other man. He stilled himself and found his calm "You've done this dance a thousand times, he reminded himself as he assessed the situation. The beast holding him was a menari, a brutish race of demons that employed disguises of seductive women to hunt and kill unsuspecting men and women when they were particularly famished. If a man vanished off the streets with no trace, chances are a menari found dinner.

But they had one weakness: their eyes were a loose fit in their sockets, and if you could pluck them out, the menari would be half as dangerous, but, half-dangerous was plenty dangerous too. Besides, no one ever made it past a menari's claws unless your name was Crabbe H Appleton.

In an instant, he wriggled out of her grasp, and using her swinging arm as a fulcrum, he swung onto the back of the beast and dug his hands into her eye sockets up to his wrists. When he pulled them out, he was clutching two spasming goey sacs that were once eyes.

The menari screamed, a sound heard all the way in hell, and flung Crabbe off her back, slamming him into the windshield of the white Honda. The other demon stood off to the side, watching the scene like a gambler at a dogfight; she did not attempt to join. Crabbed groaned to his feet just in time to jump out of the way as the menari slashed in an arc around her. He stood out of arm's length, he would not survive another bear hug, and he was getting dizzy again from the stench of demon breath in the air.

"Hey demon, over here," he called as he positioned himself in front of the oak tree at the end of his driveway. The menari turned her head towards him as she caught a whiff of his blood.

"I can smell you," she growled in a guttural voice, and swiveled her head in his direction.

"I'm counting on it," he smiled.

The menari charged, but without eyes, it was impossible for her to see that the trunk had been carved with runes that now glowed brighter with each thundering step she took. At the last moment, Crabbe rolled out of the way, and the demon plunged into the tree, horns and all.

The spell activated as every bone in the menari's body snapped all at once, and she lay in the grass, shuddering as her lifeform descended into the depths of hell.

Crabbe heard a loud sigh and looked up, the rainbow-haired woman/demon shaking her head. "Looks like it's up to me now," she said with a slimy sensuality that made Crabbe gag. He hated when these demons played at being humans.

"Are we gonna talk all night or..." he sneered, closing his fist around the eyeballs of the fallen menari.

Oh, baby, you want me, don't you?" She began to toss her clothes; any other man would stare, but Crabbe knew what she was before she finished transforming: a Sepr, a serpent demon that, like the menari, fed on human flesh.

Her lower torso and legs fused into a snake trunk that undulated as she moved towards Crabbe, who bid his time.

The Sepr had seen what Crabbe was capable of. She was more cautious. She darted in fast as a flash, striking Crabbe across the belly and knocking him into the pavement. He was back on his feet in a jiffy. He could not afford to lose any ground to this particular demon. The Sepr opened her mouth impossibly wide and vomited white lumps that sizzled when they hit the ground, then bounced at Crabbe, who dived behind the oak tree. He could feel; the Oak's life force absorb the burn of the acid bomb exploding against its trunk.

"Thanks, buddy," Crabbe whispered He was pinned behind the tree without a way out that didn't involve an acid bath. He needed a distraction.

"Just a minute, honey" he yelled at the Sepr, his fingers drawing a spell in front of his mouth. The Sepr would hear Crabbe's voice on the other side of the driveway. He was counting on the fact that Sepr eyesight is dogshit. It worked; the Sepr spun on her trunk and hurled more acid bombs, craning her neck as she slid closer for a better look.

"Don't keep me waiting, darling," she cooed in between regurgitations, then the moment Crabbe was counting on came.

She burped, and for a moment, there was nothing to vomit, Sepr were prone to burps in snake form. He rolled out from behind the oak and sprung to his feet, a pair of menari eyeballs hidden in his fist. "Surprised to see me?"

The Sepr spun around, momentarily confused to see Crabbe behind her at that moment, she was off guard with her mouth hanging open..

Most people who encounter a menari eyeball don't live long enough to learn that once detached from its life source, it becomes a deadly acidic poison that eats away at humans and demons alike, except for beings like the devil and Crabbe who has the devil's blood in him.

This serpent demon was about to find out the meaning of pain.

In that split second, her mouth hung ajar, two well-aimed menari eyes flew into her mouth, and she bit down in shock.

"What have you done..." she gasped, then realized just exactly what was in her mouth. A curse rose to her lips as she clawed at her face, but it was too late. The demon acid ate her head first, then her body. dissolving the Sepr into a puddle of foul-smelling green liquid.

"An acid demon destroyed by acid-how poetic!" Crabbe scoffed.

Everything had occurred in less than 5 minutes, and not a single soul saw a thing-perks of living in a business area where the business people arrived late and left early.

"So much for clearing my head," Crabbe Appleton sighed as he assessed the damage: the driveway was relatively undamaged, the oak tree had been gored where the menari had crashed into its trunk; some melted stone from where the acid had hit; a half-destroyed Honda Civic; and two putrid puddles that used to be demons.

Crabbe summoned power from within and spoke a single word, "Irazo."

The puddles disappeared along with every accessory the demons arrived with except the Honda. He was too tired to transport it through the dark dimension. He would call Bob to get rid of it for scrap value.

"All in a night's work," he muttered as he trudged up the steps and inserted his key into the lock.

CHAPTER 2

Crabbe was beyond tired, he'd had a long day and all he wanted to do was crawl into bed where the warm arms of unconsciousness awaited him As he unlocked the door and made his way to the back of the house that also doubled as his office/shop, he thought about the irony of calling his house an office what a way to spin the burden of the curse in his blood. Work from home yay!" he muttered under his breath as he reached for the light switch and flicked it on and stood still.

A werecat the size of a pitbull and black as night, came surging through the hallway, Crabbe braced himself as the flying mass of fur entangled his knees and rubbed against his shins. Mr Kit The resident feline of the Crabbe household.

When he meowed, there was a worry in it, the cat had heard the commotion outside. "I'm fine, Kit, they didn't stand a chance, now stop worrying" Crabbe stopped short as Mr. Kit let out a rippling growl and swiveled his head towards the door. Two seconds later, there was a knock. Mr Kit's preemptive warning meant one thing, whoever was at the door was supernatural.

Crabbe sighed. No rest for the wicked indeed, but this time he would not be taken by surprise.

His business card introduced him as a clairvoyant or herbalist, but he was not just all candle and incense. Amongst other tools of the occult, he possessed a cane of the finest pinewood grown on the bank of the river Jordan capped with a gold top from the lost temple of Solomon and branded on the bottom with a seal that vanquished demons with a touch. Perhaps the easy slant with which the cane stood in the corner bore testimony to the battles it had been through. This time, Crabbe scooped it up with a practiced swing, and as the cane arced through the air, it hummed with a crackling energy.

He crossed the hallway and swung the door open, his feet firmly planted on the threshold. For a moment, there was no one there, then the air shimmered, and there stood a grey-haired couple. They could pass off as the friendly neighborhood grandma and grandpa-heavyset, Hilda clad in a blue, red, and white polka dot dress with the handbag to match, Elmo in faded khaki overalls and spotless work boots.

Crabbe knew who they were, they were harmless, at least to him, With a mental command, he depowered the cane.

"Hilda, Elmo, fancy seeing you here tonight," he stepped aside. He didn't need any clairvoyant skills to know they were in distress, their faces were drawn and Hilda's make-up was marked with a facsimile of tears.

"Sorry to bother you, Mr. Crabbe, but we didn't know anyone else to turn to, please, you have to help us." Elmo said earnestly.

"Can't it wait till tomorrow. It's been quite a day." Crabbe grumbled.

"It's Jenny! She's gone missing! Sweet little girl, just gone!" Hilda spoke up for the first time, she sounded like a woman in grief. Crabbe could feel the onset of a headache.

"We think she's been kidnapped!" Elmo added quickly.

Yes, this was a headache now alright, Crabbe waved them in a single motion that disabled the wards guarding his door. He led them past the second bedroom he'd turned into his consulting room, through some beaded curtains into a lounge area, a circle of couches with a fireplace, and an enclave Crabbe had long appropriated into a minibar. This was where he entertained his clients sometimes.

He motioned for them to sit down and perched himself on the edge of his favorite couch. "When did you notice that she's missing?"

"Joan and Robert haven't tucked her in, in two weeks. and we can't detect her presence in the house at all."

"Did it possibly occur to you that she might have been at a friend's, or a grandma's, or vacation, something of that nature?" Crabbe said as gently as he could muster

"We thought that too but she just disappeared one day she did not pack anything, not even her favorite book."

Elmo started before Hilda finished "Plus she didn't say goodbye to us, that's unlike Jenny."

"Maybe someone from school, perhaps." Crabbe thought aloud.

"Her grandma is dead, she told us she has no friends because all the other kids want to talk about stupid stuff," Hilda burst into tears again.

Crabbe studied the spirits seated before him, while they played with human appearances and emotions, even he wondered how they could feel so deeply for a human.

Hilda and Elmo were the kind of spirits most humans were not aware of, those who clawed their way up to the surface world through a million illegal paths from hell. The tunnel in Yugoslavia was seeing a ton of traffic these days. Spirits that simply wanted a better existence than sulfur and brimstone. These spirits and demons could be as human as they needed when they needed, after all, they'd been studying humans for millennia.

Hilda and Elmo were simple inhabiting spirits, the basis of tales of monsters under beds and closets told to frighten children in bed, but if a child tuned into the supernatural like Jenny looked under her bed, she would find a friendly face like Elmo's who would introduce himself and start a friendship that would last the duration of that kid's childhood.

Unfortunately, these spirits could and did grow attached to their momentary wards and sometimes grew vicious in their desperation to keep themselves connected to the children whose bedrooms they inhabited, even though the bond was supposed to weaken as the children got older.

"C'mon guys, you know how this works and how getting attached helps no one, I'm sure Jenny's fine. Are her parents panicking or anything as such?"

Crabbe inquired.

"That's the thing," Hilda was getting agitated again.

"They act like nothing's happened, like she never existed, it's odd, I can feel it."

"Something isn't right, Appleton. We know it might sound like we're two crazies who've forgotten their place in the grand scheme of things, but please will you at least look into it?"

Crabbe had dealt with Elmo and Hilda long enough to know they would cry him to death if it would get him to agree, besides, it wouldn't hurt to check.

"Yes, I believe you. I'll swing by tomorrow and see them."

"Sixteen-twenty Sharon Road." Hilda's tears faded into a sweet smile. Crabbe groaned, they'd gotten him to commit

"Yeah sure, I remember." He stood, and they followed suit. He led them to the front door, and just before Crabbe shut it, he saw their forms shimmer and disappear like water vapor on a winter night.

There was another spirit floating in the hallway as Crabbe turned toward his bedroom. Morocco, the in between so named because he was caught between this world and the next and would have been subjected to wandering the 7 dimensions had Crabbe not created a home and purpose for him.

A fortune-telling booth Crabbe had taken off the hands of a circus operator who filed for bankruptcy, had quickly been converted into a home for Morocco with the help of a tethering spell. He dwelt in a 6ft mannequin and flitted between crystal balls positioned strategically around the house. If you've ever consulted Crabbe and asked for your fortune to be told, chances are, you were probably dealing with Morocco.

The form the spirit often chose to appear to Crabbe was his earthly form before his demise, tan skin, black slacks, red dress shirts, a black vest and a white turban from his days wandering the streets of Marrakesh.

"Do you think it's serious?" He asked as he floated towards Crabbe, flanked by Mr. Kit.

"I guess we'll know by tomorrow, won't we?" Crabbe was ready to drop, and as he turned off the lights in the hallway, his eye caught the shimmering portal at the end of the hallway undulating in the low light. Most people would have seen a mirror shimmering with light and they would have been so wrong. Crabbe smiled to think of the deadly duel to the death he had fought with a wizard from the dark dimension to win that portal Now, it stood in his hallway shimmering with power. If anyone had looked closer, they would have seen an ornately carved team in the form of entwined dragons.

Except they were real dragons in their idle states; Sira and Sera.

Little hatchlings he had rescued in Siberia soaking up a ton of radiation. These days, they were content to guard the portal against nasty intruders from other dimensions who were often drawn to the pulsating power of the portal.

Since we're on the journey of the Crabbe household dependents, perhaps it's right to mention that Mr. Kit was freed by Crabbe from the fighting pits of Tartarus. When a fracas that had broken out after Crabbe's brawl with an especially powerful demon bounty hunter spilled into the pits, Kit who had been biding his time had transformed into his werecat form and tore through his chains like paper towels and joined Crabbe in vanquishing the demon. They had been inseparable ever since.

Crabbe hit his bed with the force of a nuclear missile and in the time it took for the bedframe to stop bouncing, the man was fast asleep.

CHAPTER 3

Most people would not associate a 1984 Quasar Geo Metro with the status of a favorite car unless you were Crabbe Appleton, he was a man in love with the classics. But this morning, as he turned the ignition and pulled out of his driveway, he hoped that Hilda and Elmo were overreacting again. If he had a dime for every time the pair cried wolf, he would never have to work again but he could appreciate their hearts and intention. Yet he couldn't shake the niggling feeling at the back of his head, that same feeling that had him looking over his shoulder lately, he shook his head to clear his thoughts and gunned the engine.

That's when it happened For a second, the monotony of the highway persevered, suddenly, a green Honda Civic came roaring off the ramp and cut off a white BMW with chrome rims, forcing the driver of the BMW to slam on the brakes to avoid a head-on collision.

It might have been another case of reckless driving, but the BMW was one to hold grudges, tires screeched as it accelerated, quickly closing the gap and smashing into the Honda which careened off the road to come to a violent stop against the curb, but the BMW driver was far off from finished. Crabbe watched in horrid fascination as the driver's door flung open and the driver, a big burly brute in an armless jean jacket emerged, he reached back into the vehicle, hefted a baseball bat, swung it once like it weighed nothing, and stalked towards the still steaming Honda swearing unprintable curses.

The other guy was still getting his bearings when the bat smashed into his window and an arm covered with tattoos caught him by a fistful of his shirt and dragged him out through the window knocking off his glasses in the process, the Honda guy didn't stand a chance, the brute socked him in the jaw before laying into him with the bat until he lay prone, only then did the brute finally let the bat fall to his side.

No one had stopped to intervene, slowing down a little to record for their TikTok before rolling up their windows and speeding off.

What happened next was straight from a horror movie. Just as the raging driver, finally exhausted of his blood thirst, turned to enter his vehicle, a speeding Corvette slammed into him and sent him flying into the air in a horribly perfect arc of death to come slamming onto the trunk of a screeching Ford Tacoma, swerving to avoid the scene. In the ensuing chaos, his body was run over by 4 cars as they all tried unsuccessfully to avoid the pile up.

From the moment the Honda appeared, to the last tires which bumped over the driver of the BMW, barely 5 minutes had passed, Crabbe had pulled over to watch, but more than anyone else, he had seen the spirit of the BMW driver staring at his mangled corpse in what might have been shock. It was hard to be sure, seeing as his form undulated and shimmered like a Nevada mirage.

Crabbe put the Geo into gear and drove on, it was days like this that reminded him just how much horror he'd seen for such a violent death to barely register. One day, he was going to get away from all of it and find somewhere to find his humanity, if there was anything left of it. He'd heard good things about a monastery in Tibet, but until then, Crabbe Appleton at your bloody service.

Joan and Roberts lived in the nicer part of town where there was still enough land to attempt landscaping and artistic lawns. In its lazy tranquility, it could have been a scene from an idyllic movie. Crabbe hoped it was a tranquility that ran deep. There was enough bad stuff going on in the world already.

He adjusted his suit and patted down an errant strand of hair in the reflection of his car window. "Here goes nothing" He took a deep breath, walked up the driveway and depressed the bell button.

He waited.

He glanced at his watch. Two minutes, still no answer.

He was about to try again but the door was already opening. A woman in a simple jean dress and flip-flops was standing in the doorway, her eyes slanted in suspicion "Can I help you sir?" she asked. Crabbe smiled. "I'm Mason Briggs from the school board. Are you Mrs. Joan, Jenny's mother?" She hesitated, caution deepening the furrow between her brow. "Any problem?"

"We've received reports that Jenny has not been in school for the past few days, and we decided to swing by and see if everything is alright." Crabbe's face was hurting from the disarming smile he was trying to maintain. He was not sure it was working either.

"Of course everything is alright, why wouldn't it be?" She tried to toss her hair in what should have been a sensual nonchalant gesture, but it was forced and awkward.

Crabbe's smile slipped a fraction. She was definitely hiding something. "May I come in?"

"Oh! Please come in, forgive my manners," but she remained in the doorway for a fraction longer as if hoping Crabbe would change his mind, then she turned and led him into the sitting room that felt and looked sparse. Crabbe noticed the dust gathering on surfaces that should have been clean from regular use. This room was for show.

"Lovely home you got here, a nice place to raise a kid." Crabbe noted as he sat down, Joan looked around her as if she was a guest herself then nodded, "Yes, it's nice."

"Is Jenny home?"

"Ummm, no, she's not"

"And your husband? Mr Long, I believe," Crabbe was studying the row of pictures of a smiling Jenny and her family arranged above the cold dusty fireplace. Something about them puzzled him.

"I'm sorry Mr. Briggs, what is it you do again?" He could feel her eyes burrowing into him.

"I'm here on behalf of the school, Her teachers are concerned she hasn't shown up in class for the past..." he made a show of studying the empty notepad he carried, "..2 weeks. Wanted to be sure..."

"She's visiting her sick aunt in Tampa, she specifically requested Jenny, her favorite niece" she shrugged.

Crabbe made a show of writing down what she said. "Is it terminal?"

"What is?"

"The illness"

"Sadly yes, anytime now. The doctors say she won't make it past summer so one can only hope, right?" She threw up her hands in false resignation.

"I find it strange that none of this information has been filed at the school"

"I'm sure we did. They must have forgotten all about it, maybe I should call my husband, he's at work right now, but I'm sure he can provide the details you need."

Crabbe rose to his feet, "Unfortunately, I still have a list of parents to visit this morning, can I indulge you in that glass of water now?"

"Sure, give me a minute" and turned into the kitchen.

Crabbe waited till she was out of sight and touched the dial of his watch and turned it 180 degrees and time stood still.

The Watch of Sloth was a tool forged as a gift by the Archdemon Lucrel, a demon known for its perverse wantonness and lasciviousness. Two years ago, Crabbe put a Drakensword through its heart and claimed the watch of sloth as his prize.

Rumoured to have been assembled outside of time and space itself, the watch granted the wearer the ability to significantly slow down the passage of time and operate at normal speed Crabbe didn't enjoy messing with the watch, especially with the reality-altering effects it could have on the real world.

Crabbe made a beeline for Jenny's room, the room had a fine layer of dust over everything, Crabbe stood in the middle of the room and soaked up Jenny's dormant energy for a few minutes, then sent out psionic waves, a second later they came pinging back, Jenny wherever she was, she was alive. Crabbe didn't want to risk using more power than he'd already done. It's said the watch of Sloth pulverized any mere mortal who tried to use it but it still exerted a whole lot of energy, even for someone like Crabbe. Of course with the devil blood inside of him, he should have been able to use the watch at full blast all day but tapping into that raging boiling storm of blood in his veins would drag him closer to his demon form. A thought that made him shudder.

Crabbe twisted back the dial and life resumed at 1.00x speed again, he felt dizzy for a second, he would never get used to the raw power the watch could channel and the toll it often took on him.

The glass of water arrived. "Thank You Mrs Long. I'll be in touch."

He was unlocking his door when he realized what puzzled him about the pictures in the sitting room;

on Jenny's jaw just below her chin was a little brown bandaid. The same bandaid appeared in all the pictures from Christmas to summer to Easter to recitals. Unless she had the world's most stubborn graze, all the pictures had been taken within the same time frame and adjusted to fit whatever the Longs had going on.

They would hear from him.

CHAPTER 4

As Crabbe drove home, he mulled over the home he'd just visited and how he would handle the Longs. He hated when children were involved in shady business, even worse when their parents had a hand in it. It rang too close to home.

His thoughts were interrupted by a psychic warning, a spirit was in the vehicle with him, out of the corner of his eye, he saw a form materialize.

Most people would have veered off the road in shock. Crabbe was not most people, he was used to visitations from spirits recently deceased, who were drawn to the devil in his veins hoping he could offer them a way out, others just wanted the company. He mostly ignored them until they left him alone. That was the strategy he planned to adopt now.

He kept his eyes firmly fixed on the road ahead as the spirit finished taking form. It was the driver of the BMW from the accident earlier, his black T-shirt hung in tatters, his left eye hung loosely in the sockets and he looked like he'd been put through a meat grinder.

"I need your help." He said.

Crabbe ignored him.

"Hey, I know you can hear me, I need Your help!" his voice, more insistent.

"I can't help you," Crabbe muttered.

"Then why were you lighting up like a beacon from miles away?" There was confusion with an undertone of anger in his voice, clearly his brutish ways carried over even in death.

Crabbe sighed, he was tired of explaining his curse to every ghost that dropped into his passenger's seat. "Let's have it then," he made a mental note to renew the cloaking spell that hid him from roaming spirits.

"My name's Jeff, Jeff Stout and I died-"

"I know who you are, and I knew everything about you as soon as you breathed your last. You're a mob enforcer very familiar with that bat of yours, and have put a ton of helpless store owners in the hospital or worse, when they default on your protection money, did I miss anything?"

"I was also the wrestling champion in high school and boy, was I vicious?" Crabbe had never heard anyone so gutsy.

"Now I know, happy for you. Now can you go to hell?"

"See, that's the problem, I'm stuck here."

"What do you mean you're stuck here?" Crabbe turned to face the spirit. He knew of spirits that were condemned to roam the earth to and fro, for eternity. Chief amongst them was the biblical Cain, but Stout's should have been cut and dried, a bad man who did bad things, send him down below. Case closed.

"I can't explain it." For the first time, Crabbe saw a hint of fear in Stout's mangled face. "I don't know where to go, the others avoid me like the plague, then I saw you glowing. I thought you might have a clue."

There was a red light up ahead and as Crabbe pulled up, it started to make sense, the Devil was at it again with one of his twisted jokes, every once in a regular while, the Prince of hell would send some of the despicable spirits his way to test his patience, anything to make him lose control.

It was a sick twisted game that's played out for 30 years. "Mister..."

"Crabbe, and no relation to the crustacean," Crabbe answered as the light turned green.

"Crusta what? Look, Some people will say I've done some bad stuff-"

Crabbe's head swung around, incredulous. "Some people?! Some bad stuff?" Crabbe's voice was a quiet whisper but the angry power it carried caused Stout's spirit form to wilt a bit.

"Okay yes, pretty messed up stuff but I don't have a choice, I either did these things or I'd lose my post and in this line of work, your retirement plan is a coffin, but I'm here right now and I can't even cross over. You have to help me!"

"Listen, dipshit! I don't have to do anything for you, you hear me?" but Crabbe knew this soul wouldn't go anywhere if he didn't do something about the situation. Another cruel joke from the underworld.

"Can you help me?"

Crabbe sighed. "I guess we'll see about that, won't we?"

....

"You what?!" Robert was livid. "Don't scream at me, he looked the part, what was I supposed to do?" Joan wasn't meeting her husband's eyes. He shook his hand and fished about in his pocket for a phone. "Just because a man looks the part doesn't mean that he's the real deal!"

Joan threw up her hands, how many times did he want her to apologize. "I didn't know, okay?"

Robert found his phone and hit the speed dial. "Yeah, it's me, what can you tell me about a Mason Briggs? He says he works with the school board."

. . . .

Down at Crabbe's apartment, there was a spiritual disturbance. Crabbe was on the sofa, a half-drunken Pepsi can in one hand and his eyes fixed on the midway point between the ceiling and the ground where two spirits glared at each other.

"Morocco," Crabbe sighed "Do we really have to do this?" Crabbe groaned.

"This piece of shit does not deserve our help!" Morocco was furious, the lightbulbs flickered with every word he spat.

"Who the hell do you think you are?!" Stout bellowed right back.

Crabbe shared a look with Mr Kit who was curled up near the fireplace, his eyes glittered in the fires he yawned and went back to sleep.

Crabbe wondered if letting Stout into his house was a good idea after all, the shouting match that started as soon as stout phased through the door and lasted the next 15 minutes seemed to suggest otherwise.

"Okay, cut it off you two!" he'd had enough. "What are you gonna do? Kill each other?" the spirits glared a second longer, a moment longer and the flickering light would have burst.

"Do you always have spirits roaming around your house? Stout hovered a few inches above the ground. "Spirit Singular. One. His name is Morocco. Two, he lives here, the rest is none of your business"

"Mr Appleton, this-" Morocco was trying his best to ignore Stout.

21

I know, I know Morocco, believe me, I want him out of my hair too, but you know who is playing one of his stupid jokes again, we have to figure out a way to unbind him from this plane, if not, he's stuck with us."

"I'd die a thousand deaths than set my eyes on that uncouth creature even a minute more"

"Yeah, my thoughts exactly" Crabbe sighed and sunk back into the sofa.

"But he's a waste of time, he can't even pay you," Morocco said, seeking a way out.

"I think I can help there" Stout brightened. "I have a tidy sum in a Bank of America account, it's yours if you want it." He was smiling coyly at Morocco. Crabbe suspected Stout was doing it to spite Morocco but money was money.

"Don't you have some family that need the money?" Morocco wished he would shut up.

Stout shook his head. "Nobody to miss me."

"What's there to miss?" Morocco whispered snidely.

Crabbe glared at the turbaned spirit then turned to Stout. "There has to be somebody." Stout hesitated for a second, "There's an aunt in Florida, but she refuses to take money from me. Shit, I don't even remember what her voice sounds like. She's probably forgotten that I even exist, so yeah, no familia."

The room was quiet for a moment, and then Morocco's laughter shattered the scene. "You believe this guy?"

"Does it matter, when this is said and done, we'll find the aunt and give her the news. Now Stout, will you please go do whatever it is ghosts do? I'll summon you when I know something that can help." Crabbe pointed to the door. The spirit looked like it wanted to say something but thought better of it and vanished in a poof.

"This is a bad idea." Morocco drifted down to the couch where Crabbe sat.

"Maybe, but the last thing I need is a spirit hounding me.

"Using your powers draws you closer to the brink remember?" Morocco pointed out.

"I know, Moe you worry too much, it won't get that far, I have a lot of juice left." Crabbe didn't like talking about what would happen if he had to dip into the lake of fire boiling in his veins and the uncertainty of what would happen after.

"I'll help you find the guy who killed Stout, but it'll take some jumping around." Morocco sighed, he knew better than to argue with Crabbe, his powers were surpassed by his inability to listen.

"Be careful, we don't want last summer repeating itself." There was laughter in Crabbe's words.

He knew without looking up that Morocco was rolling his eyes.

"You're never going to forget that, are you?"

"You bet I won't," Crabbe sniggered as Morocco disappeared in a pop.

Last summer. Crabbe and Morocco had run into a sticky situation when Morocco mistimed a body jump and ended up in the body of a hyperactive 5-year-old girl, whose mind was as tenacious as steel.

CHAPTER 5

Sal's Diner was a thorough American experience; underpaid and overworked staff, greasy food and plenty of coffee. It also doubled as an outpost for Sal's criminal activities.

His father had come to America on a cruise ship with nothing but the gators on his waist. He would have been shocked to learn that his pudgy son now ran a mafia of proportions who contributed to keeping the hospitals well stocked.

In the back of the dinner, a part of the storeroom had been demarcated and furnished to Sal's malodorous tastes; low light in the ceiling, lots of blue cigar smoke in the air, and a ton of food on a picnic table covered with a greasy table cloth.

The mob boss called Sal reached his bejeweled fingers into the bowl of smoking hot chicken just delivered 5 minutes ago and plopped a drumstick into the cavernous jowls he called a mouth, drumsticks and all.

Three other men sat around the table shuffling cards and smoking cigars, if the loud chewing from the head of the table bothered them, they did a good job of hiding it.

Murray Child the enforcer, built like a 6ft tank and rumoured to have killed a man when he was 14 with his bare hands, he positioned himself far away from

Sal, his boss, he would take a bullet for the man but he couldn't stand a minute of the mustard whiffing off the overweight Italian.

Pitt, a human rhinoceros, short and stocky with more muscles than he could fit in a T-shirt, and a cigarette between his abrased lips.

Ralph 'The Mouth' Murphy, also called Ralph Malph. He was neither muscular nor particularly intimidating, but he made up for it in snark and an ability to talk himself out of any situation, he was the man Sal sent when the situation called for more finesse, he was also a pain in the ass.

"Pitt, heard your man got whacked, you didn't teach him some skills?" Ralph grunted, he loved riling up Pitt and Pitt loved falling for it.

"I could teach you some right now," Pitt glared at him, but his mind was on Sal. The man hadn't said anything since he got the news, he just ate and ate. Pitt found himself comparing his boss to a human trash compactor, he quickly shook the image from his mind.

Sal could see those kind of thoughts on a man's face.

"Stai zitto!" Sal snapped, his head was throbbing from all the wine at the mayor's ball last night, he was not in the mood for chitchat. For now, he would eat, and then he would address the elephant in the room.

Ralph flashed his grills at Pitt who scowled and muttered, "Told that bonehead to go easy on the swing. Stupid motherfucker think he Schwarzenegger or something."

"I wonder who must have taught him that sort of behaviour," Ralph breathed as he laid out a royal flush, Murray chuckled as Pitt's scowl deepened. Everybody knew how Pitt had pestered Sal until he let Stout wear the uniform.

"Fuck you, Ralph." Pitt spat. "That kid's got anger issues, I done told him to get his noggins looked at."

Sal finally took his eyes off the TV as he sucked oily crumbs off his fingers and let out a belch that was almost a yell, he fished in the cooler at his feet for a beer, and he held the frosty bottle above his head. "To Stout, a dumb son of a bitch!"

"Poor sonofabitch he was." Ralph raised his glass.

"Pitt, we now have a vacancy." Sal grunted.

"Really, where?" Pitt brightened at the opportunity to impress Big Man Sal.

"You're even dumber than Stout, but at least he knew to use a bat," Ralph sighed. Pitt turned red when he saw that Sal chuckled at that.

"I'm telling you Ralph, one day, I gon' put my Glock up that big mouth and see how you like it!"

"Sorry amigo, I don't roll that way," Ralph was enjoying this.

Sal reached under his chair and when he straightened, he was huffing, his chest wobbling as he panted, but in his hand, he held that cane. The one Stout used to drive fear into the hearts of the residents of NewCross. The heavy price they paid when they didn't have the little white envelope stuffed and ready, as the BMW came roaring down the street.

Pitt flinched at the sight of the bat, "Boss, I don't know, I'm more a point-and-shoot type of guy."

Sal let the bat fall in front of Pitt with a ringing clang. "Stout may be stupid but he got one thing right, amigo. Bullets are bad for our business. Break some bones, make it dramatic and bloody so everyone else learns, but no guns. Every time you shoot someone, I have to pull strings, and I hate to pull strings!" There was a menace in the last word.

Pitt picked up the bat.

"Stupid sure looks good on you." Ralph smiled, and for a moment, Pitt wondered how many minutes it would take to beat Ralph to death with the cold bat in his hand.

None of them saw the shadow hanging in the corner, seething. Stout had come visiting and each time his stupidity was mentioned, he got angrier. He had busted his ass for Sal's gang, taken the fall many times and thrown everything into being the perfect henchman only for them to act like he was just some thug, easily replaceable.

He would show them.

....

Crabbe was having a rotten day.

The stench that often tipped him on the imminent presence of demons had pervaded his nostrils as he shifted into gear and pulled out of the drive but he soon forgot about all of that as he tried to process the nightmares he'd been having especially the ones he woke up to, with his sweat steaming.

He was standing on a cliff overlooking black burning clouds, raining down liquid fire on a scorched hellish landscape, a horde of demons on his heels, gnashing and slashing as they thundered towards him. A voice clashing like a thousand cymbals repeating one word 'jump' and just as always, just before the demons could reach him, he would wrench himself awake and awash in steamy sweat.

The demons he could handle, but that voice scared him to admit that if you really listened, that voice sounded like his own.

He shook his head to clear his thoughts, and that's when he spotted the two jaywalkers weaving through honking cars with their gaze burning in his direction, he didn't need to smell them to know they would stink to high heavens, their jerky movements gave them away as demons still adjusting to their human disguises.

They clocked that he had spotted them and cast away the act and broke into a maddening run on all fours. Crabbe checked his side mirror and threw the cranky S-10 into reverse spinning into a tight U-turn, he cringed at how many traffic laws he was breaking at the moment, but he knew if those demons got any feistier, he would have a lot more to worry about than a traffic fine.

He glanced at the mirror now, the demons were sprinting hot on his tail and boy! Were they livid?

He saw a gravel road up ahead and accelerated, the demons were gaining on him, their human disguises dropping off their frames like wax, allowing Crabbe to get a good look at them for the first time. His blood chilled at the tell-tale black fur of the Njiantis

He twisted the steering suddenly, bearing that he wouldn't choose this moment to sputter out. The S-10 whined, kicking up gravel as he turned into the road. The turn had slowed him down.

The demons closed the distance in a dash but they were going too fast. Crabbe slammed the brakes, and braced for impact, their feral strength and momentum carried them into the back of the truck. Crabbe groaned, how many more favors could he call in with Billy before the man got tired of saving this heap.

But now was no time to worry about that, he fished out his cane from the passenger seat, and sprang out of the car, tucking into a roll and coming up a few meters away from his car. There was no one there. Half of the car's rear was crumpled but there were no demons in sight.

Puzzled, Crabbe spun in a circle as he sent out psychic feelers searching for the Njiantis. Nothing.

The monsters known as the Njiantis are a special breed of demons bred for the sole purpose of seeking and destroying, they are ferociously efficient in their ruthlessness. Not easily fazed by magic and untiring, their sense of smell was stronger than a shark's, their talons razor sharp.

They look like really buff upright jackals covered in jet black fur.

Crabbe sent power coursing through his cane and its brass head glowed with intensity and lengthened in his grasp, he spun it in a protection circle around him and mounted its obsidian tip into the gravel at his feet. He knew the kind of demons he was up against.

Just in time, out of the corner of his eyes, he caught a fast approaching movement and spun around in time to deflect the swipe of razor sharp talons off with his cane that glowed hot on contact.

Crabbe's mind was racing, he had never dealt with the Njiantis before, he had good reflexes but these beasts made him look like a tortoise with an arthritic knee. Worse, there were two of them.

He looked around him, this was a little used path but it wouldn't be long before someone came along. That someone would not survive it. He had to end this quickly before it escalated into a bloodbath. As these thoughts raced through his mind, a tinier voice hidden deep within the recess of his subconscious pointed out that he could end this fight with just one word. One command was all it would take and these beasts would bow before his feet- - Crabbe crashed into the side of his already battered truck, he would be surprised if he didn't break something and he would deserve it too for getting distracted.

He rose to his feet, the Njiantis now in full glare, they never spoke a word thanks to nonexistent vocal chords but they didn't need to, they were pure killers.

The first one let out a rippling growl and hunched to the ground, in a second he was going to put on a lightning spurt of speed.

Crabbe was hoping on that. Njiantis may be fast but they had poor maneuverability at full speed.

Even though Crabbe was expecting the rush, he barely saw it, he only had time to mutter "Defrendo!" and send power through his cane which pulsed and sent a blinding pulse of light at the fast approaching beast. The Njianti didn't know what hit him, a solid crushing wall of power that spun him off his feet into the trees. The odds may have evened but only barely.

The other Njianti barely glanced at his companion before launching an attack. What unfolded was a chaotic scene of flashing talons and flesh ripping injuries as the Njianti slashed and swiped over and over.

Crabbe could barely keep up as he parried glancing blow after glancing blow.

He knew that once the other Njianti recovered, he was as good as dead, he was already bleeding from several deep cuts to his chest and thigh, his arms felt like lead and the Njianti's foul breath was clouding his senses.

He tried to parry one more blow but to his horror, he realized this arm refused to rise, the exhaustion was finally taking over, the Njianti snarled at the chance and lunged, talons flashing in the afternoon sunlight

Time seemed to slow for Crabbe as he imagined those talons eviscerating his insides, there was nothing he could do, he had done his best, every battle that had come his way, he had managed to win. Maybe this was the end of the road for him. Out of the corner of his eyes, he saw the other Njianti emerge onto the gravel path. The beast was beyond enraged.

This was it, or was it?

"I can save you," the voice in his head spoke up again, this time, it was insistent.

"No.." Crabbe started to say, but the voice repeated, "I can save you now, release me!"

Crabbe was too weak to resist, and in that moment for the first time in 30 years, Crabbe tapped into the devil's blood in his veins and hell was let loose.

One moment the Njiantis were sure of lunch, the next, they felt a wave of power crashing into them, brutally forcing them to their knees and filling them with a dread they had never felt in their existence.

Crabbe was gone, for a fleeting second, the being that stood in his place emanated a fierce evil magnificence, the cane in his hand lengthened into a spear with a burning tip.

The Njiantis were simply helpless as he swung the spear in one measured arc, dispatching the demons from existence on all planes and dimensions.

And just as suddenly, it was just a wounded broken Crabbe bleeding out on the gravel, a truck caved in on one side and a puddle of demons. Smoking among the carnage was a blackened cane burnt nearly to a crisp. The surge of dark power was too much for the cane's magic to handle.

Crabbe gritted his teeth as he reined in the demon and slammed the door, that exertion blurred his vision, threatening to swallow him. With the last vestiges of strength he could muster, he fished out his phone and dialed a number.

He was unconscious before it rang.

....

Crabbe woke up with a banging headache, the intense light spilling onto his face only made the throbbing worse.

"Get that light out of my face, Lester!" He groaned. "How am I supposed to sew you up if I can't see what I'm doing?" The man standing over Crabbe shot back right on cue, the past few hours came rushing back and in tow was the pain of a dozen slashes and cuts.

Crabbe grunted as Lester finished the last stitch with a snip, he tried to sit up, but Lester pushed him back down on the gurney. "Easy man, this is not one of those movies where you can hop straight back into the action." Lester turned to wash his hands.

"Thanks," Crabbe finally said.

"You're lucky I still have that tracker thing on your phone, how the hell would I have found you?" there was affection in his voice.

Crabbe didn't respond, they had had this conversation a million times, he didn't need clairvoyance to know that Lester was into him, and sometimes he felt guilty for using him, but without Lester, Crabbe would have bled out several times over the past nearly 10 years, too bad he didn't swing that way.

He reached into his wallet and fished out five 100 dollar bills and laid it on the cold metal beside him. There was a full-length mirror across from him but he didn't look at it, he knew what he would see. His body criss-crossed by fading burn marks like someone had taken a burning pencil and drawn haphazardly across his body. His healing factor left burn scars all over his body. He didn't like the aesthetics but at least he was alive.

Lester was back to fuzzing over him, reasoning with Crabbe was a lost cause and he would rather save his strength. He checked the stitches and applied the bandages, then double checked. He knew it was a wasted effort, Crabbe would tear them off as soon as he could.

"Alright, I've tried my best to prevent any type of infection but it would help if you rested for a few days, after all it's 87 stitches but who's counting?" He picked up the money and shoved them into his back pocket. "You do know you don't have to give me money every time I sew you up right?"

"Thanks Lester, I appreciate it." Crabbe pointed at his jacket draped over a chair, Lester tossed it to him. "You really should slow down."

"As the great Thomas Shelby would say, maybe in another life." Crabbe staggered to his feet, his vision swirled for a moment before it settled into a haze, he felt like he was going to burn up.

"I'll drop you off," Lester said softly, the little he knew about Crabbe left him with more questions than answers but he kinda liked the guy anyway.

"No, thanks. I got the sure-you-love work to do," but Lester was having none of it.

"All of my patients are dead anyway, what are they gonna do? Get up and leave. C'mon I'll drop you off, it's almost closing time anyway." He started turning off the lights.

"I said I'm fine, I'll walk, I need the exercise." Crabbe gritted his teeth in pain, struggling not to let it show, his healing factor conveniently did not include pain relief.

"Like hell you do, not when you're carrying enough stitches to make a dress, c'mon." He helped Crabbe outside the door down the parking lot and into a blue Prius, each step, an explosion of pain for Crabbe, but the pain was the last thing on his mind. The beast within was still struggling to surface, he had tapped into the blood for barely a second but the rush of power he felt was like nothing he had ever felt. He looked out the window at the neon lights coming on as the bars and restaurants opened for business, for a moment, he thought he saw it all in flames. Then it was just neon lights again. He drifted off to sleep.

He came to just as Lester killed the engine in his drive,

"Thanks Lester," and before Lester could try to stop him, he hopped out of the car and came over to Lester's side.

"I don't even know why I bother." Lester grunted in frustration.

"Really, I'm fine, it's just a few scratches." Crabbe laughed.

"Scratches?" Lester looked like he would have a stroke.

"C'mon, I'll be careful, that reminds me, that BMW dude that got whacked, did someone claim the body?"

"Yeah, his aunt or something. Look, what are you doing tomorrow evening?"

Crabbe smiled. "We'll see about that."

CHAPTER 6

Perhaps it was the destiny Crabbe had been cursed with, but the moment he walked through the front door Morocco was on him.

"You did it, didn't you? I felt it!" Morocco's fierce stare was equal parts accusations and worry. Mr Kit, curled himself around Crabbe's shins.

"At least, let me take my coat off before we start the interrogation, don't you think?" Crabbe sighed, Mr. Kit growled in agreement.

"This is serious, Appleton!" Morocco was frantic "You think I don't know that? But can we do this some other time. I just almost died." Crabbe was taking off his shirt, he glanced over his shoulder at the floor to length mirror edged in purple obsidian, his stitches were already fading into blood red scars across his back, even without turning, he knew his chest and abdomen would look the same. So much for a beach body.

"It's only a matter of-" Morocco started to say before a large explosion from the sitting room, one of Crabbe's household wards had caught something. Crabbe sprinted in the direction of the noise, his wounds already forgotten, Morocco hot on his heels.

The flickering form of Stout glitched around the room as the invisible wards zipped after him in a magical whirlwind as he whirled around in confusion, his mouth twisted in a silent cry of alarm.

Crabbe waved a hand and the spells dissipated, Stout flickered some more before his form solidified like a high resolution hologram.

"Give me one reason I shouldn't lock you in a time loop with a thousand more of these wards right now?" Crabbe's voice was icy.

"You still need a reason?" Morocco almost screamed.

"I want to make them pay!" Stout snapped, taking Crabbe aback, even Morocco flinched.

"Make who pay?" Crabbe asked.

"Old Sal and the rest of them, they were mocking me like I wasn't ever there? Stout's eyes were clouded and faraway like he was still back at the diner. Crabbe shared a look with Morocco, "Stout tell us what's going on."

So he told them them of Old Sal and everything he'd been through to ascend the ranks; houses he'd set on fire, the policemen he'd bribed and then set up, the shops he'd looted, he probably would have gone on about the people he shot, but Crabbe had heard enough. "We're not killing anyone for you, Stout. That's not how we roll around here."

"Really? And what about the idiot who killed me? You ain't gonna make him pay too?"

"We're working on it, kinda have our hands full at the moment"

"With what? What's more important than this? I thought you wanted me out of your shit faces?"

A low growl rippled through the room as Mr. Kit padded into the room, there was no mistaking the bared teeth, even Stout stepped back a few feet. Crabbe smiled.

"Heaven knows that I'd eat wet jeans if it'd save me a minute without setting my eyes on you but for god's sakes, go away!" There was no smile in that last word.

Perhaps Stout would have stayed to argue the finer points but at that moment, the doorbell rang, the one dedicated to customers.

"Scoot Stout, time to earn my rent, I think I might have a way to bring your guy to justice-"

Stout snorted "To justice? Don't make me laugh." And then he was gone, in his wake, the nose tickling whiff of sulphur.

"That guy is getting on my nerves!" Morocco sighed.

"You don't have nerve endings, Morocco, you're a ghost. Now, get ready while I get the door." Crabbe was already off to his wardrobe, he had an appearance to maintain.

First he fetched the black coat with shiny chrome buttons that also served as charm stones to channel his energy. It was heavy as hell but he felt comfortable in it and he looked like those wizards in the movies, people ate it up. Then he looked for the top hat with a metal seal against psyche sneak attacks and telepathic compulsions, he'd learnt after an old flame, a Salem witch who had compelled him to strip down to his underwears as a Valentine's gotcha moment, he was able to break the hold before it got too risque two weeks later, he had the hat smothered in spells but since he grew out his lustrous afro, he never wore the hat these days instead choosing to weave the physic wards through his hair itself. There were the random sparks and tingles but as he soon discovered to his delight, the spell kept his hair quite moisturized. Today, the hat would be a prop and a conduit. He snapped a finger and muttered a drying cleaning spell he'd invented and put on a magic speed dial, his pants straightened out and his shoes instantly gleamed with polish.

The shooting pain in his back was coming back with a vengeance but he had to see this final appointment through, he had a hunch to confirm that might get Stout out of his hair even sooner.

Around him, Morocco was changing. The tweaking of the light, changing colours, lowering and increasing intensities, this was the moment Morocco got to shine and he carried out his duties with relish, by the time Crabbe laid his hand on the door knob, barely a minute had passed but the house, precisely the part the led to to physic lounge was lit up in hypnotic hues and aromas, clients often paid more than they bargained to, but Morocco would swear that had nothing to do with it.

"Ummm, Mr Appleton?" The man at the door was unsure of himself, he squinted repeatedly at the house number. "My name is Jason Fuller, I'm not sure I have the right address," he had a square face that was going soft. From the initial reading Crabbe had of him, he could tell that the man was struggling with loss and additional responsibilities but determined to make the best of it.

"Spot on, Crabbe H. Appleton, at your service. Come in please." Crabbe swirled around and led the way, a habitation spell locked the door behind them, Jason hesitated as he oriented towards Morocco's playground. "Is it just me or does it smell like sulhpur in here?" The man asked as he took his seat opposite Crabbe who sat with his coat spread out around him and found it all a bit dramatic especially the carved table in between them that held tarot cards, incense holders, an ouija board and more stuff Jason had never seen in his life.

"Don't worry about that, just some spell we're cooking for the police, helps them catch drunk drivers before they can get lead footed on the pedal." Crabbe said casually, he had just made that up, now he prayed he would remember it after this session so he could run it past Silva, maybe she might just pay him more. Business wasn't exactly thriving this month.

"Would you like tea, coffee or a soda?"

"Er..." he seemed unsure.

"A beer perhaps?" Crabbe sensed that Jason feared judgment on his drinking and the man had been indulging a bit more.

He hesitated for a second. "Something stronger would be nice."

"Whiskey 99 it is, and a fine blend too." He didn't need to say anything, Morocco was already on it.

As they waited, Jason seemed to withdraw into himself, but Crabbe caught on. "Jason, when we met on the bus two weeks ago..." Crabbe remembered feeling slightly nauseated by the pulsating black aura from Jason who sat morosely staring into the distance.

Crabbe would have been content to switch seats and let that be, had he not caught the reddish hue of Jason's aura, the telltale sign of brewing malevolence.

This man would soon be a danger to himself and others if nothing happened. So Crabbe had reached out and given him a card and offered to listen to him. Surprisingly, he had called later that night and booked an appointment, if only it was this easy to get clients... "there was something wrong with your aura."

"If you hadn't given me that card on that bus, I would have..." the man shuddered and looked away, "I don't know, but it probably would have made the national front pages."

The drinks arrived, floating on a silver tray. Crabbe watched with satisfaction as his client's eyes widened, that trick never failed to impress.

"What exactly do you do here, I'm not sure I understand Jason's eyes were still on the hovering tray, Crabbe flicked a finger and it floated away bobbing a little, he still needed to work on the balancing spell.

"I help you find answers. Let's just say I possess a specific skill set that allows me to probe inwards and beyond, to find the answers you need. I can talk to a dead relative for you, I can look into the future for you, I can look into the past amongst other things."

"What of these?" Jason gestured at the table where the black tarot cards lay face down. "Go ahead, pick one."

Jason turned over a card and flinched at what he saw, a tower struck with lightning and two people falling from it. "That doesn't look good."

"The Tower card which often represents sudden change, destruction, and an upheaval of sorts, you've recently gone through something that's-"

"Yes yes, My divorce one year ago," Jason was talking quickly now like he'd been waiting for a prompt. "It blindsided me out of nowhere, we'd been married for 17 years, can you believe that? Out of nowhere, I just can't...then I lost custody of the kids, I can't have my children everyday, do you know how much that hurts?" The man was miserable, his stone-like features were starting to crumble as he really began to process bottled up emotions. Just like many people who came to see Crabbe, they often needed a therapist more than the magical solution they sought.

"I understand how you feel Jason. Sometimes you feel like you have a part of your life all figured out, and it all just falls apart and it's hard to make sense of it. I understand this." Crabbe's mind flashed back several decades ago to that Saturday morning in the kitchen when his parents had told him about the curse in his veins and what it would mean for him and his life. All his dreams of going on to become a doctor or a lawyer or something, he couldn't even remember now, he remembered how bitterly he had cried as he tore down the metallica posters off his wall. "Pick another card Jason."

Jaosn was more hesitant this time. "It's a woman tied and swords I think."

"The eight of swords." Crabbe took the card. "You're struggling to move forward, you feel stuck and you think this is your life now, but that is not true, pick another card."

Jason did. "It's a compass, of some sorts."

"The wheel of fortune, to remind you that change is inevitable. What you do with it, matters even more than what has happened. Are you going to sit around feeling sorry for yourself or are you going to do something about it? The marriage is done, perhaps it's time you move on."

"I'm trying to, I am," Jason muttered.

"I'm clairvoyant, Jason, but I hardly need that to sense that you're one more sighting away from a restraining order."

"I just wanted to see my kids, she has no right to keep my children from me." His fists were balled up so tight, Crabbe was half worried he'd crack them.

"Yes, yet there's a way to go about it. Do you want to not see your children at all instead of once a week, Jason?"

He was quiet for a while. "No."

"You came here to see what lay ahead, the future is a blank slate Jason, you can either choose to write the story you want or you can let life write it for you."

"Jeez, you sound like my mother."

Crabbe chuckled. "I'm sure she's a lovely woman."

"Yes, I miss her so much, she often gave the best advice and baked the best cookies."

"Would you like to get a message from her?" Crabbe wanted to do something nice for the man.

"Like right now?" Jason was coloured with disbelief.

"Yeah, right now, you think I just read cards? Come on!"

Crabbe was already on his feet and heading to the back of the room where an ATM stood. It was painted in hypnotic swirls of colours that changed as you looked at it, a keypad with a palm read had been added.

"What is this?" Jason asked.

"Think of them as teller machines, but for communicating with passed away loved ones." Crabbe pointed out the features. "You put a bill in that receptacle by the keypad and place your palm on the reader and think of the person you'd like to talk to.

"You're kidding me!" Jason scoffed, "You're messing with me."

"Am I now? You haven't even tried it."

"Fine, how much?"

"A 20 is fine."

Jason reached into his wallet, pulled out a bill and stuffed it into the receptacle which immediately retracted and the machine came to life, actually. Morocco just activated it, he lived-ghosted for moments like this.

"Please place your palm on the reader and think of the person you'd like to reach," a voice ensured from the machine startling the daylights out of Jason who complied. The machine beeped rhythmically for a few seconds then there was a whirring sound and a slip of paper was slowly ejected.

Jason took the paper and his eyes widened in shock, "This is my mom's handwriting, this is a sheet from her favorite notebook, How did you do this?" He still could not believe his eyes and in that moment it would have taken all the angels in heaven to pry that note from his hands. As the man read his mother's note, the smell of freshly baked almond cookies filled the room causing him to frantically look around, when he looked up at Crabbe, his eyes were filmy. "Thank you," he whispered.

"You're welcome Jason, take your time, I'll be in the lounge."

When Jason emerged, he stood taller and seemed more sure of himself, Crabbe idly wondered what was in the note, but as a matter of professional ethics, he never asked.

"I didn't know what I was expecting when I booked this appointment but I'm happy I came," he sat down still treasuring the note in his hands. "Can I write you a check?"

"Of course, one more thing," Crabbe placed a business card on the table "If you're really serious about moving forward from everything holding you back, call this woman, Dr Penny, she's a therapist that I-"

Jason cut in "But I'm not sick in the head or anything... .I've just been going through stuff," he was ruffling through his pockets for his checkbook.

"I know Jason, this has nothing to do with being sick in the head or psycho, we're all going through stuff and sometimes we need someone who's trained to help us work through these issues so we can live a satisfied life."

"But, there's...it's just-Jason was struggling with the idea."

"Okay, think about this Jason, when you get a toothache, you go to a dentist, right?"

Jason nodded.

"You need surgery, you go to a surgeon right?"

Jason nodded, slower this time.

"When you needed a lawyer for the divorce, did you go to the dentist?"

"Of course not Mr Appleton." There was a little smile on Jason's face.

"And when you needed a haircut, did you go to your lawyer?"

"Okay, okay, I get it. I'll call her," he handed Crabbe the signed check and picked the card, slipping it into his shirt pocket. "Thank you once again, looks like I have work to do."

Crabbe grinned. Don't we all, I'll see you out."

The two men headed towards the door.

They were in the corridor when Morocco suddenly whispered, the spirit's voice tuned to the Octra, a frequency only demons and Crabbe could hear.

"He's had some contact with the Corvette driver. The psychic scent is faint and fading but I'm sure of it."

Crabbe groaned. "Are you sure?" His voice equally tuned to the Octra. A psychic scent was a powerful way of finding people without all the shiny tech gizmo.

Everyone you interact with over a period of time, gains a fleeting bit of you like a perfume that only certain noses can pick up.

If the scent of the Corvette driver was on Jason, he could be the missing link and this gave Crabbe a lot of trouble.

"You know what you have to do, you'll know when to make the jump."

"Yes. Crabbe, in position."

"In position? What are we? The marines?" Crabbe chuckled, but the spirit was gone.

Morocco hated making a jump via touch as opposed to crystals. With crystals, he had a clear path of entry and exit but humans were a literal hot mess with their psyches all messed up, you never know what to expect inside the dark dimension that was a human host. They could look all put-together and amazing but when you jumped inside them, you find the walls of jericho falling apart brick by brick, a neural cacophony of consciousness running as one big engine to keep everything in balance, they were the worst hosts because the presence of a spirit was a parasite that plunged through humans like a big clumsy dog stumbling through a doll house.

Plain catastrophe.

The spirits who knew how to make the jump and inhabit a human host could come and go, quiet as a whisper and stealthy as a mountain cat, leaving their hosts with as little neurological impact as possible. Morocco was one of those who was good at jumping because he'd had hundreds of years of experience.

Now, it was second nature to him. As the humans walked to the front door, he surged through the house from one crystal to another like a leaping gazelle, as he cleared the last crystal, he braced for impact before he slipped into Crabbe's consciousness like an expert diver into clear calm water except Crabbes' was a tumultuous wave of boiling water. Morocco hated being in here, the rate of raw power was like being tossed and turned out at sea in a raging storm in a little ferry. You could barely hold on for dear life. But he'd been here enough to know what to do. He settled in the raging storm and waited.

Crabbe was reminding Jason to call Penny and to take action in his life. Jason was nodding.

Crabbe extended his hand for a handshake, Jason clamped his hand and in that moment, created a human portal, a neural Panama Canal that Morocco swam through in a flash, bracing and impacting Jason.

It was like jumping into a tumultuous but unmoving lake.

The man staggered back, his eyes blurring for a second.

"Wow! That was powerful, I feel... full." Morocco settled into a lazy swim acquiring the psychic scent of the Corvette driver, all he had to do now was wait.

"I've heard it feels like that sometimes, farewell Jason, don't forget to call Dr Penny." Crabbe waved as the man turned towards his car.

"It really does reek of sulfur here," Crabbé sighed as the door swung shut.

If only he knew how right he was.

In the shadows of the oak, Stout shimmered and smiled. His current predicament came with a few perks, he could see into ghost planes and he had seen Morocco switch into Jason. The things he could do with a power like that.

CHAPTER 7

For a man who didn't make a lot of money, it was ironic how much many favors he owed Billy the repair guy, if billy could turn these favors to Benjamins, he would be able to retire far away from Crabbe and his rickety babies, but since that was out of the question, it had to be him rolling out of bed at six o'clock to open to the insistent knocking of a certain Mr. Appleton.

"So sorry to wake you up Bill, I ne-"

"Where?"

"What do you mean where?"

"Where's your car all bashed up this time, Appleton?" Bill grunted, he'd done this a thousand times.

Crabbe sighed "Don't be like that Bill, this has to be the first time this month."

"One day I'm gonna have a stroke and it'll be because of you, then we'll see whose door you're gonna be knocking on," Bill grumbled.

"I heard Jimmy is amazing with engines."

"Don't be a smartass, I'll get my bag."

The drive to the site was uneventful, but Crabbe was perched right on the edge of his seat. Billy's wife would kill him if anything happened to her husband.

Billy's jaw dropped off its hinges when he laid eyes on the mangled S-10; side caved in, headlights busted and a thousand other things exactly where they shouldn't be.

"Didn't I just replace this fender?" He kicked a piece of metal that looked like it used to be a fender.

"I should think so"

"How do these things even happen, Appleton? Let me guess, A drunk driver?" he reached into the back of his tow-truck for the chain.

"They just find me, I'm unlucky like that. Can we wrap this before your wife kills me?"

The scent of the demons was mostly faded, but Crabbe could still catch a whiff or two, there was no sign of demon remains, the earth's sunlight had a cleansing effect on demon corpses.

He muttered cleansing spells, the magical version of wiping fingerprints.

"I'll tell Emilia you were thinking of her," he double-checked the hook. "We're good to go."

"Can't thank you enough for this," Crabbe was quick into the passenger's seat.

"You owe me fourteen hundred bucks Appleton, but who's counting?" The S-10 grated along the gravel in a harsh moaning that bit at Crabbe's ears.

"Yeah, I keep hearing that a lot. I'll pay you. I promise."

"And I keep hearing that a lot. Maybe I should let Emilia know you ain't paying me."

"C'mon, don't do me like that Billy, Don't do me like that. I'll have your money, I'll drop off at Maries and Saints right near the grocery store."

. . . .

The Longs were in this time, Mr. Long opened the door with an eponymous face.

"Can I help you?" He stood squarely in the doorway, he was neither a tall nor imposing man, but he wore a terrible scowl that pulled the muscles of his face in a twisted arc towards his receding hairline.

"I'm Mason Briggs, I was here a few days ago to talk about your daughter, Miss Jenny Long."

"Yeah, what about her?"

"We haven't seen her in school?"

What did you say your name was again? The menace was starting to creep into his voice.

"Mason Briggs. I-"

"I called the school, they've never heard of you." The menace in his voice was there alright.

"Maybe they got the name mixed up, I don't know, Just checking in on your daughter?" Crabbe showed his palms in the classic non-verbal I'm not a threat sign.

"I don't appreciate you all up here asking questions about stuff that don't concern you, Mr. Briggs, is that even your name?" He took one step forward.

Crabbe didn't move, but when he spoke his voice was icy. "There's a lot of wrong and rot in the world, and there's nothing more I hate, than children being mixed up in that, especially by people who are supposed to protect them." The last word was almost a growl, Mr. Long didn't realize when he took a step back.

"Get off my property or I'll call the cops"

"I'll go, but I'll be back." Crabbe spun on his heels.

"What are you, the Terminator?" His voice had a slight tremor to it, he watched Crabbe till the man was out of sight, then he dug in his pants for his phone. It rang once.

"Yeah?"

"That man is back asking questions about Jenny, you said to call if he showed up again."

"I'll handle it."

The line went dead.

Two blocks away, a green van peeled off the sidewalk and raced after Crabbe as he walked to the bus stop.

....

A man lay dying on the pavement, the morning sun just beginning to poke out. He was dying from a brain aneurysm, one moment he was taking a brisk walk as he had done for thirty years, the next moment, he felt like he had been stabbed in the chest with a block of concrete, then he was on the ground losing consciousness.

Someone had called 911 but he would be dead before they arrived. Just another unfortunate life lost.

Except the man had died from a botched attempt at body jumping.

Stout had rushed into him like a whale jumping into a pool, shattering the man's neural delicacy into a thousand shards in the process, it would be a mercy if he died, his mind was shattered beyond repair.

It wasn't all roses for Stout either, a true brute even in death, he had learned the hard way, the jump left him simply through the tether, the multidimensional space that allowed ghosts to coexist with humans none the wiser.

Even as his ethereal being floated fractured and refractured, a plan was forming.

What was the plan?

What was one more human?

It would be like learning to shoot a gun.

He would master this and he would make them pay.

Everyone of them.

....

Across town Morocco was having a good time.

You don't always get to choose your host, least of all a host that's trying to get his shit together. It's like dredging a river of filth and watching the sun get all to the surface.

Any good jumper can make a host take any actions they want but an expert jumper was even more subtle, manipulating the threads of thought and action in a fine puppet show that left the host wondering why they did what they did but, blaming these actions on themselves. Mediocre to fairly good jumpers are the reason, 'the devil made me do it exists.'

Now that Morocco was on the inside, he initiated a scan of Jason's memories trying to pinpoint the psychic signal that was the Corvette driver. He dug carefully. This man was already emotionally charged, one wrong turn in this maze of a mind and he could drive him mad.

Carefully, he worked, sifting and searching.

As Jason scrambled his breakfast eggs, he suddenly wondered why he was thinking of that night at the club La Rozar. Last time had been a disaster, none of the women were looking his way and all the drinks were expensive.

So why did he want to go again?

Just as suddenly, the urge faded.

Morocco had found the memory, Jason and the Corvette guy had briefly been in the rest room for all of 5 minutes but that was more than enough.

Jason didn't know it yet but he would be clubbing tonight.

Crabbe loved to walk, it helped him think. The thing is, walking often got him in trouble, from the bullies who wouldn't let him be, to the demons who were just as annoying. Sometimes he didn't know which he prefered.

He had seen a lot in his lifetime, he had seen bone chilling horrors that would make the most hardened US Marine flee in terror, he had traveled to universes where the very soil itself ate your flesh as you walked and the air was poison, he had fought the very lieutenants of hell and yet, nothing got him angrier than involving children in this mess.

He often fantasized about retiring and raising kids, driving them to school, ball games and recitals, the American experience, and everytime he would shave his head and focus on the present, a dark world creeping with horrors that would have him for lunch just because they could.

He shook his head and turned up his collar. How was he going to find a little girl whose parents were complicit in her disappearance?

Was he even sure she was in danger? What if they sent her away to live with some relative?

Could he really trust Elmo and Hilda's judgment?

All it takes is one thought for you to get distracted even if half of your DNA is of hellish origin, one moment, he was taking a stroll down Marie's and Saints, the next, he was tumbling down a ditch. He heard someone scream but the pain exploding in his side was all he could think about.

Some idiot had hit him in the side with a car, sending him down the side, off a road into a glade. As he struggled to his feet and took in his surroundings, an uneasiness settled. That was premeditated. Right on cue, the green van tore through the glade headed straight for him, but this time he was ready, he flicked his arm in a redirection spell and the van's front wheels jerked violently to the side. The brakes squealed as it came to a stop and his assailants emerged.

They were humans through and through, Crabbe smiled and channeled his magic, they were at least 5 men in total.

They didn't know it yet but they had chosen the worst person on the planet to pick a fight with.

. . . .

It was first the perfume, a heady sensual scent that cut through everything else in the club to tease your nostrils.

Heads were turning, searching for the source, then he walked in, clad in a business suit and silk shirt that hung open at the neck, his attire was simple but conveyed a charisma that was new to him.

As he walked past one of the dozen mirrors, Jason wondered who that guy was, he looked so smooth, then with a jolt, he realized that that guy was actually him. His heart rate spiked.

WHAT WAS HE DOING?!

All of a sudden, he wanted to run and bolt but just as suddenly, he felt a calm permeate him and he continued walking, if he wasn't so absorbed in putting in trembling leg after the other, he would have realized that at least 4 ladies he normally would think were out of his league were sneaking glances at him, Morocco grinned to himself He'd had more fun than he expected making this night happen.

In the days of his humanity, Morocco had been quite the explorer of the sensual art, but getting Jason to follow through like it was an original thought had been tricky.

You never wanted to force a thought or action onto a host, especially acts in parallel with their personalities. With Jason, Morocco was able to dig up repressed college day exuberances and then refine it into a style that was uniquely Jason, at least. Morocco could only hope..

Of course it took a few credit cards and driving around all day to barbers and malls, but the end justifies the means, eh?

"What are you drinking tonight sir?" The barman quickly took in Jason at a glance, he looked like big bucks, he hoped he would be generous.

"Sir? C'mon Timmy, I'll have a b-" at that very moment Morocco snatched back the reins and jayson found himself saying "a perfect manhattan"

Timmy's smile was puzzled, "Right away...sir" he reached for the ice. "Do I know you?"

"C'mon Timmy, it's me, Jason, I drink beer here every Thursday."

"Jason!? That's you?!!" Timmy leaned in for a closer look. "No way! DO a little spin for your boy"

"C'mon man, just give me the drink." He could feel the eyes on him.

"You cleaned up nice, you smell like it too. You got a date here?"

"Nah, just stepping out for the evening." Even as Jason said it, he didn't know why he was here, he shook his head.

Morocco settled in and waited, as his influence receded from the fore of Jason's consciousness, he felt the man's panic simmering as his self image struggled to come to terms with his new physical appearance and the attention he was getting.

A Latina with a mane of black hair simmering in the soft lights and a gown that it looked like she was born in it twirled into Jason's sights and his heart stopped, then restarted in a panic fluttering, it was like he was staring at perfection and he had been cut adrift from time.

Then a sadness overcame him, he would never talk to this woman, she was miles away in a different league Timmy placed the drink in front of him. "Hey, that beauty over there has eyes on you."

Jason glanced over his shoulder, "What? No! She's definitely looking at you."

"Suit yourself" the bartender turned towards his next customer.

At that moment, Morocco sensed the man he was after entering the club, his psyche scent wafting into Morocco's equally psychic nose.

He unfurled like a tentative sail, his consciousness seeping into Jason's, binding to every molecule of the man's mind.

It was time to hunt.

The next 10 minutes remain a fuzzy blur in Jason's mind, so we'll look at it from Morocco's perspective.

To jump from a human to another human with finesse required something more than just momentary touch, that touch had to mean something, toucher and the touchee had to share a moment, no matter how small. No easy task when it's a stranger you're trying to take over.

Jason's heartbeat spiked as his body stood up, he didn't know why he was working towards the hot lady, it's like his body was thinking for him.

"You're expecting someone?" he leaned in to ask, his nose suddenly filled with a heady sensual perfume he knew must be very expensive.

"It depends, you wanna sit?" Her accent was European with a little Mexican chile, she looked like a woman who had grown into her female graces.

"Actually, I'd like a dance, they're playing the samba." He stretched out a hand with the cleanest nails in a hundred yard radius.

"Oh was all she said. Then she placed her perfectly manicured hand into his and stood up.

CHAPTER 8

Morocco was in full control now, Jason knew nothing of the samba As they whistled onto the dance floor, Morocco led the dance with a controlled abandon, the lady herself wasn't a slacker, she knew where to put each foot and she was dainty about it.

The locked and separated in unison, spinning and cycling and tapping to the rhythm with each step, Morocco led the dance in a direction only he could see, but brought him closer and closer to his target, a man in a blue beach shirt was dancing with a fierce lady, her red heels flashing and slashing.

This was the moment that would mean the most, as Morocco spun his partner, he positioned himself beside the man he'd been looking for, the song ended.

"Hey nice technique, your dancing is impeccable." Jason, reaching out for a handshake.

The man took the hand. "Thanks buddy, we do what we can."

The moment had lasted less than a couple of seconds, but it was enough, the Corvette driver who Morocco was learning about now as he diffused into the man's psyche was Alan Miller, his close friends called him Al, but most people knew him as Alan.

He had gotten the 1999 Corvette as a gift from his Dad, and since then, the sleek beast had been his one true love. On the day of the incident, he had been racing to meet up with his friends.

The switch was less smooth, Alan spasmed as Morocco rode the stormy haphazard waves that was Alan's mind, this mind was always racing. He had to tame it without breaking him. Alan was startled a bit.

"You okay fella?" Jason asked, placing a steadying arm on Alan's shoulder allowing the last vestiges of Morocco to transition.

Yeah, I suddenly feel... full"

"You know I've been feeling that way myself. Take care now."

I will. You too" Alan walked back to the woman who Morocco knew was named and was in a complicated situation with Alan, they fought a lot about everything but they also had the most passionate sex ever.

"Do you want to get out of here Al?" She asked as they finally took their seats.

"Umm yeah, where do you have in mind?"

"Goergians I'm in a mood for steak she was already grabbing her bag.

As they left the club, Morocco caught sight of Jason, he was at the bar chatting away with the lady who told Jason her name was Lya. They looked like they were going to have a good time.

Time to refocus, Morocco flitted through Alan's experiences searching for the day of the hit & run.

It was not there, he trawled through the library of recent experiences, nothing.

Alan and Lori were in the underground garage now. He pressed the keyfob and a black Corvette flashed its lights. For a brief moment, he thought about the paint job and how much it cost.

That was the thread Morocco needed to pull, but slowly.

"You've been awfully quiet," Lori noted as they picked up speed. He didn't reply.

The thread Morocco was pulling on took him into the deep recesses of Alan's mind and echoing chamber where the man had locked his most traumatic experiences. Morocco touched that memory and was hit by an onslaught of emotions Alan felt then and still now, a potent swirling storm of fear and guilt. He was trying his best to forget.

Morocco wanted him to remember.

They pulled up to an intersection, the left turn was down Valley Avenue and eventually Goergians. The right turn would take them down Shingle street and eventually the police station.

Morocco needed to make Alan make up his mind by himself if not his mind would be broken and all this would have been for nothing.

Morocco pulled on that thread, guided the guilt like a newly formed river to bleed into Alan's stream of consciousness. This time, this river was inked with a simple thought "turn yourself in now."

Alan gasped as the scene replayed vividly in his mind, then he fought it, throwing rationale and logic at the pictures playing in his head.

"It's not my fault that he wasn't looking I didn't mean to kill him"

"People die every day."

"Your hands are shaking? Are you okay? Lori was puzzled.

The lights turned green.

"There's something I need to do." He jerked the steering left and stepped on the gas pedal. Now Lori was alarmed. "What are you doing?! Georgians is the other way!"

"There is something I need to do!" Alan's knuckles were stretched as they gripped the steering lighter.

"What do you mean there's something you need to do? You always do this!" Lori half-screamed, she was fed up and tir-.

"I killed a man." Alan's voice, a shaky whisper.

Lori shrank away from Alan."You what?!" "Remember when I told you I hit a lamppost?"

Yeah? What does-" she trailed off as she put two and two together. "That was a man?"

There was fear in her voice. Alan saw it.

"I promise, it wasn't intentional, but I need to make this right."

"And how do you plan to do that?"

He didn't reply, he didn't need to, she followed his eyes, the Glencrest P.D. building was looming into view. More two and twos were put together.

"You can't be serious Al!"

"I need to make this right?"

"Alan, can we talk about this for a second" she was nigh hysterical. "It's already done baby, if they haven't picked you up now, You don't have to do this, don't do this!

Alan's face glistened with tears, he was fighting his conscience. A conscience powered by Morocco, Alan didn't stand a chance.

"I'm sorry" He slowed the car, then pulled into the parking space.

"Alan, you don't have to do this" She clutched at his shirt as he opened the door, trying to stop him but his mind was made up. "Walk with me?"

"Of course." What else could she do?

Morocco had to be careful now, he didn't want to overload Alan's neural pathways and trigger a meltdown, but he didn't have to do much. This man had a conscience even if he didn't always use it.

The policeman sitting behind the counter was half-asleep, today had been a slow day. He eyed the couple sauntering in, he wondered if they were coming to place bail for the man they had arrested this morning for breaking and entering. It was a little guessing game he liked to play.

No, they looked like they-

"I want to turn myself in." Alan said.

"What did you do, son?"

"I killed a man."

The policeman sprung to his feet, all traces of sleep vanishing, his wary eyes already assessing the situation.

"Can you say that again?" he rose slowly out of his seat, signaling two other police officers.

"I killed a man two days ago, A hit and run on the freeway, a red Corvette-" he saw the light come on in the officer's eyes.

"Please follow me", the police officer whose name was Jones stepped aside for Alan, they would need to ask him some questions, read him his rights and make an official arrest

"Al. You don't have to do this" Her voice was breaking. "Alan! Al!!" she called out as she reached for his hand one last time and in the brief warm contact, Morocco made the jump.

Afterwards Lori would be escorted and Alan would come to in a holding cell as his consciousness regained control, the last shred of Morocco guiding Alan to write a full confession, but leaving a part of his essence like that came at a cost.

He was getting weaker and needed to get back to his mannequin or risk well, he didn't exactly know what lay after the asciudation in that came as more of his essence fractured and dissipated

Lori's consciousness was a choppy mess that Morocco rode, he made no attempt to take control, instead he sent out psychic beacons that only Crabbe could detect, then he settled in again as his host retrieved her bag from the Corvette and it was driven into evidence lockup.

She picked a direction at random and started walking. Crabbe was leaning against a sign as she approached, and as she made to pass, his stepped into her path and they collided, she dropped her bag, he dropped a glistening pendant. "Miss I'm so sorry, didn't mean to knock into you like that." He picked her bag, ignoring the pendant that lay next to her feet. "No, No, I'm the clumsy one, I should have been looking." She pointed at the pendant. "Is this yours?"

"Ahh there it is, It must have fallen out of my pocket," Crabbe made to reach for it, but she scooped it up, stared at it for a second and handed it over to him.

The exchange was fluid, all she felt was a sudden shudder that rippled through her frame as Morocco exited into the pendant where he would be safe.

She suddenly looked disoriented.

Are you okay, miss?" Crabbe asked, he wondered if he should call a taxi. "No, I'm fine, I've just had a weird day. See you around stranger." She continued on. Crabbe watched her go for a moment, then he put the pendant around his neck and locked the clasp, which in turn completed the circuit that allowed Morocco to speak into his mind.

"Good job Morocco!" Crabbe whispered as he tucked his hands into his coat and trudged along. "Why do you stink of human blood?" Morocco asked.

"You don't want to know!"

"Of course I do, that's why I'm asking!"

"Doesn't mean I have to answer."

"Don't be a dick, why do you reek of blood?"

"You're a spirit, how are you able to smell?

"Blood drinks on more than one dimension

"What does that even mean?"

"Did I stutter?

And on and on and on they bickered, two friends happy to see each other again.

CHAPTER 9

What does a man with the blood of the devil coursing in his veins do on a Sunday?

The answer is; He goes to church.

Must be shocking that a man of the occult would find solace in the house of the Lord.

Except he wasn't there for solace, he was there for family.

Perhaps it is time we take a tour down the Appleton family tree, after Obadiah's fury demise, Sarah moved town twice before settling down in Texas where she set out to raise her two children as best as she could.

Elijah and Caleb Appleton would grow up to be strong brawny men, but we'll follow the breach of the family tree that leads straight to Crabbe Appleton, in this case..... Elijah.

He would eventually tow the part of his father and become a salesman while he played as a part of a jazz quartet on the weekends in the few clubs that let black people in.

It's in one of these clubs that he would meet Sortiana, a bright eyed biracial woman who taught at the local school. Elijah would offer to buy her a drink as the band setup which in turn would kickstart a whirlwind romance that would end up at the altar and lead to 5 children.

2 of those children, a sweet boy Daniel and his twin sister Grace never made it past the age of 7, and so again, leaving behind Samuel, Beanie, and Marcus. Again, direct line to Crabbe, so we focus on Samuel, who would grow in the midst of the civil rights movement and become something of an advocate himself, sowing the first seeds of philanthropy the Appleton family would eventually be known for. Samuel would die of a heart attack in 1961 leaving behind a son, Marcus Jnr, named after the little boy's flamboyant uncle.

Marcus would eventually father and raise 5 children in relative comfort thanks in part to a modest inheritance bequeathed by Marcus Snr.

Crabbe was the last of these 5 children and the one in whom the blood had boiled hot after running cold for decades.

Perhaps it was a comical irony that Marcus's first child and son would end up a Reverend and his last son would be locked in eternal loggerheads with the devil.

Crabbe chuckled at the thought of that as they all rose to sing a hymn.

"When peace like a river attendeth my way...."

....

Halfway across town, A man was seething. This is someone we would soon be familiar with, and went by only one name Hiram and he was the leader of a movement.

A movement that you've most likely never heard about unless you were more than casually interested in the occultic and something even more sinister.

He was annoyed for other reasons though.

When he had gotten the call from Robertson, and was told of a certain school inspector, he knew whoever the caller was, he was a liar plain and simple. He could not have known Jenny was not in school because Jenny did not exist, the girl who went to school was Maryam.

Calling her Jenny was his first mistake, but he had extended the benefit of the doubt because he was occupied with a more burning problem now the man had made a return and Hiram had tried to put an end to it, but maybe he had put his trust in the wrong people. He had played just the right amount of college football to be disgusted at the men who sat before him, unable to meet his gaze, five men was plenty enough to deal with one man. How hard could it be?

"Drew, can you go over the story again, I think something's wrong with my ears." He made a show of fiddling at his ears, but it was enough to convey his displeasure. "It's either that or this is the most batshit story I've ever heard."

"We don't understand it either, it's like the bushes came alive at once and..."

"I'm going to stop you right there. Have you been messing with those stupid drugs again?"

"Hiram, I'm telling you.." Drew looked to his gang for support. Guys back me up here"

"He's right Hiram, this is some voodoo shit" Ellis, the brawny dude who scoffed at deodorant, spoke up.

"Voodoo? That's nonsense! All I hear are excuses!" But you see, it wasn't nonsense after all, even if these men don't understand any of it, something incredible had happened to them. It was supposed to be a routine shake-up, they did this kind of work all the time. The boss didn't like somebody and wanted you to let that person know they weren't liked, violently of course. But this man with the afro and the trench coat was different, they had followed him down a side road and into what could have only been a glade.

Of course they hadn't wondered why a lone man walking had suddenly diverted off road. Why would they? He was just one man and would be making it easier for them anyway.

If only they had known. But perhaps it was for their own good that Crabbe was in a tolerable mood. A man who fought demons to death against a bunch of humans, you can guess how horribly it could possibly end.

So indeed the bushes did come alive, lashing and grappling at the men as they jumped off the van, and in the middle of it all stood the man they had come for, hands akimbo in the storm of leaves and twigs.

When it was all over, they had more welts than they had hair, a truly sorry mess, itching and scratching as several cocktails of sap permeated their skin, it would be several hours before they had the strength to even flee from the scene.

Let's come back to the room, Hiram, even as he blew hot, knew voodoo was not nonsense. That same voodoo or a variation of it was the reason he was dealing with these knuckleheads.

There were terrible households that should have never been allowed to have or even worse, raise children then there was the household that he grew up in. A catastrophe, a father who told everyone he was an army vet but anyone who bothered to look at his records would have seen he never made it past basic training before he was kicked off for being a slovenly slob, he was not the kind of father any child would have wanted.

The situation might have been salvageable if Hiram's father had not taken up with a woman who was having trouble raising herself from a drug addled haze never mind raising a child but somehow these unlikely duo managed to procreate and raise a child Hiram, for all their slobbery and drug use, Hiram turned out mostly alright. He loved them as parents but despised them as people.

He was a huling fellow who didn't know what he wanted to be, but he sure knew what he didn't want to be, and that was broke, dirty, and living in a slovenly apartment with the doors half hanging off the hinges. A football scholarship had taken him across the country from Iowa to THIS CITY but just a few weeks into his sophomore year, he was caught boosting tires in the parking lot, the next month, a security officer stood at his dorm door as he threw his meager belongings into a duffel and left the university premises for the last time.

He would disappear for several years before reappearing 4 years later as the leader of a shadowy underground club that no one knew exactly what they did.

The rumors were Hiram was the man you meant when you needed something that no one else could give you, all you needed was a collateral. There were also the rumors about a man who used to be his roommates but suddenly disappeared. The police department had dropped the case due to lack of circumstantial evidence, but he still got the look, unless you needed his help.

If you wanted a case dropped, an election won, a bet won, a little this and a little that, if you asked the right people they could point you in the direction of the man known as Hiram.

Sometimes you had to part with your Bentley, or your vacation house or maybe those stocks you had in Facebook or something, it didn't matter, if your need was important, you had to cough up something.

....

There was a time that Appleton questioned God and everything sacred, those days when he fought demons and slew monsters from the bottom of hell who sought to vanquish his soul. In those days, as he slashed and

65

stabbed he wondered if this was his God ordained purpose, it made him laugh sometimes.

As his brother Tomas who led this congregation stepped up to the cherry oak pulpit, a little jig in his walk and the microphone gripped tightly, Crabbe found himself chuckling but stopped almost immediately, the white haired granny a pew away was glaring at him. She wouldn't understand.

As the church dropped to their knees for prayers, Crabbe did a cursory look around out of habit, he didn't expect a demon here of all places but old habits die hard.

The church was an old castle that had been bought and renovated as a community project, with arches and curves that soared and intersected in a dome, the church had never had more than a few hundred attendees at any time, but as Tomas would say, "quality over quantity." But Crabbe was on the lookout for a phenomenon more sinister than any demon; the twins; Brian and Brandy, also known as the police. Two scrawny brats afflicted upon his sister Blossom as children and who earned their nickname for their insufferable antics, chief among them stirring laxatives into the communion wine. They loved Crabbe to death and swarmed over him like ants whenever he decided to drop by. He would battle a thousand demons before he let any harm come to them, but just like everyone else, he was wary of the devious ingenuity they could collectively come up with. He scanned the pews at the front where his family had by force of repetition enforced as the Appleton area.

A fiery headed woman froze as his eyes fell on her, then she turned, met his eyes, and her face broke into a smile, Lilac, the youngest sibling who went and came as she pleased. She waved at him to join her, patting the space beside her, nevermind that the entire church was caught up in the mumble of prayer, Crabbe blew her a kiss and shook his head while gesturing with his eyes to the fidgeting man beside her, she rolled her long-lashed eyelids and stuck out her tongue in a retching motion that man was a big reason she didn't attend church as regularly as she preferred. As he rose into his seat, he spotted Brian, one of the twins crawling under the pews with the most wicked of smiles on his smug face.

Oh boy!

....

The man stumbling down the sidewalk was going through hell, his head was on fire.

Not literally of course, but as he staggered through the sea of bodies, he felt like someone had lit a fire in his head, that burned as it yanked and pulled, a pain that was like nothing he had ever felt in his life.

But there was really nothing he could have done, he was the victim of a vicious inexperienced jump.

He crashed to his feet and tore at his hair, pulling out bloody clumps that he shoved into his mouth, a look of pristine terror etched on his face and reflected in the face of passersby.

Stout was having so much fun actually, he was body jumping like a pro and he didn't even need that snotty nosed Morocco after all. Of course it had taken a few trials and errors, but no one would find the broken bleeding bodies of those homeless folks with their neural synapses fried to a crisp from Stout's forced entry, nobody cared about them that's why he had chosen them.

The first person Stout had possessed, he had barely taken a step before the man's mind snapped and the man crumpled into a heap, before he had hit the ground, Stout had already jumped into the woman gawking at the body spasming at her feet.

This man's name was Billy, a construction worker and father of three, when he arrived for work this morning.

he had an idea of how his day would go, his mouth was watering at the thought of what his wife had packed for him to eat at 1, he had reminded himself that he had to leave work earlier today to beat the rush downtown so he wouldn't miss Richard's recital, his first son would hate him if he missed it again, but as he jerked and thrashed, his head splitting in pain, every thought recitals and pastrami sandwiches forgotten as Stout ran rampage across his mental landscape, fracturing his consciousness.

"Hey Buddy, you okay?" someone asked. Billy swung his inflamed head around, his eyes were bloodshot and glaring, actually, Stout was doing the swinging, the spirit tottered on legs he hadn't managed to walk properly with yet, but he could smile and he smiled widely. The man who had asked the question had something he wanted so badly. The access that the shiny badge clipped to his belt gave him.

"Yes, I need help." Stout still didn't know how to work the vocal muscles yet, and his voice came out cranky and guttural,

The man stepped closer, "Sir, how can I assist you, you do not look okay."

"You can help me get revenge, officer" Stout croaked.

"Sir?"

"Come closer"

The man hesitated, the man tottering in front of him had no weapon, he looked drunk as seven bars, but in his eyes, there was a menace that had the police officer's fingers inching closer to his holster, then he shook himself out of it. This man was only a danger to himself, he took a step forward.

Stout jumped into him.

CHAPTER 10

For all his experience evading and battling demons from all planes and dimensions, he still could not avoid being cornered, as the services had winded up, he had kept his eyes peeled for Brain, but he couldn't have prepared for Brad dropping straight from the galley above onto his shoulder, the only forewarning he had was the collective gasp of the church a split second before the boy dropped. Crabbe had looked only in time to get a faceful of ass. At that very moment, Brian sprang up from under the pew Crabbe had just vacated and sprang onto his like a four limbed spider.

"You are now in the custody of the police!" The children yelled in unison flashing the wickedest of smiles. Crabbe fell to his knees and raised his hands in fake surrender. "Please officers take it easy on me" he was flashing an equally wicked smile.

"We want chocolates, lots of it!" Brad managed to say as he tried his best to maintain his perch on Crabbe's broad shoulders. "Or we'll have to bring you in for trespassing"

"Oops!" it was Brian who first got a whiff of real trouble, a very pissed blossom was stalking towards them, "Seek cover! Seek cover!" and with speed and agility that would color a US Marine green with envy.

they scrambled out of sight leaving Crabbe to deal with their mother.

"Crabbe Appleton! What do you think you're doing?" Her voice was quiet but cut through all the noise and her face was a mask of displeasure.

"Hey sister! Can't you see I just had a run in with the police?" Crabbe said with the straightest face in the history of straight faces.

Ugh! Why do you encourage them?" her mask slipped a little.

"We should all strive for law and order and of course chocolates," Crabbe said solemnly.

"Preach!" one of the twins yelled from a safe distance. Blossom rolled her eyes, her mask cracking into a tired smile, "you're a bad influence on those boys, I hope you know!"

"I wouldn't have it any other way." Crabbe grinned and pulled his sister into a hug.

"Your hair smells nice B."

She blushed.

"Where's Harold? I haven't seen him since last Thanksgiving." Crabbe threw an arm across her shoulder in a familiar motion, she was a feet shorter than him but twice as fierce, auburn hair framed her face and her sleeves were always folded, a pastime from her work as a high school chemistry teacher.

"He's been deployed to the Black Sea for a drill, the SS Beauchamps I think." As she spoke, she guided them towards the front where the rest of the family were chatting.

Tomas spotted him first and came over to hug him, "Hey Lobster, you look like shit."

Crabbe laughed. "You're supposed to be the reverend Tom!" His voice effecting mock shock. "Where are your rascals?"

"Sage and Randy are off back-packing in Europe, but you know Parker, where Randy goes, he has to be, now's it's just fancy but she's back home with a fever sour as a puss cos she couldn't go with them" Trudy said from behind Crabbe, smacking him upside the head and darting out of the way, Clover went after her.

"Clover and Charles will be home this Christmas with the children, that should give me enough time to find a coffin that'll fit you" Tomas said as they watched the women go.

Crabbe shook his head in confusion, "why would I need a coffin?"

"When was the last time you called her?" Tomas asked.

"Oh Shit!"

"Yeah, you'll be staying for lunch, won't you?"

Of course, I won't miss your terrible pot roast for the world"

"That's how you end up with a empty plate boy"

Tomas growled before he was caught up in a crowd of parishioners.

Crabbe made his way towards Lilac, the church was emptying out as more worshippers filtered into the sunlight

Crabbe smelt him before he saw him, Milton, the deacon who had taken it upon himself to torment Crabbe with his existence.

"Look who showed up today, thought you had forsaken the congregation of the bath voices," was a rasping staccato that reminded him of falling tiles

"Milton! Have you managed to pull that stick up out of your ass yet?"

Milton blushed a deep red, started to stammer a response then thought better of it and stormed off.

"Crabbe, one day that man is going have a heart attack and it's gonna be because of you"

"C'mon Sis, it's a war out here, it's either me or him"

"C'mon, I'm starving, Trudy swears by the pie, we'll be having lunch." She picked her bag off the pew and laced her arm into Crabbe's.

"When are you not thinking of food Li?"

"Look at me, I eat anything I want and I don't add an ounce, and you think I won't milk this blessing" She smiled a truly devilish smile. "No pun intended."

"Blessing indeed, you're not the one who has to fight a ton of demons" Crabbe pretended to sulk.

"Don't be so grumpy, all that exercise, you must be in pretty good shape, I'm sure officer what's her name must be swooning all over you

"First, it's Silva, second, isn't the dear Deacon Milton the one God Almighty has promised you?" Crabbe was sensible enough to free his arm before he said that. The murder in Lilac's eyes was the only warming he got before she lunged at him, intent on cudgeling him to death with her Chanel handbag, he saw it coming and took off down the aisle, she streaked after him...

Just like old times.

....

The leaves rustled like a thousand vipers as the Mazda snaked down the path that led down to the factory that used to be a mine, no one with a bit of sense came here these days, there have always been a dread around this place, some people said the place stank of death and decay but it could have been just talk The six men definitely felt it. Hiram's fist clenched the steering wheel like he wanted to snap it off and beat someone to death with it.

But these men were each lost in their own thoughts, Drew with the scraggly jean overalls he washed once a month, Wally with a face like he was sucking on lemons, Levi who seemed to have forgot how to shave, Ellis, the guy with only one life concern, where he could get his next bottle of beer, Stan, former dealer who was trying to save up some money to go big in Hollywood. They were all lost in their individual thoughts but if they could hear the thoughts in Hiram's head, they would have been chilled to the bones.

A curse escaped Hiram's lips as they crept forward, he cursing himself for picking up that damn book when he should burnt it or thrown it out looking back on it now he should have seen the signs, a bidding site with no ads and only one item, a book that swore was the lost script of Lilith, first wife to biblical Adam and supposedly the mother of all demons to roam the earth.

The book had been dirt cheap too at 35 dollars, he cursed the fingers that clicked the BUY NOW button. Yes, he reveled in the mystery around his personality and the power it offered him but the day that book had arrived and he had held it in his hands, he could have sworn he heard a soft moan escape from the book as he ran his fingertips over the leather that felt strange and warm to the touch. But he had concluded the wind. Now he knew he had just been stupid.

Over the next few days, as he he read the book, a dread fell over him as he uttered those words, feelin the darkness forming in the air around him but even at that point, Hiram should have been fine until that night when he grew restless and went into his room to find the book open to spell so faintly written that he had to draw the dark shades to read it but as he uttered the first sentence "oh Orci incola.o esse tenebrae Graecae..." a sudden haze of heat blew into the room and try as he might, he couldn't stop the words flying out his mouth "amator carnis, potator corporis mortalis..." a jagged hole was burning in the center of his room, the wind was now howling with hot winds that rivaled a sandstorm in the Sahara. Hiram fell to his knees, tears in his eyes as he realized that he was in over his head yet his mouth refused to obey, chanting manically "ad haec te mortalia regna voco, o dea doloris" he had paid enough attention in latin class to realize that he was summoning a demon.

The howl that was a gravelling shriek was the cue that his unintentional invitation had been accepted. His roommate, Brown had chosen that very moment to walk into the room.

"Dude what the fu-" was all he managed to say before the abomination from hell had descended on him, razor sharp talon that dug into his gut ad ripped open his stomach like wrapper off a Christmas present, the demon reveled in the spray of blood and with an unearthly shriek, had dug into what once was a human being, Hiram cowered in the corner of the room convinced that he was the next item on the menu but after it was satiated, it had turned to him and spoken to him in a voice that reeked of evil the consistency of molasses and just as sensual, "are you the sorcerer that summoned me?" When Hiram raised his head, his eyes widened in surprise, a woman stood before him, her form flickered like a mirage, her shadow, a horde of swarming tentacles, she used what looked too much like a finger bone to pick her teeth. "You humans taste rubbery, is it, ummm, what do you humans call it?"

Hiram was too terrified to say a word.

"Are you lacking a tongue too?" she paused to survey him with bored feline eyes.

"What do we humans call what?" his voice, a hoarse croak.

"The thing that makes your cities hotter, and melts your glaciers" she bent to pick a scrap of flesh off the ground and tossed it into her mouth.

"You mean global warming?"

"Is that what you call it these days?" she stared at him for an answer.

"Are you going to eat me?" his voice still a croak away from breaking.

"Nothing would delight me more, but no, I'm bound to you in this realm and I'm rather liking my stay here, the air is much fresher here" at that moment, she had inhaled, a huge gulp of breath that seemed to draw all the oxygen in the room into her, a wet disgusting sound that made hiram's ear lurch.

"You're stuck here?"

"Not much as stuck but bound in covenant to you, to provide your heart desires if I so please, in exchange for....." she stepped into the glare of the light, and he finally saw the demon he had summoned. What he had thought was a gown was globs of mucus that hung in strands from her body, she moved like she didn't have joints and from every end of her spine protruded long tentacles that stiffened behind her, swishing and slashing with a mind of their own. "...food, lots of it, even now, the aroma of you humans is pleasantly overwhelming. Is something wrong with your legs?"

"No?"

"So why aren't you standing?"

Hiram rose to his feet but never really stood, inching away from her until his back bumped into the wall, she regarded him with contempt, and turned away

"What is your name?"

"The people born to this land called me Tsonokwa, the wild woman, I feed on blood, flesh, entrails, you know, your sort" she waved a dismissive hand in his direction.

"Tsonokwa, Did you eat Brown?"

"That was his name? The one that tastes like rubber?"

"Yes! Yes! Yes!! That's his name. Oh my God, you ate Brown?!" He wanted nothing more than to wake up from this nightmare, he didn't like the guy but he was decent enough to wish he would be hit by a truck or something, not mauled and devoured like bloody cheese sticks.

"What do you want, mortal? I'm growing impatient

"Can you bring Brown back to life?"

"As manure, yes"

"Then we have to get out of here immediately"

"I like how you think" Then she started to spin in a tornado of flesh that shrunk into an orb the size of an egg. As Hiram scooped to pick it, he already knew what suitcase he was gonna pack and the buses he was gonna take.

....

"A little child?" Tomas tapped his unlit cigar thoughtfully against his head. "I hate being stuck in between these things but they seek me out like flies to honey."

Tomas sighed. "Bees to honey, brother

"What?" Crabbe was hiding a smirk, he liked annoying his elder brother.

"Dickhead

"It would break our mother's heart to hear you cuss like that Crabbe nodded at the cigar, "why do you carry that thing if you don't even smoke it

"You don't look so good C, you've been sleeping well?"

"It's not so much the sleep but as what I do when I'm awake, something is brewing I can feel it"

"I know I can feel it too" Tomas shook his head and set the cigar aside. "Do you think it has to do with this missing girl?"

"That's what I'm trying to figure it, but i fear it's even much bigger, also something-"

"There you are!" Lilac was standing at the door, her petite frame looking even smaller in the doorway, she had changed into a yellow sundress fluttering around her in the afternoon breeze. "What are you boys gossiping about now?"

"Oh nothing, just the googly eyes that Milton was giving you today

"Crabbe, i will stick my fingers up your nostrils till i scratch your brain"

"Cmon, he likes you, Tomas back me up here"

"Leave me out of it" Tomas scooped up his cigar and kissed Lilac on the cheek, "I need to run the dishes before Trudy wakes up" He shared one last worried look with Crabbe as he opened the door. Lilac saw the look but she didn't say anything.

"You know it's crazy how much here has changed but somehow still looks the same" she looked wistful for a moment, "sometimes, I can't believe we all grew up here" "Remember that night Tomas and blossom snuck off to that concert and you jumped from the window and went after them in complete darkness and somehow thought you could walk all the way to Ashtown at 2 in the morning..."

"And of course, I lost my way and you sneaked out too to come find me and bring me home, of course! remember" she was laughing now.

"You're not still thinking of moving back here are you?" Lilac glanced atkin, why do you say it like that? If I recall you thought it was a brilliant idea at the Sin even though I suspect it's because you'd get me to run all your errands.The Lord hateth false accusations darling, but It's just something's been happening in the city, a dark presence that has me nervous.

"Does it make your blood boil? That was her way of asking if it had something to do with the double dose of the Appleton curse he had received which left him much more sensitive to the rumbling of the underworld but everyone in the family still had a drop of it which manifested in several ways, it helped Tomas with the premonition win a modest lottery at 35 that allowed him to focus on his love; helping people through his church and foundation, Lilac's was physical speed, once she hit it off, she was unstoppable and a mantlepiece full of track and field medals could attest to that, Clover had an uncanny intuition for reading people Blossom was the who had the healing touch, there was not a scar on her body, and she was never sick, Lilac was fast, a mantle piece full of track and field silverware could attest to that, when she got moving, it was like the winds were with her.

And of course, our dear dear Crabbe, a man in whose veins surged hell's blood, it was a wonder how he didn't spontaneously combust as a child, he was the child who had nightmares and weird stuff around him, except that time demons invaded his elementary school or that other time, he almost accidentally warped the 7 dimensions, you know, pretty regular stuff.

Now let's give these siblings some privacy to catch up, as we take a spin back to the sordid affair of Hiram.

CHAPTER 11

"What's that horrible smell?" Drew was the first to ask, his face scrunched up even further.

"Smells like really dead meat," Stan muttered.

"What's up boss, where did you say we were going anyway?" Ellis asked.

"I said we're going to solve a problem, you drunk punk." Hiram spat.

Ellis chuckled. "Reckon we can get a cold beer, I'm not prickly, I could settle for a natural light at this point, and may-"

"Man, shut the fuck up!" Someone snarled in the back. Ellis was not one to back down but there was an ethereal chill in the air that wouldn't let him say a word so they all fell quiet again, giving us a chance to escape into Hiram's mind.

Maybe Hiram could have reached a compromise of sorts with Tsonokwa that allowed him to get even a semblance of what he wanted. Even now as he thought of it years later, he shuddered, as a chill ran through his body.

That night, he had stirred to find Tsonokwa sprawled, staring at him under hooded eyes, her spiny tentacles undulating in a nauseating hypnotic motion.

He remembered how he had surged from the bed in fright and the whiplash spread those tentacles that latched onto him and threw him flat onto the bed covers.

"Where do you think you're going boy?" Her words were a slurred hiss that crawled over his skin leaving a trial of goosebumps erupting.

"Get the fuck off me!" He fought the restraints that bound him but for all the good it did him, he could have been pushing a wall.

"You're not happy to see me" she slid up him, her skin cold of the touch, a layer of mucus dripping off her fingers as she ran them across his cheek. Hiram snatched his face away.

"I said, get the fuck off me!" He was bucking like a mad man now, but this seemed to only excite the demon, this was the part she never told any of her hapless victims, she had an insatiable sexual appetite and the summoner was bound to oblige at Tsonokwa's discretion.

Hiram was a man who prided himself in being a pureblooded stallion between the sheets, that first night, Tsonokwa thoroughly abused that notion from his mind. At first he had to be bound and gagged to get going, then slowly, he didn't scream or fight as much anymore, on some days he just lay there, numb and sore everywhere that mattered. She was not jealous, but she didn't leave much for anyone else, his then girlfriend had called him an empty husk before she promptly dumped him.

She in her own way had taught him how to speak and what to say to build a following, how to talk the money out of their pockets and how to have them, he strayed on the gray line and after fleeing across the country to escape the scandal about his brother, here he was in Glencrest, and this is where it all started to fall apart. Tsonokwa would eat nothing but flesh. All the butchers in the city knew him. Since they arrived in Glencrest, she had grown haughty and insufferable. Apparently she now yearned for the blood of a descendant of the fallen. A child born from the line of the Nephilim, they came as rare as diamonds because their blood held the potency to bind Tsonokwa to the mortal realm and finally do away with her bond with this earthling.

Hiram found out the later part in a library hidden in a little town in Nashville, a little book that could fit in a pocket, where a man that had been deemed medically insane had scribbled that if Tsonokwa drank of the blood of the fallen, she would have have freedom to wreak havoc on earth.

Hiram had trembled as he read the scribbled words, he had made a mistake.

Back in the present, he shook his head. They had long arrived and now he had to find a way to do what he needed to do.

....

Uptown just past the ridge, if you take your right and continue straight ahead, you're sure to come up on the Glencrest police department building, a former bank building that had been taken over by the state and gifted to the police department as part of an expansion drive.

It was big, ugly and presented a mean face to all who would err on the side of justice. Perhaps that was the plan all along.

Our story takes us deep into the bowels of this building where the holding cells are located. Alan was the only one in the cell, an airless box that smelled like mold and rust, he cast a sullen figure as he sat hunched over in the chair provided for him.

Since he first wrote down a statement he had refused to say another word on the advice of his lawyer who was on a trip to Vegas and was going to jump on the next available flight back.

Alan had no way of knowing that a man had just walked into the building, well, more like staggered, the navy blue shirt of the Glencrest P.D. uniform hanging limply off of him was the first sign that all was not well but he had never been a model officer to begin with.

His name was Corporal Lorne, a loud, brash man who had already been suspended twice for improper conduct, these days most of his colleagues gave him a wide berth so it's hardly surprising that anyone glanced at him twice, if anything they gave him an even wider berth, Lorne was unpredictable when he looked like that.

"Hey Lorne, fancy seeing you here, though you were out on patrol?" the officer at the reception island called. Lorne staggered past without a word. The officer shrugged, it was probably for the best.

10 years ago. He used to have an office, until everyone came to work on Monday and found out that he had thrown a party in the same office, along with a demotion came a desk on the floor, it was a wonder how he had still managed to last in the force this long. His colleagues would never admit it to his face but he was a damn good patrolman.

When the investigators from Washington would look over this case later, they would attribute what happened to a laxity of rules and general oversight, but if they had been there that day watching Lorne stumble across the foyer to the elevator, you would have thought he was in another one of his sour moods, or at worst, he was inebriated on duty, and it was a matter of which higher ranking offer saw him first and subsequently kicked him out of the building None of them could have any way of knowing that Officer Lorne was little more than a puppet in the hands of a spirit who had no idea what he was doing but learning fast.

Stout rode his hosts the same way he rode his BMWs rough, hard and easily disposable, unlike Morocco who tried to go with the flow and not break them, Stout wanted to see them break. Now he was excited and while Lorne may have cut an apprehensive figure, all that was Stout's excitement bleeding into Lorne's nervous system. It was taking all of Stout's skills to keep the man's feet in a straight line as he accessed his memory searching for what he needed, Lorne walked over the elevator and hit the -1 button that led to the first sub-basement floor which served as the holding cell as well.

Lorne hardly ever went down there, he was the guy who brought them in and let someone else take it from there, even now, as he stood in the empty elevator as it hummed down the shaft, he still didn't know why he was going down there, he was even more surprised that his hands were taking his sidearm out of the holster, and taking off the safety, a cardinal crime in the Glencrest police building since the infamous shooting incident ten years ago, when a suspect had grabbed a gun from the sergeant who had brought him in and went on to shoot and kill 5 officers, before a SWAT sniper had taken him down.

As the doors slid open, he swallowed hard, his heart pounding in his ear, he didn't know it but he was sweating profusely and his blood pressure was already through the roof. He took a step forward and stumbled to his knees, his cap flew off his disheveled hair, Stout was taking a toll on the man's body.

Across the foyer a man was lounging in his chair, legs up on his desk with a nameplate that said Sgt Henry who was apparently lost in a paperback Sidney Sheldon, brows furrowed in concentration, it had taken him years to tune out all the usual rabble that ensued on this floor and concentrate. This would form the basis of his defense later when questioned as to why he hadn't seen Lorne till it was too late, the truth was much simpler, Henry like everyone else didn't give a shit about Lorne

Alan heard the elevator open and for a second he thought his lawyer had somehow managed to get here, he shot out of his seat but it was only another police officer. Alan hissed, he was turning when out of the corner of his eyes, he saw the man stumble. "Hey officer, you good?!" he called.

Henry raised his head at the suspect's voice, then his eye fell on the figure hunched in front of the elevator.

"What are you doing here, Lorne?" his voice a drawling echo. Lorne waved, that was all Henry needed to return to his book, but Alan was not confused, he pressed his face between the bars to get a better look. The man on his knees didn't look good.

Lorne raised his head and met Alan's eyes and for the first time in his life, Alan felt true fear, he had never met this officer in his entire life but he could swear that the man hated him with a passion, but even as he watched on, the man started to twitch and rise to his feet at the same time. Jerky spasms that rippled through him like an electric pulse but through all of it, Lorne's eye never left Alan and try and as he might, Alan couldn't look away, not even to look at Henry for help, but that would have been futile, Henry was engrossed with the book in his hand.

What Alan was witnessing was real-time destruction of the Lorne's remaining neural defenses. With each spasm, Stout forcefully took control of every motor function that would allow him to do what he needed to do now. Instead of putting the thought of walking towards a particular direction and compelling his host to walk, he took control of those very limbs and walked -twitching and all- towards the terror stricken Alan, it was time to settle the score.

Poor Lorne, no part of his law enforcement training could have prepared him for this mind bending torture that could break grown men in half without breaking a sweat but the thing in his head raged in his head and the synapses in his brain snapped one after the other under the overload of vile hate that even his loathing for that dipshit Suprintendent Murphy paled in consideration to. This was pure distilled hate pouring from eyes that used to be Lorne's and Alan was trapped in its dark light.

Henry turned a page.

The twitching stopped. Lorne was gone. Stout smiled, and that broke the spell on Alan, he reeled back. clattering into the side of the chair and sent it screeching across the cell, the sound echoed in the silence.

Henry looked up sharply, "for goodness sakes! Be quiet, will you? What do I look like? Your babysitter?" He barely glanced at Lorne before his head bowed again. When he would be questioned later, he would say the book was hard to put down.

Lorne was standing right outside Alan's cell, he peered curiously at the man sprawled on the floor and felt an immense satisfaction in his helplessness. "Get off the floor!" Stout's tone was cold and angry. Alan found himself complying.

"You're the lackey who likes to hit people with their shiny cars, yeah?"

Alan remembered the words of lawyer screaming over the phone "don't say a fucking word till I get there!" He would not give this man the satisfaction he wanted.

"You like to go voom voom in that daddy's car and hit people huh?" Lorne was snarling now.

"Shut up!"

"Yeah, I know your type, you have everything in the world, hakuna matata, no worries, I bet your fancy sleek talking lawyer is on his way here to bail you out and probably found a loophole that'll let you remain the asshole that you've always been.

"You know nothing about me, " Alan's face had turned red with anger, he couldn't help himself now. "You know absolutely nothing about me, " he was screaming now.

"You know nothing!"

"Lorne, can you stop being an asshole to our guest? Henry put down his book, "What are you even doing here, shouldn't you be out in the streets finding perps to put in here?"

If Lorne heard Henry, he did not move, his entire attention was on the angry man separated by steel bars. "Did it feel good when you killed me?" He pressed his face between the bars, there was pure madness in his eyes. The confusion on Alan's face was priceless, all he could say was "What?!"

Lorne smiled and in what was an impossibility, his facial features morphed into a face Alan thought he would never see again. Last time he had seen that face, it had been twisted in death.

"What the fuck!" Alan reeled back, clattering into the poor chair again but this time, he scuttled even further backwards, when he looked again, Stout's face was gone but he knew what he had seen.

Time seemed to stand still, and in that frozen moment, Henry was running towards Lorne, but he might as well have been running through jelly for all the good it did. Brandon was paralyzed with fear, his eyes locked on the barrel of the gun, his voice caught in his throat.

Lorne's finger tightened on the trigger. The gunshot echoed through the holding cell, a deafening explosion of violence and death. A plume of red blossomed on Alan's chest, and he crumpled to the ground, his life extinguished in an instant.

Henry reached Lorne just as the metallic tang of blood and gunpowder filled the air. His hands closed around Lorne's wrist, wrenching the gun from his grip and tackling him to the ground. Henry was screaming into his radio, But it was too late. Alan lay lifeless, a crimson pool forming beneath him, and the taste of bitter tragedy heavy in the air.

Henry would never know it, but the man he was now putting the cuffs on was innocent Stout was long gone.

CHAPTER 12

There's a story that when the founding fathers of Glencrest arrived to lay the foundation of this city, they drank a toast in the Bull's End bar. Of course, you'd best take that tale with a pinch of salt, sugar, or whatever condiment you fancy. The point was Bull's End had always been around in the city, everyone of drinking age had had a beer or two there. During the second world war when there had been a shortage of men of drinking age, the bar was always full.

The Bull's End bar had a charmingly rustic interior, with weathered wooden beams and dimly lit chandeliers that cast a warm, inviting glow.

Tonight, it was roaring, a band from out of town, the Timothies was playing; a shimmering cacophony of tunes that were quiet enough to talk but melodious enough to tap your feet to.

Perhaps that was why most people didn't notice the man who sat in a private booth, nursing a bottle of scotch with hands that trembled every now and then. He was not deaf neither did he hate music but tonight, the only sounds he could hear was the ripping and shredding and screaming.

Hiram hadn't been able to sleep, the images of the gore he had witnessed, -no, he had facilitated- flashed before his eyes like a broken reel. Finally at 2am, he got dressed and took a cab to Bull's End where he had ordered the strongest whiskey in this damned place.

Even now, he could still smell the blood and the guts. He gulped down another fiery mouthful, it was a miracle it didn't go down the front of his shirt, he peered at his fellow drinkers, did they know what he had done? Could they smell the blood on him? Was that guy by the bar looking at him?

Then he started to laugh at the ridiculousness of it all. A laugh that quickly turned into a hacking cough that drove him to his knees.

His eyes were watery when he finally managed to breathe without a cough, a waiter came over with a glass of water.

"Sorry buddy, here you go."

"Thanks man."

"That's a nasty one there, you should get it looked at." The waiter peered at the angry red welt glistening on the back of Hiram's neck. "Did you get into a fight with a bear?"

"Mind your business," he said gruffly and turned up his collar.

The waiter raised his palms in a gesture of surrender. He knew better than to exchange words with a man who had drunk a bottle of whiskey by himself. "Well, we've got some nuggets cooking in the back, do you want some?"

"Sure, bring another bottle too," he hadn't eaten in days.

"Gotcha, be right back!"

When the steaming plate of chicken arrived, Hiram could not bring himself to eat a bite.

Was this who he was now? A murderer? Tsonokwa's laughter swirled in his head, toying with him, teasing him, calling to him, taunting him. Yes, he was a murderer.

He shook his head dully and pushed the plate away, he took another swig of whiskey, the alcohol bringing back the memory of Tsonokwa's tentacles lashing out hungrily, latching around the men's knees so hard they had snapped one after the other in a sickening crunch that was barely audible over their screams of pain and confusion that echoed in the tiny space. Ellis was the first to go, he was still screaming when Tsonokwa reached into his mouth and using his jaw as leverage ripped his head clean off and tossed into a corner, she liked saving up brains for later, she plugged her lips to the spurting fountain of blood and drank long and deep. One by one, she tore through her victims and as they flailed in the darkness.

One by one, 5 grown men were reduced to a pile of bones. Hiram remembered flicking on the torch to see nothing but a pile of rags that used to be clothes, then slurping sounds had drawn his attention to Tsonokwa scooping the brains out of what used to be Piper's head, she smiled at him and the bile that had been threatening his throat finally unleashed and he didn't stop retching till his stomach was empty.

Afterwards, he would drive back into town and crawl into bed but the night was far from over.

It was that rotting smell he'd come to associate with her that alerted him that Tsonokwa was in the room. He lay as still as he could, maybe she would leave him alone.

"You fed me well today Hiram," she toyed with his name, drawing it out, he felt her climbing into bed. He rolled over, might as well get this over with.

"Isn't this better than the Nephilim you're always going on about?"

"Nothing even close mortal, you have no idea." She licked her lips hungrily, and in that moment Hiram knew that his plan to keep her occupied with human flesh would not work.

"Now, I'm in a mood."

She ripped off his pants.

....

Lily was flying back that morning and of course she wouldn't stand for a taxi, nothing short of her big brothers dropping her off at the airport, Tomas and Crabbe were grumpy but they hopped into the their pants and lugged her luggage into the back of Tomas's Highlander,

"Young lady, Do you have a whole store in here?"

Crabbe grumbled as he pushed open the front door. "Losing your touch old man?" Lily fired back, Tomas laughed but got a glare for his troubles.

It was a chilly quiet Monday morning but not for long. If they hoped to beat the downtown rush, they would have to leave immediately. But the men knew better than to rush their little sister, even the end of the world couldn't get her to hurry up especially not when Trudy was wrapping up leftover pie for her. It was a miracle she ever got on her flights at all, they were content to wait, they sat in the front seat sipping hot coffee "How's that thing not taking your tongue off?" Last time Tomas had made the mistake of sipping Crabbe's coffee, his tongue had been raw for a week, everyone knew to stay clear of his cup now.

"All I can hear is that you're a wuss," Crabbe gulped down a mouthful, he didn't think it was all that hot anyway but it may have been the fire in his veins.

Crabbe's phone rang, a persistent thrilling that shattered the quiet, Crabbe glanced at the ID and hit answer immediately.

"Answering on the first ring, I'm flattered." a low female voice floated through.

"Don't be, are you calling to tell me the rest of my money is coming in today?" Crabbe had a smile on his face, Tomas noticed.

"Oh, you're insufferable," the woman on the other end groaned, Crabbe knew she was rolling her eyes and smiling and that made him smile too.

"Good morning Detective Silva, to what do I owe this torment?"

"Nothing good about the morning, Appleton" she sounded more tired than he'd heard her in a long time. "There's been a murder, several of them actually, well, that's what we think for now but it's hard to tell."

Crabbe was all serious now, "forensics gone over the scene?"

"Yes, and they're just as baffled, you'll see when you get here."

"Woah woah, when I get where? I can't be starting my day with a murder scene, Come on Detective"

"I'm sorry, did I make it sound like you have a choice?" her voice was steel?

"C'mon! You guys still owe me for services rendered."

"Take it up with the bursar."

"I wanna take it up with you. Wait, you're asking for my help aren't you?"

"Appleton!"

"Fine Crabbe sighed, send me the location, what time?"

"We're still trying to get clearance from Cravenhill as the property falls right on the boundary. I need you there by 1pm pronto."

"Yes Ma'am"

"Good boy." Crabbe heard her laugh as the line went dead.

"Wow, she's so bossy"

"You have no idea" Crabbe sighed again, but he was thinking of the murders, Silva was not a woman who asked for help easily, if she was calling him on a Monday morning then it was bad bad.

"I need to get home soon."

"Just a sec!" Tomas revved the car, leaned his head out of the window and bellowed "Lily! Get your ass out here immediately at this very moment or your luggage will be at the airport without you!" He turned back to Crabbe with a mischievous twinkle in his eyes and slowly pulled away from the driveway.

"Wait for it..." A second later, they heard the sounds of furious running through the house and the front door was flung open.

"You wouldn't dare!" Lily screamed at them.

CHAPTER 13

A man was waiting outside Crabbe's door, he was seated on the steps flicking a deadly knife between two rough calloused hands, he'd had practice with this. As Crabbe got out of his S10, the man stood up but he did not move, he didn't stop flicking the knife back and forth.

"You're gonna need more than that to take me down," Crabbe smiled.

"What?" The man seemed confused, then his eyes fell to the knife in his hands and he stopped mid flick and sniffed. "You're too skinny, I prefer choice rib"

"Ouch, that's cutting." Crabbe smiled now, the men shook hands, "Good morning Motor?"

Motor sniffed again, "Good morning Mr Appleton, Have you had breakfast?"

Crabbe pretended to consider it for a second, it was true Trudy had stuffed him to his gills, but "I could eat" it's not every time someone offers you breakfast for free.

"In that case, follow me." Motor turned away, and crossed the road to the next house, a renovated townhouse painted in a peeling red varnish and high windows that reminded Crabbe of Victorian times. The entire ground floor had been converted to a dining area, with chairs and tables arranged around a central serving island,

Crabbe noted absently that most of the chairs were covered in a thin layer of dust.

"You like coffee?" Motor pointed in the vague direction of a shiny coffee maker that looked well cared for, snapped up an apron and disappeared in the back. As Crabbe poured his coffee and found a seat to perch on he heard the tinkling of a man who knew what he was doing, and in case he was deaf, his nose was tickled and delighted by spices and aromas he had never perceived before. He made a mental note to get the names of these spices from him and make a gift of them to Trudy.

"How do you like your steak?" Motor called over the angry sizzle of frying oil.

"Well cooked please." Crabbe called back.

"What kinda answer is that?"

"The only type that I got, what do you want from me bud? I got things to do.

"Mr. Appleton, I got a niece, you know that right?"

Crabbe heard him chuckle.

"Ha ha, very funny Motor, but what about this niece? I'm no Sunday school teacher."

"I think she's been possessed."

Crabbe sighed, he heard this one before, are you sure she's not epileptic or something? Has she seen a doctor?"

"She's in an asylum, so yeah." Motor's voice was coming closer, then he emerged carrying a feast in his arms, Crabbe's belly grumbled in appreciation.

There were eggs, scrambled and boiled, bacon strips, stewed beans, some jollof and a slab of tenderloin that made Crabbe almost cry. "You have quite the eye for prize cuts if I do say so myself".

....

To say that Stout enjoyed his new host, is an understatement. The man whose body he hopped into, was his kind of guy.

A drinker, who eye-balls women, and loves sports much like he did when he breathed. The spook thought about his arrangement going to the depths that wasn't exactly Hades, but he had to pay for his sins, breaking one of the ten commandments. Thou shalt not kill, but he did, becoming a member of the deceased club. He had all the time to think about his wrongdoing.

He put people in the hospital, broke limbs, cracked skulls with a swing of his bat. Through all that, he couldn't comprehend why he beat a man to death during a road rage. The man didn't come at him with animosity or threat. He approached with a question: "Why?"

Stout didn't know what the why was, because he didn't bother to find out. He got an adrenaline rush grabbing the bat and when he raised the bludgeon, he saw fear in the man's face which turned to pain once the clobber struck bone.

The bad man kept at it, after feeling the rage building inside his body. The bop struck the man's skull and blood flowed down his cheek, he got a distant look in his eyes followed by a glossy film, meaning death was moving in and he would no longer be a part of the living. The man fell hard to the pavement; his head bouncing, opening up a bigger gap in his skull letting out more plasma. Stout saw a puddle. He decided he'd done enough damage, and it was now time to get to his car.

Then the unexpected happened, when he did a cartwheel upon getting hit by a red roadster, landing hard on the concrete with his head busted from the impact. He got run over by another car, but the red one did the damage. Stout inhaled, wishing he had kept a cool head. But it's too late for that now. He'd settle for the body jumping and forget about the driver of the red car because he enjoyed his new found talent.

Crabbe never said anything, but he felt night came fast to him. The spell-caster wondered if it was because he anticipated his nightly encounters with demon bounty hunters, lurking in the dark, waiting for him. Either way, he felt as if daytime was short, and even in the time change, sunlight didn't last long enough.

All the kids were tucked in bed. Crabbe knew a few were awake, talking about boys and girls they thought were cute who attended their school.

He smiled within himself, the cousins were all like brothers and sisters which made him feel good despite knowing different parents, his siblings made sure the children formed a tight bond and they would stay in touch when they became adults. Not like his cousins who are strangers because of his situation, but have called upon him when it suited them, and because of family ties he helped. He nodded thinking, not his nieces and nephews. They will always be as tight as a boy scouts knot.

"You agree brother-in-law?" Harold asked.

"Huh... what?" Crabbe responded wearing a dubious look.

"This is serious, you got to pay attention," said Charles.

Crabbe gave a salute. If he regretted anything beyond coming to church and the family dinner, it was the Sunday night family talk. What was the world coming to? Law and Sage wanted to join in, figuring now that they were young adults they could weigh in on the conversation. Their parents won the debate that they still weren't old enough to have an opinion that would matter. The two towering cousins looked at each other before heading upstairs and Crabbe read them like a book.

Their body language told him it was but a matter of time, before they'd get the chance to voice their opinion. Crabbe cleared his throat. "I told you before, yes there are demons at your jobs, schools, supermarkets, and so on, but they know if they broke the rule exposing themselves, that it would be an express way back to hell."

Charles made a fist touching his mouth with it giving a stern look. "Why don't you just vanquish them with a blink of an eye?"

Clover inhaled, filling her breasts up like balloons waiting to pop. "Charles!" She caught herself fearing she'd wake the children even though some were not asleep. "We talked about this and you know Crabbe has to keep his cool and besides he ain't no damn bewitched."

"Or I dream of Genie," Crabbe remarked. "Aren't all demons bad?" Harold intervened.

Crabbe thought of Blossom's husband as weird Harold, though there wasn't anything weird about the man, but the nickname came to Crabbe's mind from a cartoon character back in the day.

Harold joined in as usual, backing Charles as if to say we brother-in-laws have to stick together, and from time to time he'd get a nudge from Blossom to be quiet, and he'd give her a look as if to say this is a family discussion.

"Not all demons are bad," said Crabbe.

"Say what?" Harold questioned getting moon-eye. "You must be crazy," Charles remarked.

"The word demon gives them that reputation like the word devil makes you assume he's evil because it sounds that way," Crabbe retorted.

Charles frowned. "He is evil."

Crabbe bobbed his head rolling his eyes."Well, yeah... but you don't put all humans who commit murder in the electric chair,"

Crabbe watched the brothers-in-law nod their heads in agreement and took time to survey the room. Tomas sat with his arms folded, sturdy in his lazy-boy pose, doing his usual observe and wait to speak when needed. Trudy sat behind him on a bar-stool chair with one hand in her lap and one on his shoulder playing the stand by her man wife. Charles shared the love sofa with Clover and Crabbe chuckled knowing how uncomfortable he was with Clover staring right through him.

Big sis always got his back. Crabbe exhaled when he looked at Lilac. Milton was gone and Crabbe wasn't sorry, Lily sat on the couch with Blossom and Harold wedged between middle sister and the wall hugging herself. *******Crabbe knew she did that because hearing them talk about demons and the devil frightened her. He wished she could be excused from the talk, but it was mandatory for all family members to attend.

Blossom knew too, how frightened and kept a hand on her knee for comfort and at the same time nudging Harold.

Tomas cleared his throat. "It's late and the conversation has gone around in circles and when that happens that means their nothing more to talk about,"

Crabbe gave a sigh of relief, The reason they had these talks was for the in-laws to have their say since they agreed to become part of this cryptic family and Crabbe was fine with that because they could have tucked tail and ran, but instead proved love conquered all. Crabbe watched them all head up stairs. Lily will sleep in Harold's and Blossom's room. Harold had to abide since no sex allowed a policy Tomas put in play since this his house and Blossom wouldn't have sex anyway because she respected big brother, Crabbe pulled out the sofa bed making it with the pillow and sheets Trudy gave him.

Crabbe got comfortable and smiled knowing he didn't have to fight with any demons tonight.

CHAPTER 14

Hiram parked the van twenty yards from an old looking large round metal corn and feed holder with a cone shaped top. He checked his rear view and the five that failed him look as though they were on a special ops mission, but no such luck.

"Explain again what we are supposed to do out here?" Drew questioned.

Hiram didn't like Drew. He contradicted him when he could, making the other cult members question his authority and he smirked thinking Drew will get his for being a smart ass.

Hiram cleared his throat. "You ever done something on your job and instead of getting fired you get put on probation to prove your worth for keeping around?"

"That happened to me once," said Wally.

I'm sure it has, thought Hiram. "Well that's what this is—a test to prove yourself that you are worthy of being a member."

"Okay, but why out here and the feed container... what's that all about?" Drew asked.

"Yeah." said Stan. "You want us to fill it up or something?"

"That won't be a problem for me," said Ellis.

"I'll do whatever it takes to be a part of the club," said Levi.

"This is stupid." said Drew. "We're not farmers and I'm about to reconsider why I joined in the first place."

Hiram heard the others talking among themselves agreeing with Drew. "What better way to test your courage than in the dark?" Hiram questioned.

"What's with this courage shit?" Stan asked.

Hiram didn't like Stan either. He felt Stan and Drew were two peas in a pod just to irritate him. "One guy took out the five of you and I'm sorry that just don't cut it and for the record your ass ain't going nowhere because you know what we are all about... don't forget about the little girl."

"I was against that from the beginning," said Drew.

"What's done is done and you are a part of it. When the task is completed you may talk to me about your departure from the club." said Hiram.

"That goes double for me," said Stan.

Hiram sat up straight realizing he was losing control. "No problem I don't want anyone who second guesses being a part of my group, but since we all participated in keeping the girl on the down low we are in this together."

"When this is done then I'm done," said Drew.

"Sure, but in the meantime I want you to prove yourselves. I can't give you a slap on the wrist and let the other members think I'm soft."

"What do you want us to do?" Wally asked.

"Spend the night inside the container," said Hiram. "And if we don't then you all will get kick out and pay a fine on your way out." said Hiram.

"Now hold on," said Drew. What fine? I don't recall reading about paying any money."

"You didn't read the fine print of the membership?" asked Hiram.

"I read it thoroughly and I don't recall any fine print." Drew stated.

"Neither do I," said Stan.

Hiram exhaled. Two peas in a pod.

"Well there is a clause you two overlooked," said Hiram.

"You know what—fine I'll just wait five minutes inside that damn thing and start pounding for you to let me out." Drew remarked.

"You do and you all will be out and I don't think everyone wants to leave the club."said Hiram,

"He's right," said Ellis. "Yeah." said Levi.

"Don't ruin it for the rest of us," Ellis replied.

Drew swallowed hard. "Okay guys... fine, When we get inside I will go fast asleep and before you know it, it will be morning and those who want to still be members will be. But I will pay my fine of whatever and be done with this shit."

"You won't be alone," said Stan.

"How about you Wally?" Drew asked.

"If it's okay with you two, I'll sleep on it." Wally remarked.

"That's fair," said Drew.

"Thanks," said Ellis. "I appreciate what you're doing, Drew."

"Let's get this shit over with," said Drew.

Hiram stepped out of the van smiling. "Gentlemen, follow me."

Hiram led the five men though tall weeds to the rusted feed container. He opened the creaking door and they all duck their heads stepping over the lower base to fit inside.

"I'll see you in the morning, sleep tight." said Hiram.

The container smelled of mold, rust, mildew, decay, and a stench none of the men wanted to find out where it came from. Neither man could see each other in the pitch black, but their bodies touching from forming a protective bundle told them they were all afraid. And jumped when they heard the latch lock.

"I'm with you Drew, to hell with this," said Wally.

"Wish you had said that when we were out in the clear and we could have rushed Hiram," said Drew.

Hiram climbed the attached ladder to the feed container; he tried to be quiet, but was sure the men heard him. He took out night vision goggles and when he got to the top he twisted the circle vent big enough to look through. The hole meant to keep the container and what it contained fresh till it needed to be used. Hiram exhaled looking down on the fateful five.

"That you Hiram?" Drew questioned. "Let us out of here... I think Ellis and Levi have changed their minds and I'll pay their fines so let us the hell out of here."

They got startled when hearing a thump sound out through the feed container.

"What the hell are you doing Hiram?" Drew yelled. "You've made your point scaring us for screwing up the job, now cut the crap and let us out of here."

Hiram laid on his stomach peering down through the hole watching the fateful five squirm and the demon move toward them.

"What's that smell?"Stan asked.

"Damn it Levi, did you cut one?" Ellis asked.

"Hey! Wait a minute you guys have asses too," Levi remarked.

"It ain't none of us," said Wally. "There's some loud footsteps coming this way,"He sniffed. "And whatever it is, it smells worse than a fart." Wally reached inside his pocket taking out a lighter. "Forgot I had this," He flicked the lighter, a little flame appeared for a brief moment. They all saw the monstrosity before Wally dropped the lighter.

"Hiram you son of a bitch! What's going on here?" Drew questioned.

"Damn it guys, don't you see it's a naked woman and I get first dibs?" said Ellis.

"Are you crazy?" Stan questioned. "Yeah I saw boobs, long hair, but shit, I saw a face a mother wouldn't love."

"Well I like my women big and strong like me." said Ellis.

Drew cleared his throat. "Ellis I hate to break this to you, but I don't believe that's a woman."

Ellis huffed. "We all can't have a pretty little wife like you and guys like me got to take what we can get so fuck you and you guys get some sleep and I'll try not to wake you."

"Ellis don't..." said Drew, grabbing the big man's arm. Ellis snatched away from his grasp.

....

Drew and his companions cringed when they heard bones snapping and limbs sounding like they were being pulled and liquid splatting on the floor they all believe to be blood.

They knew something was wrong before the disturbing noises happened when they heard Ellis shriek. Wally got down on all four trying to find his lighter. Drew felt him down around his ankles knowing he wasn't praying but Drew doubted that would help. They were all in hell and about to pay for their sins for joining a cult club.

Hiram watched from above, getting sick to the stomach. What did he do? He thought, shaking his head at the horror he witnessed so far. He saw Ellis move in for a kiss and got the ultimate French kiss when the demon's mouth opened wide enough to devour his head and from there she tore his arms and legs from his torso turning Ellis's limbs into a beverage bottle drinking his blood to wash down his flesh. The demon wasn't done, she grabbed poor Wally screaming and pleading for help. Hiram watched a train wreck and couldn't look away.

His eyes glued to the carnage of the men he sacrificed to protect a little girl from a monster he conjured. He realized the demon planned to eat the girl and he instead fed her five men who did not deserve this. Wally squirmed so much and screaming like a child the demon ripped him in half and continued to feast. Hiram watched Drew instructing Stan and Levi to spread out which Hiram knew would only delay the obvious. Buying time for more scrutinizing pain to come.

Hiram watched Levi landing blows strong enough to put down a man, but this was no man. He threw haymakers at a demon and though it pushed her back it was not enough as she caught his wrist then ripped his shoulder out of its socket.

Levi fell to the floor in pain and she pounced on him feasting on his face.

"Levi! Levi!" Stan called out. "Are you alright? Levi!?"

Hiram watched in horror seeing claws like knives thrust into Stan's chest pulling out his heart. Hiram shivered watching the demon devour it. Drew stood with his back against the wall and unlike Stan he had no plans to call out his name so see if he was okay. His gut told him Stan died a horrible death. He wanted to call Hiram and feed him every curse word possible but was scared to silence hoping for a miracle inside the dark abyss.

Drew started getting sick on the stomach from the smell of blood and body waste.

He assumed the blood came from his dead comrades and they shit themselves after witnessing the monstrosity that took their lives and unless he can find a way out he'd be next.

Drew shook his thinking he should have joined a country club instead of listening to his cousin Larry about what an adventure to join this cult or secret society that he wouldn't classify as a Freemason.

It got quiet; the slurping sound of blood, the crunching of bones had ended. But Drew still kept his head trying to find an escape. His foot landed on something; he feared it would be a hand or fingers from one of the guys but it felt solid so he crouched down to pick it up. He reached under the sole of his shoe. The lighter, he found it., Wally's lighter. Drew pondered whether to flick it to see if he was near somewhere inside the death hole to get out. He swallowed hard, turning on the lighter. Drew saw the monstrosity not even a mother could love.

Hiram almost fell off the chair, as he woke up with a start. He was drenched in his own sweat, and despite it being cold and with the air conditioning turned on, he was sweating profusely.

This wasn't his first time reliving the events of that horrendous night, and even in the silence of the night, he could still hear the screams of those five, he could still hear his heart pounding in his chest, as he scrambled away, trying to get to the van, knowing he'd have to explain what happened, but at the moment, he wanted to leave behind the carnage and think about his next move another day.

CHAPTER 15

Crabbe stretched and yawned, greeting the morning which for him couldn't have come fast enough. He adored his family, but knew they felt uncomfortable around him. Lily didn't hide her uneasiness. Blossom used to tease her saying she was jealous of Crabbe, because he took her thunder since she was the baby for six years, until her question was answered asking their mother why her stomach was so big, because it didn't get that way from eating.

Crabbe laughed thinking about the childhood days that were not always cheerful.

He got up and went to the linen closet. He got a towel, bath cloth, and Harry's body wash from his travel bag.

Crabbe's Monday ritual at his brother's house; get up early and be the first to shower then get back on the couch and go back to sleep because his youngest nieces and nephews would wake him up for breakfast. Crabbe toweled off and got dressed in his white pullover shirt, relaxed fit blue jeans and high top black Converse sneakers.

Then he stretched before parking himself back on the sofa, closing his eyes, catching up on his sleep.

Hiram drove all night to his sister's house. He needed some strong coffee. He didn't want any booze in hope of drinking away the horror he witnessed, of men being eaten alive by a monster he conjured from the bowels of hell.

Hiram took a deep breath releasing it easily through his nostrils and even though he didn't do the actual killing, he committed murder.

He got out of the van using his key to open the front door of his sister's abode.

Fresh coffee greeted him. He made a beeline to the kitchen to get a cup. Hiram walked in brushing by Lisa, a single mom with two girls of 12 and 10. Hiram became the man of the house taking care of their bills, though he didn't live with them and for that, he told Lisa if he ever needed a favor, he'd cash in.

"You look like shit," said Lisa.

"Don't start," Hiram replied, pouring coffee in a large mug. "I need this, and some peace and quiet."

Lisa snorted, then took a sip from her own cup. "You're in luck the girls stayed up all night and I'm not about to wake them."

Hiram held his cup with both hands sitting down on the kitchen chair like it was a soft bed. He was relieved the girls were still asleep because for now, a cup of Java was all he needed. Lisa leaned on the counter tapping her foot.

"What did you do?" She asked.

The twins Brandy and Brian known as the police are 11 years old (Blossom and weird Harold's kids). Chauncey 12, Charity 10, and Pierre 8 (Clover's and Charles). Randy 14, Fancy 10, and Parker 9 (Tomas and Trudy's)

They all played their part waking Crabbe up for his late Monday breakfast. Sage and Law outgrew the ritual and Crabbe was happy because to have two 18 year-olds play with his hair, tickling him would be awkward. Wait for it he thought, Blossom came to the rescue.

Crabbe sat at the table with what came to be a family tradition; sitting at the breakfast table after everyone else had eaten.

Clover and Trudy did the cooking, he didn't know which one prepared the still warm fluffy eggs, bacon and sausage, stack of pancakes, bowl grits now metamorphosed into cement, coffee, orange juice, with the company of Blossom and Lilac.

"You being careful, baby brother?" Blossom asked.

Blossom like Clover, were like bookends showing their concern. He appreciated it, Lilac never asked and he hoped it was because she didn't want to sound like a tape recording. Crabbe ate like it was going to be his last meal.

"You've touched everything except your grits," said Lily winking at Blossom. Crabbe swallowed with the help of orange juice.

"I don't eat cement."

Blossom snorted. "They would be soupy if you ate them fresh from the pot."

Crabbe grabbed a napkin. "Grits are tricky and..."

"You prefer them mixed with bacon, broken up, butter, salt, and pepper." Blossom and Lilac replied in unison giggling.

He frowned. "Once they get like that, you might as well trash them and to answer your question, you know me I got to play superhero."

Lily glared. "You act as if this is a game."

Lilac never minced words, taking the family curse a lot more seriously than her siblings and Crabbe tried walking on eggshells for her sensitive nature.

"Relax Lil," said Blossom. "He has to stay loose."

Crabbe combined sausage and pancake smothered in maple syrup, shoveling it into his mouth. Blossom, the sibling who could comfort Lilac. Ever since that day when they were kids, Crabbe attacked Lilac over a toy and she never felt comfortable around him fearing he might lose it again despite them being kids. It bothered Crabbe if she walked into a room seeing him and no one else she left, unless they were outside and others in earshot.

He had her pinned down and his eyes glowed red. Crabbe understood how that could have a lasting effect, but hoped one day she'd understand he was a child and at the time did not know how to control his demon powers.

"Lil," said Crabbe, glad she cared about what happened to him. "What I deal with is more afraid of me than I am of them." He looked smiling at Blossom then Lilac. "You guys... My family is my motivation not to fail.

He gandered at Lilac. "I got this."

He took a bite of his bacon, swallowing hard.

"So Lil, what's up with you and Milt?"

Lilac straightened in her chair, batting her eyelashes, shaking off the surprise question. Blossom leaned forward using her elbows as support with her hands cupping her chin. "Yeah, what's up with Milton?"

"I feel comfortable around him. He makes me feel safe." Lilac replied.

Crabbe lost his appetite, almost falling off his chair. Lilac spoke with a serious expression, a piercing look that she wasn't joking. He wanted to know how deep, but vowed he'd never use his clairvoyance on her or any of his siblings. Their thoughts were their own. He would not trespass unless asked.

Blossom saw Crabbe rattled. She winked at Lilac thinking she could not be serious about the nerdy deacon though she noticed they talked and sat with each other after service.

Blossom cleared her throat. "A future brother-in-law?"

Lilac shrugged. "Could be, I mean I'm not getting any younger, might be time to settle down."

Crabbe studied his sisters. They were playing him and it was not the first gang up with the three of them together. It kept the kid in all of them. He'd join in with a jolt of his own.

"Bad enough we have weird Harold in the fold." Crabbe remarked.

The round brown table was small enough for Blossom's long arm to reach and smack Crabbe on the back of his head. They inherited their father's height though Blossom had his features like Tomas and Clover, the hue like Lilac and Crabbe from their mother.

Thanks to Crabbe's Afro it felt like a glancing blow. Blossom followed with a punch to his shoulder and felt satisfied watching him wince.

"First... ow." Crabbe frowned. "You were always a tomboy."

Blossom leaned back folding her arms giving a Cheshire cat grin. "Don't talk about my man, the father of my children."

Lilac giggled. Another sign Crabbe enjoyed hoping she'd use laughter to crawl out of her trauma hole he put her in.

Crabbe nodded. "All jokes aside, would he accept our family?" He glanced at his sisters. "The others excepted are credo, but will he?"

A question Blossom and Lilac knew had to be asked.

Tomas told Trudy and she didn't believe a word. Till she sat down with Tomas, Crabbe, and Clover, giving her Appleton history 101. Tomas clutched her hand confessing how much he loved her and understood if she found it a burden.

When Trudy saw how much he loved his baby brother, she knew she couldn't let a man with a heart as big as his go.

Charles looked into Clover's big crystal clear brown eyes and said he dreamed of having a big robust woman to match his girth and he would not lose her over anything.

He validated his commitment giving Crabbe a bear-hug. Crabbe joked he felt and heard his ribs cracking. Then Clover snatched him, delivering a bruin-embrace of her own for his comment. Harold paced around the room, looked out the window as if expecting somebody, checked the door, and blew in a paper bag like having an anxiety attack and Crabbe labeled him weird Harold.

He too couldn't let go of his flower Blossom. Lilac, like her older sisters with flower names, was afraid she'd scare off any suitor who took the old maid route, the aunt destined to grow old with a house full of cats.

She and Blossom were two peas in a pod. Lilac told her confidant everything troubling her. She worried about having children and one of them inheriting Crabbe's curse. Blossom relayed the message to the others and they all hoped and prayed she would take the chance Tomas, Clover, and Blossom did, but so far the younger two were still single. They all have the devil's blood inside of them passing their DNA to their own children. Crabbe won the lottery and thanks to a loving family and holy water he contained the demon powers to keep his humanity.

"Would Milton be able to handle it?" Blossom questioned.

Lilac swallowed hard. "It's not serious, but I don't think I'd be a good wife worrying about passing our genes to our children."

"Sounds fervent if talking about having children." Crabbe remarked.

Lilac looked toward the floor. Her posture slumped, looking like a deflated balloon. Crabbe hated seeing her drown in self-pity.

"He called me the devil," said Crabbe. Blossom and Lilac got moon-eyes.

"Yeah, that's right so let's kill the headlights and put it in neutral." Crabbe suggested.

"You two are like oil and water." Lilac replied.

"Like you and Milt are peanut butter and jelly." Crabbe gave a look.

Blossom sat moving her eyes back and forth. Crabbe didn't want to tell Lilac he thought of Milton like gum stuck under his shoe. He wanted her to have a life, be with someone and not grow old alone. He patted his belly.

"Time to journey home," said Crabbe.

Blossom and Lilac helped clear the table, giving him a kiss and a hug. Crabbe stepped out on the patio with Clover making eye contact. She knew the drill, grasping him in a firm embrace. She let him go, turning away, wiping her eyes. Trudy came next followed by the brother-in-laws with less drama to their good-byes. Tomas gave the combo hand shake and half-hug. Crabbe stepped on the grass getting a bum rushed firm embrace by the nephews and nieces forming a college world series dogpile. Clover's thunderous voice rescued him. The older of the children acting more adult, no longer running to get a hug. Sage and Law stood together waving.

They said their good-byes that way fearing they may never see him again and he lived far away protecting them from his enemies. Crabbe didn't let it control his life, he intended to see them as much as he could on Sundays and holidays when he could.

CHAPTER 16

Hiram pointed. "Don't judge me!" He downed his Java and poured another cup. "Look around you; a roof over your head for you and the girls. You show some respect."

Lisa hugged Hiram, thankful for her brother's help, they'd waste away, she and the girls without him, but it didn't feel right if the money came from blood. Hiram never held down a 9 to 5 job, always scheming or coming up with schemes to live for today and worry about tomorrow.

"I appreciate everything you've done, but I don't ask where the money comes from because..."

"It ain't from blood." said Hiram.

"You never had or worked a genuine job, Hiram." Lisa replied.

"I did." Hiram glared. "It almost killed me."

"You can't blame me for asking, in case the authorities..."

Hiram snorted. "It ain't clean, but nobody gets hurt."

Lisa swallowed hard. "Now you're scaring me."

She held herself to keep from trembling. "Tell me you don't have blood on your hands."

"Where's Tom, huh?" Hiram questioned. "Yeah, laid up in a roach infested motel with a bottle in one hand and cheap women in the other."

"He's a good man." Lisa replied, tearing up.

Hiram shook his head. "Hell you said the same about dad. Guess you got a thing for sorry ass men."

He snapped his finger. "Maybe that's why you love deadbeat Tom, because he reminds you of the old man who gave mom a fat lip more than once and fractured my jaw."

He put his hand on his chin.

He pointed at Lisa. "The reason he spared your ass is because you said you loved him a thousand times. He looked at you with pity, then walked down the hall laughing."

Hiram slid down the wall landing on the floor burying his head between his knees then looked up. "The damn thing is, saving the three of us was cancer." Hiram choked back tears.

"He's down there in hell waiting for my ass." Hiram cried.

Lisa rushed to his side holding him. "Hiram, what's wrong?"

Crabbe made it back to Parts Unknown. The Metro came to a halt when burly Bob Graham, owner of the Carvana dealership across the street stopped him with his hands up high and legs spread apart. Crabbe heeded to the dealership owner hoping he had a good reason for almost getting run over or he had news about the S-10.

Bob leaned into the open window. "We have called a town meeting."

Crabbe gave a bewildered look. "This isn't a town... four businesses and that's all. A town meeting? What do you think this is? The wild wild west?"

"Well..." Bob cleared his throat. "Some patrons drove by, claiming they saw some weird shit." Crabbe straightened and swallowed." What kind of bizarre stuff?"

"They saw bright lights, static, and monsters," said Bob.

"Sounds like a thunderstorm." Crabbe remarked.

"They didn't mention rain." Bob replied. "And I know they ain't shooting a movie here at night because you voted against that."

Crabbe took a lot of heat from the locals, but with the bounty on his head he had to veto the idea.

"It doesn't have to rain..." Crabbe shook his head. "Never mind."

"You here twenty-four seven and you have noticed nothing strange?"

Crabbe inhaled. The wards he set up around the area were losing their mojo. Wards are magical shields or barriers to protect those within it and repel enemies. Crabbe put them up to protect innocents passing by, to keep the naked eye hidden from strange activity. The so-called town meeting told him he'd have to whip up a stronger spell.

"Where's the meeting being held?" Crabbe asked. "Burgers Brew and Pizza 2." said Bob.

Hiram rose to his feet with Lisa's arms wrapped around him. He eased them off by nodding to her saying he was okay.

"How are the girls?" He asked.

"They're fine, why?" Lisa answered.

"I mean Jenny too." said Hiram.

"Lisa frowned. "I don't understand."

"Her foster parents are shit." Hiram remarked. He refused to tell her why, fearing how she'd judge him. Though he admitted his money was not clean, but selling children, especially young girls would lose his one true family member.

Lisa shrugged. "Except for mom, we know something about bad parenting."

Hiram stared into his kid sister's eyes. Their mother, God rest her soul. He felt guilt having God in his thoughts after the sins he committed. She played the old man's punching bag. The battered woman had a smile of peace when she died. Hiram shook her out of his thoughts, knowingly feeling her disappointment from above.

"She has two and I'm not taking her back to them," said Hiram. "Don't ask me to explain." He bought and paid for the girl for a demon sacrifice. He inhaled, keeping two things from Lisa.

"I've been meaning to ask about your intentions for her." Lisa folded her arms.

Hiram exhaled. "I told you not to judge me. I deal with some shady people, but no blood on my hands so rest easy on that." He hoped he took Lisa's mind away from thinking he killed for the money he provided for her and the girls. His sin was witnessing murder by a demon and he might as well have held a gun and shot the victims. Hiram led them to the slaughter and a bullet would have been merciful.

Lisa observed Hiram's face. "You sound like you're in trouble."

Hiram bit his lower lip. No way he'd tell her about conjuring a demon and the vile creature wanting the girl as a morsel. What he witnessed in the grain storage was not for the faint of heart, and he hated that his heart had gotten dark, and he blamed it on his childhood and struggles that forced him to make a living, by not caring for human lives until now. He would not give a child to a demon. Hiram didn't want that on his conscience when he dies, and his soul making a beeline to hell.

"How well does Angie and Kimberly relate with her?" He asked.

"Like sisters." Lisa smiled. "Why do you ask?"

"How do you feel about her?" Hiram questioned. Lisa's eyes matched her wide smile. "She's a joy."

"You're going to be a mother again," said Hiram.

Crabbe followed Bob inside the eatery claiming to have the world's best burger, like so many other under the radar joints. The owner Motor Rooster, Crabbe thought with a name like that, the guy would own a chicken restaurant or a gas station.

He got his name on a rainy night when the car broke down near a hole in the wall of an auto shop before getting to a hospital. A vehicle on the lift provided them shelter for his birth. His parents named him Motor because he cried like an engine getting revved up.

Crabbe didn't question if the auto shop had an office or something else, rather than taking a chance, having a baby under a car that could have dropped on them any moment. A secret for Motor and his family.

Motor made breakfast; English muffins rival McDonald's, but the time he took to serve his sausage, bacon with eggs, didn't last long and he made it for early morning wayward travelers. Few of them, but he wanted to cash in any way he could. He set out a pitcher of orange juice and coffee to wash them down.

The men all accounted for and the ladies. The Banger sisters, owners of Banging Tattoos; Peaches and Precious. Peaches the older with a stocky, thick shapely figure, shoulder length Gothic raven hair wrapped around her full face.

Precious, hair same color, but shorter with a bang covering her left eye. She looked like a fitness model; lean long muscle tone, chisel face with the same features as her older sister, both the same height, piercings and tattoos covering their bodies. The sisters wore black leggings every day leaving nothing to the imagination if you like thick and lean. They sat side by side, but parted like the red sea when they saw Crabbe.

He took their offer sitting between them, but refusing to take a bite of their sandwiches. Bob stood in front of everyone clapping his hands to get their attention.

"Now that I have everyone's attention," said Bob, clearing his throat. "Some of Motor's customers claim when they drove by one night they saw strange things happening around our businesses."

Now the plot thickens, thought Crabbe. He shook his head after hearing Bob say everyone. He, Bob, Motor, and the Banger sisters... again not a town meeting.

Peaches frowned. "What activity are you talking about?"

Bob turned to Motor. "Here's the man who can explain."

Motor stepped to the center of the floor while Bob drifted to a corner table.

Motor, a tall dark chocolate hue, bald pointy head, with a culinary degree from Johnson Wales University.

Crabbe joked he confused him with a reverend because of his unique name. Motor thought the same of Crabbe. A strange moniker and even stranger when Crabbe took part in the annual Motor Rooster talent show.

He questioned Crabbe's magic talent saying they were too good, since he could tell how most tricks are done and Crabbe left it at that, refusing to argue.

"I overheard two of my customers talking about fireworks, bodies locked together, then a flash of light blinding them and when they got their sight back it was... spotless." said Motor.

"Well, there you go," Crabbe, a trickster remarked. "They had too much to drink."

Bob stood up shaking his head. "Now hold on Crabbe." He looked over at Motor. "When did you say they talked about this?"

Motor shrugged. "Two weeks ago."

Bob pursed his lips. "About the same time you were in terrible shape the morning I saw you Crabbe and your truck was worse for wear."

All eyes on Crabbe. He inhaled thinking, way to go Bob, no one else knew about that night until now. "Did you fix my truck?"

"As good as new." Bob replied.

Crabbe's mind boggled, thinking of a way to spin-doctor the situation. He thought about Motor's customers seeing fireworks around the businesses and his incident with the Njiantis was miles down the road. "That took place down where you found my truck and what they saw happened on this street so one has nothing to do with the other."

Whatever the patrons spotted, the light show was because the wards were weakening and it was time to weave a new spell to recharge them.

Crabbe felt hands rubbing his body. The Banger sisters.

"Are you all right?" Precious asked moving in close enough for her perfume to tantalize Crabbe's nostrils.

"Why didn't you tell us?" Peaches stroking his spine sending a stimulation. Despite the attention he gave Bob the evil eye. He got satisfaction watching the dealership owner wishing it was him getting touched by the lovely ladies.

Crabbe milked the affection given by the tattoo queens rubbing it in Bob's pudgy face.

"Your home and business is here." Bob retaliated. "You must have noticed or heard strange activities going on?"

"I'm dead to the world." said Crabbe wishing he could find a way to end the first annual town meeting.

"With that creepy ass eye pendant on your door that opens up every time you rang your doorbell when business is closed." Bob poured it on.

"To scare your ass so you won't bother me," said Crabbe. "We think it's cute." The Banger sisters remarked.

"You would." Bob replied. "Speaking of dead to the world, you almost were."

Motor gave a dubious look. "What are you talking about, Bob?"

Precious got moon-eye. "Is there something we should worry about?"

The room went silent.

"Somebody say something," Peaches demanded.

Bob leaned forward. "I dropped by Crabbe's place when he left me a message to pick up his truck and when I saw him slice and dice."

The Banger sisters gasped and Motor frowned.

Crabbe stood up. "Kill the headlights and put it in neutral." He shook his head. "There were two punks and I played nice picking up hitch-hikers and they tried to jump me. I fought them off and got scratched."

"Yeah, right." said Bob. "They bandaged you like a mummy."

"You fix my truck?" Crabbe asked. Bob inhaled. "As I said, as good as new."

Damn you Bob, thought Crabbe after hearing the Bangers gasping and go back to stroking his body.

"If you have scars we can decorate your body so no one would notice," said Peaches.

"Yeah." Precious agreed, attempting to lift Crabbe's shirt.

He grabbed her hands kissing them. "I'm shy and it's against my religion to have graffiti on my body."

"What kind of religion is that?" Motor questioned.

"Baptist." Crabbe remarked. "Ever heard of it?"

"So am I smart ass." Motor replied.

Crabbe smiled. "Amen brother."

Motor waved him off and Crabbe gave Precious back her hands with a wink. He blew a silent relief, stopping the shirt raise. His healing factor usually kicked in after fights taking away some pain and almost all the scars. He wouldn't be able to explain why his skin didn't have a pimple. The pros and cons of having demon blood. Crabbe raised his hands, getting everyone's attention.

"Look, I don't know what Motor's customers thought they saw, but as you can see your businesses are intact. No vandalism or anything stolen right?" Crabbe asked.

They all agreed.

Crabbe smiled. "So this ends the first and I hope the last town meeting. Sometimes tired eyes see strange things at night. They ate or drank too much. Meeting adjourned and Bob if my truck is ready, could you park it at the back of my house?"

Bob gave a salute. "Thank you." said Crabbe.

They left in single file with Crabbe bringing up the rear. Motor grabbed his arm.

"We need to talk," said Motor.

CHAPTER 17

Hiram sat at his desk watching and listening to the round clinging metal balls moving back and forth.

He didn't understand the fascination, yet like playing with a yo-yo or bouncing a ball, it plays its course to boredom. Hiram needed a distraction and for three minutes the balls provided it, till reality settled back in. Conjuring a demon was the dumbest thing he'd done. Thinking it would give him an easier life than he had as a kid.

He didn't feel sorry for himself, nonetheless he didn't want to do like some and join the military, then put in twenty years and get a government check for the rest of your life. Now that he thought about it, he could've done twenty and that government check would look real nice now. Hiram got kicked out of school and with no interest in picking up a book again, except to learn how to conjure a demon and Google helped him with that.

He was amazed at how many sites about devil worship and demonic information littered the internet and what he read scared him enough to abort those sites.

Hiram heard horrific stories about selling your soul to the devil. The devil would deliver what he promised, but what he gave didn't last long before he came around to claim your soul, no matter how you argue that your success didn't last long enough.

Two years tops and it was over because after all he is the devil and all he wants is your soul. Hiram took a shortcut instead, promising his soul for a short term promise. He heard unpleasant things about demons too, but the key was the demon and not the devil.

He used having a bad childhood as his crutch, becoming obsessed with get rich quick schemes, reading about starting a club with a purpose then charging membership fees. His sidebar was human trafficking, keeping some members in the dark.

The fateful five, blackmailed into doing his bidding, going after the 1970's man with the knowledge of a little girl for human trafficking. Those men had darkness in their hearts too or they would have said forget this. Though they didn't deserve what they got. He convinced them they joined a watered down Dungeons and Dragons, sending them on a quest in which the fateful five failed and became a main course for a nympho demon.

The book said to find like minded nerds and he found them; men, some with good paying jobs, needing an outlet from their corporate lifestyle. They didn't smoke or drink like a lot of white collar professionals do to fight stress, but harmful to your health. Blue collars joined too like Ellis and Levi.

Hiram swallowed hard, there was nothing helpful about getting eaten by a demon and smoking and drinking hard liquor was not a bad idea. Too late now since his demon lover had long digested the fateful five. Demon lover? He almost threw up thinking about it. Was the bitch from the bowels of hell growing on him? Hell no.

Watching the demon feast was a train wreck and he couldn't look away. Hiram took a deep breath running his hand through his thinning hair. He dreaded thinking about death since he would be like his father busting underworld gates wide open.

The club members will have questions. Hiram pondered what to tell them. He would lie, something he'd become good at; the sins just kept adding up.

Then there was a knock at the door. He opened up to see who was standing in the doorway. It was Larry, Drew's cousin.

Crabbe joined Motor at a table in a corner. They both held fresh cups of Java mixed with French vanilla. The tall bald pointy shaped head man wore eye-glasses making him look intelligent but he talked like he was from way down south. Crabbe saw his culinary degree, but the man kept his menu basic, nothing fancy.

Burgers, prepared in a variety of ways, beef, turkey, chicken, and veggie. He made pizza, thin crust with meat from all the farm animals and a vegetable pie. He served soda and beer and coffee. Motor extended his menu for breakfast and even comfort food; meatloaf with mashed potatoes, smothered in brown gravy.

Motor was married, with two daughters off in college. He, his wife, and six employees ran his bistro.

"What is it you do?" The chef asked.

Crabbe smiled. "I run a sampan unpleasant situation herbal shop." Motor sucked his teeth. "Don't bring that shit."

Crabbe gave him a dubious look. "Excuse me? You asked me to stay and talk."

Motor exhaled. "I have a cousin in an unpleasant situation and I'm desperate for help."

Crabbe saw the worry in Motor's eyes, almost going to tears. "I read palms, tarot cards, and tell them what they want to hear."

"And that doesn't bother you?" Motor questioned.

"Not when there is nothing to worry about. Many people have low self-esteem," Crabbe snorted. "Your father wanted you to play college ball, but your mother told you to follow your heart."

Motor got moon-eye.

Crabbe sipped his coffee then leaned back.

"I don't bullshit."

"You got skills," said Motor nodding in approval.

"If I had a hat I'd pull a rabbit out of it," Crabbe remarked. "Now tell me about your cousin."

"It's not Ruthie's fault the way she turned out. Ruthie's dad murdered her mother, my father's baby sister and..." Motor paused, taking a deep breath. "She was seven and the police found her naked, covered in her mother's blood from head to toe."

Crabbe went wide-eyed and straightened in his chair.

Motor swallowed hard. "That wasn't the worst part, the police report said she was holding her mother's heart in her hand."

Crabbe inhaled leaning back folding his arms. His brow furrow staring with an icy glare. Motor got nervous when he saw Crabbe's expression.

"You all right?" Motor asked. "Tell me more." Crabbe replied.

"My parents took her in and though she was my cousin, we raised her like a sister. Ruthie took to me better than my other siblings... we have a bond." Motor inhaled trying to gather himself.

"Take your time," said Crabbe.

"She never got a grasp on things, but my dad died proud, because she got her diploma."

"Where is she now?" Crabbe inquired. Motor exhaled. "Shaw Heights."

Shaw Heights, a respectable but expensive mental health facility, with a reputation of going beyond by any means necessary, to helping their patients. They recruit all doctors from the top of their classes in the medical and psychology field.

"She's getting worse," said Motor.

Crabbe frowned. "I heard they have the best doctors and facilities."

"Just because a restaurant gets a grade A, don't mean they serve the best food, except mine." The laughter gave them a brief break from reality.

"Motor." Crabbe leaned in. "I need to know everything."

Motor inhaled. "They have video footage of her doing things like she's fighting with people, but she's the only person in the room and they have her strapped down and sedated." He choked back tears. "The way she stretches her neck twisting, turning, squirming... it looks so real."

Crabbe frowned. "What do you mean?"

"Like someone is in her room smothering her with a pillow!" Motor exclaimed. "But she is alone. In the video nobody is in the room with her when she acts this way."

Crabbe inhaled. "About what time does this take place?"

Motor shrugged. "Why?"

"It's important."

Motor rubbed his hands over his face. "Doctor Parker calls me in to watch when I ask how Ruthie is doing and we sit and watch the videos, on the time, it says 1 am."

Crabbe's body straightened. He gave a stern look. "The bewitching hour." He whispered. Crabbe figured Motor didn't know that Ruthie's father worshiped the devil and sacrificed his family. A young virgin girl, child dressed like a glazed ham cooked and ready to slice. The fool cutting out her mother's heart was the cherry on top.

Demons were tormenting Ruthie because something went unfulfilled, and have been doing it, for her soul they have yet to claim. Ruthie was born of sin, but not a sinner making her a target. She got punished for her father's unfilled prophecy and the reason she never got that grasp on life.

"Where is Shaw Heights?" Crabbe asked. He had heard of the place, yet was unaware of its location.

"A five hour drive I-77 south, take exit 30 to Harrington road. A secluded area, thirty miles from civilization. So can you help her?" Motor inquired.

"That's the plan," said Crabbe.

Motor licked his lips. "What kind of doctor are you?" Crabbe remembered mentioning he owned a doctorate.

"I'm not a witch doctor."

Motor snorted. "You know Brother Voodoo is now Doctor Voodoo."

"Okay." Crabbe nodded acknowledging. Motor reads Marvel comics. "I'm not fiction."

"Yeah, well he wears a suit now. No longer shirtless and bare feet." said Motor.

Crabbe looked at himself up and down. "You don't approve?"

Motor observed the trench coat, pull-over loose fitting shirt, baggy jeans, and sneakers. "Live and let live."

"The way it should be," Crabbe remarked.

Motor cleared his throat. "Registered doctors ain't doing a damn bit of good."

"Thanks for the vote of confidence." Crabbe replied. "The faster I get there the better."

"Don't worry they'll be expecting you."

Crabbe rushed to his place and stood in front of Morocco's fortune telling booth. The crystal ball lit up.

"What do you need my friend?"

"A ghost in the machine," said Crabbe.

Hiram told Larry to give him a moment that he had a late night and Drew's cousin said he had to use the restroom.

Hiram wanted to prep himself for the flood of questions. He looked inside his desk drawer containing their cell phones and wallets. He knew he needed to dispose of the evidence.

What could he say to a man he sacrificed his cousin to his demon lover, Hiram bit his tongue for thinking of a monster as his lover, again. He gave himself a pat on the back for creating a club incognito. His rules; no phone numbers to family members, drawing up paperwork, getting signatures, and notarizing with the threat of lawsuits in the fine print.

A knock at the door and Hiram inhaled getting ready for Larry. Drew's cousin walked in, making himself right at home, in front of Hiram's desk.

"So?" Larry bobbing his head like a bobble doll. "Is my cousin back in your good graces?"

Hiram pursed his lips. "They are getting there, but you know we have high standards."

"What?" Larry frowned and shrugged. "They building you a house... knocking off a bank?"

Hiram laughed knowing nothing was funny about what happened to the fateful five. "I can't say because if I tell you and you slip up then you'll be doing the same as them."

"And what would that be?" Larry questioned.

Hiram pointed. "Almost caught me slipping."

"You said you wanted to put a scare in them right?"

Mission accomplished, thought Hiram. He put more than a scare in them; he put them inside the belly of a diligent.

"You said this was a club to help those wearing a designer noose around our necks to loosen up and unwind," said Larry.

Hiram leaned forward. "Bite your tongue. You're in deep and too late to undo the things we've done."

Larry exhaled. "My hands are dirty, but you said our activities wouldn't include all members and that's why I got Drew to join to relieve his stress. I'm getting a bad feeling."

"I didn't force him. He volunteered to go out and bash in a guy's head." said Hiram.

"You're right. He has a mind of his own." Larry swallowed hard. "Don't you think you're taking this proving thing too far?"

"You're biased because he's your cousin." Hiram stated.

Larry rose from his chair. "His wife is hounding me, asking questions and his job called her saying he hasn't shown up for work." He gave a stern look. "I can't cover for him if I don't know what's going on."

Hiram glared. "Does his wife... "

Larry returned an icy stare. "Only members know this number."

Hiram nodded thinking. "Fine. I'll take you to them so you can see for yourself what has them occupied."

"That's all I ask and then I can tell his wife..."

"He can tell her himself when you take him home."

Larry acknowledged what he heard. "It'll be like a surprise."

"I'll contact you."

"Sounds like a plan," said Larry on his way out.

Hiram leaned back, breathing a sigh of relief. "An ambush," he whispered.

CHAPTER 18

Crabbe hit the road at 7 pm, testing Motor's theory of a five hour drive to Shaw Heights and he was right. A guard big with bulk greeted in a gray black trim uniform holding a clipboard. "Yes sir," he said.

"I'm here to see Dr. Margo Parker." Crabbe answered. "May I see your ID?"

Crabbe handed the guard his license. He checked it then looked at his clipboard. The guard handed the license back to Crabbe.

"A moment sir," he went to the shack and the gate opened.

"Drive up and another guard will instruct you on what to do."

Crabbe nodded then drove through the split provided by the gate. He parked the S-10 Bob souped up like new. The damage the jackals put it through, a memory like the scars they inflicted on his body. A guard waited for Crabbe, escorting him inside the building where a thick stocky middle-aged woman waited. But her face gave a thirtyish look, despite gray strands dominating her once black hair in a bun.

She wore glasses, red lipstick, a white blouse containing her breasts, black skirt at the knee and pumps showing her defined legs with thick muscular calves. Her handshake potent as a man's, making Crabbe match her strength.

The touch activated Crabbe's clairvoyance showing the woman in action handling patients who got out of control, including males.

"Crabbe Appleton." He announced.

"Dr. Parker, and I have been expecting you, though Mr. Rooster left out some details."

Crabbe raised an eyebrow.

"Like what?"

Parker smiled. "Please follow me to my office." She waved off the guards letting them know she didn't need them.

Inside her office she motioned for Crabbe to have a seat. He sat in front of her desk and she got comfortable behind her ebony grand davenport. She leaned forward clasping her hands.

"He said you were a doctor?" Parker questioned.

"What gave me away? My hair?"

"Cute, but we are serious here." Parker remarked.

"Sorry, but I get judged a lot and no, I don't own a white coat, but I have a doctorate not a PHD."

"I see." She said.

"But I am equipped to help patients like Ruthie."

Parker pursed her lips. "Mr Appleton, I don't doubt your credentials, but I don't need a malpractice suit."

Crabbe nodded. "Looks can deceive."

The burly woman studied Crabbe's afro, sideburns, youthful face, and dress code of a trench coat, pull-over shirt, jeans, and sneakers.

"I've heard your medical staff have been unsuccessful."

Parker gave a look of contempt. "That may be so, but if Mr. Rooster told you anything then he should have informed you my staff graduated either near or top five in their class."

"I'm not here to question you or your staff's credentials, but if you want me to sign papers relieving you of any wrong doings I have no problem giving my John Hancock."

Parker sat up straight with her hands together. "I hate paperwork, but Ruthie is an unusual case and I will roll the dice on you. I'm at a loss and don't know what else we can do for her."

"I'd like to observe the videos you have on her," said Crabbe.

Parker reached inside her desk grabbing a remote. She pressed a button and the wall parted revealing a wide flat screen TV. Crabbe studied the time, 1 am when Ruthie had her fits looking as if attacked, but like Motor said she is alone in the room. She twists, squirms, trying to free her bound hands. The way her chin stretched as if her head was under something or worse someone sitting on her face. All the tapes showed the same time, 1 am, the bewitching hour.

Crabbe glanced at the clock, 15 minutes till 1 am.

"Why and how long is she restrained like that?" Crabbe questioned.

Parker saw the furrowed brow, and icy glare Crabbe gave her.

"She has attacked my staff and to keep from sedating her, we felt it would be better to restrain her," said Parker, returning some animosity of her own.

Crabbe inhaled and nodded, respecting Parker for not shooting Ruthie up with drugs, but the restraints made it worse to fight her demons, with vampire abilities not caught on camera.

Crabbe rose from his chair. "Okay, I need you to trust me and not intervene no matter what happens." He saw a dubious look on Parker's face. He pointed to the video.

Parker inhaled and exhaled. "We will watch."

Crabbe glanced at the clock. 10 minutes till one. "Understood."

Crabbe got off the elevator on the sixteenth floor. He turned off the lights, five minutes before the bewitching hour. Ruthie's head restrained. He walked over to the tortured woman releasing her bonds. Crabbe caressed her head. "Rest easy." Ruthie inhaled then fell into a relaxing deep sleep. One minute to go.

Crabbe reached inside his shirt taking out his red and black snake eye pentacle necklace.

"Morocco, I need a ghost in the machine." A spark of energy ran through the outlets and the complex went black. Crabbe stood across the room focusing on the near side wall of Ruthie's bed. He chanted.

"Creatures of evil far and wide, from this spell you shall not hide. Heed these words and heed them well, show yourselves before I send you back to hell."

Three green luminous demons crouched down in the corner cowering together next to Ruthie's bed.

"Good." Crabbe nodded. "You know who I am."

He studied the trio; one demon, lanky, looking like a praying mantis with oval shaped amber eyes, black serpent slits, and elf ears. A human face on the second demon, black spiked hair, beady dark eyes, hunchback , developed arms and legs like a linebacker, and a beer gut. The third should've stayed down below looking like a factory mistake Mister Potato head, with stubby arms and legs attached to his enormous noggin, swollen slit eyes as though he took the worse of it in a boxing bout, with lips to match.

Crabbe stormed toward the threesome making a beeline for spiky hair, grabbing his arm and slamming him against the wall. He clutched his genitals. His anger allowed him to bear the demon's stench.

"You disgusting, foul, perverted pariah," Crabbe squeezed. "Let me hear you scream."

The human faced demon was the one tormenting Ruthie. He sat on her face, grinding and twisting his extremities on her nose and mouth. Crabbe banged the demon's head against the wall four times. Three punches to its abdomen then bashes to the face that would have split a watermelon. He refrained from using his demon powers for strength that came naturally from the devil's blood in his veins. His rage fueled him, forcing the goblin to slump down to the floor.

Crabbe gritted his teeth, thinking how spike hair sat full weight on top of Ruthie's head, the reason she twisted and squirmed trying to get out from under his putrid body, and the other two watched feeding off his enjoyment.

Crabbe's fury grew upon seeing visions of residue on Ruthie's face after she got out from under the demon's ass. He placed his foot on the demon's head, pressing down hard to make him squeal. His partners in crime winced and cringed on seeing their companion in pain.

"This is not to your liking, huh?" Crabbe questioned looking at the duo snuggled together in the corner. Pointing for the demons to stay while he walked over to Ruthie's bed. He touched her forehead and she closed her eyes to rest. Crabbe turned back to the demons, focusing on the pervert.

"I would love to do worse to your disgusting carcass, but what I am about to do to you and yours will have to be enough."

Crabbe couldn't help kneeing the pervert in the groin, watching the other grimace. Pervert bent over, holding his testicles and took a kick to his face. His partners in crime whimpered. Crabbe decided enough, giving the pervert a beat down.

He stood in front of the threesome putting his hands together forming a triangle shape touching his thumbs, forefingers . Pinkies together and folding his middle fingers pressing them together at the knuckles chanting a spell:

"I BANISH INCUBUS, ZEALOTS FROM TORTURING THE SOUL OF THIS WOMAN, TO DWELL DEEP IN THE BOWELS OF HELL-SPAWN AND NEVER SURFACE EVERMORE.

GO FAR AWAY! SHAMED! SHAMED! LEAVE HER, DEPART FROM HER, FLEE I COMMAND. TURN AWAY, GO AWAY, DO NOT RETURN.

COMMANDED BY THE MIGHTY, COMMANDED BY THE LORD OF ALL, COMMANDED BY THE GREAT MAGICIAN OF THE GODS,

COMMANDED

BY THE FIRE AND BRIMSTONE, YOUR DESTROYER. FOR EVER MORE, SO MUST IT BE."

A portal hole in the middle of the floor opened with flames inviting the ghouls shivering like they were in the arctic. Fear draped their faces and like a vacuum they got sucked in and the hole disappeared. Crabbe cast the trio deeper into the bowels of hell. They would never surface to the topside ever again.

He then went to Ruthie's bed to untie her bonds. She pulled him down on her bed with her mouth pressed to the side of his face.

"Please help me die." She said.

Crabbe inhaled thinking about her request. She looked like death with hollow eyes, face drawn in, a night gown wearing her, twig like fingers and elbows and knees sharp enough to poke out your eyes. Crabbe pulled away looking into her brownish yellow pupils.

"Close your eyes and when I tell you to open them, look into mine."

Ruthie closed her eyes waiting for Crabbe's voice.

"Take a deep breath." Crabbe waited watching her bone hard chest expand. "Open your eyes,"

Ruthie's mouth opened wide, releasing her last breath when she saw the horror of Crabbe's demonic red eyes.

The fright was enough to scare her to death. Crabbe pulled her close, comforting her on her journey home.

He felt peace helping her on her trip from torture caused by the sins of her father. Crabbe hoped the demons he made a deal with joined the bastard and they would exact revenge on him for what he did to their perverted friend. Crabbe laid her down like an infant who fell to sleep from hearing a sweet lullaby.

"Morocco, it's done," said Crabbe.

The red serpent eye pentacle illuminated as the spirit returned.

Crabbe heard keys and Parker, shadowed by two mountain sized men, rushed in with her. All three froze when they saw the covered corpse. Neither Parker nor her men made a noise, but seemed satisfied that Crabbe put the patient's tortured soul to rest.

Crabbe held up his hands. "I know you have questions, but..."

Parker shook her head. "In this case no, but we need to talk."

Crabbe took the cup of Java from Parker, she sat down beside him on her office sofa.

"I've experienced a lot of strange things and I will not ask or question your methods, and I believe the autopsy won't reveal anything incriminating, but I want an explanation on how and why you took out my cameras?"

Crabbe swallowed hard. "Are you open minded?"

"Bullshit," said Parker.

Crabbe sipped his coffee and nodded. "I respect you and I would never insult your intelligence, but you know Ruthie was an unusual case and your methods did not help."

"She's dead."

"I didn't kill her."

"She had a stroke." Parker gave him a look.

"Autopsy I hope will reveal, but you're not off the hook."

Crabbe could have pulled an amnesia spell. He decided Parker didn't deserve that because she could have refused letting him see Ruthie.

"I have unique gifts and electronic devices that can manipulate cameras."

"You hid them well from my metal detectors." Crabbe licked his lips inhaling.

Parker stared into Crabbe's eyes "Will they enjoy you from behind bars?"

"How ever you want to handle this I won't fight it." Crabbe replied.

Parker saw Ruthie looking at peace with her eyes closed.

"Her cousin did the right thing asking for your help." She swallowed hard.

"I don't enjoy being played with," she added.

"I meant no disrespect, but what I do is not for the faint at heart."

Parker nodded and frowned. "Oh, I don't doubt that,"

"If there's anything you need..." Crabbe gestured, giving her a card.

Parker held his card between her middle fingers. "I will call you on it."

CHAPTER 19

Crabbe pulled up to his business abode with Motor waiting at his front door. He parked the S-10 deciding he'd put his reborn truck around back after talking to the man whose cousin he helped cross over. Crabbe got out not knowing what to expect turning off his clairvoyance.

Motor stepped to him offering his mitt. Crabbe exhaled, shaking Motor's hand.

"Did she go peacefully?" Motor asked. Crabbe nodded.

Motor pursed his lips. "I don't care nor want to know the details because I know it must have been better than what she was going through when she was alive."

"She's at peace." Crabbe replied.

"We're laying her to rest at York Memorial Saturday at 1 pm," said Motor.

"I'll be there."

Motor shook Crabbe's hand again then went to his restaurant needing to keep busy, while dealing with the death of his cousin.

Crabbe climbed back inside the S-10. He sat in deep thought before sighing and turning the key. Two people, Motor and Parker had gained his respect for realizing death was the cure for a woman whose life was torture.

Crabbe didn't know if Motor and Parker knew anything about demons, but the devil's children were nasty creatures and did not play nice. Ruthie wasn't the first soul he put at peace. Crabbe never felt comfortable doing it, but his conscience was not burdened, since he did it for the good of the person's soul.

He'd see Ruthie one last time at her funeral. Crabbe turned the ignition, when his cell vibrated. He touched his pentacle with Morocco inside, eager to be back in his life size mannequin. Crabbe owed Parker for allowing him to spend the night to catch some sleep, but he yearned to be in his own bed. Crabbe checked his cell. He banged the side of his head against the S-10 window.

"Damn!"

Crabbe chuckled. Bob and his mechanics did a fine job rebuilding the S-10. His text said, 'I need you, Gwyn Silva.'

Detective Silva, and she stood decked out in a hazmat costume and holding another meaning he'd have to suit up before going inside the feed container.

Silva is five-foot-seven, one-hundred-forty pounds, athletic thighs with Popeye legs when wearing a dress or tight skinny leg jeans, tiny waist, glossy raven hair, bushy on top and shaved crew cut on the sides and back. It gave her a sexy masculine look that both sexes would be attracted to, but Crabbe knew she enjoyed men.

Her creamy light skin, pout lips, big brown eyes trenched in white as snow iris, and luminous teeth solidified her beauty.

Crabbe climbed out of the S-10 strolling towards her.

"Think we got all day?" said Silva tossing him his suit.

Crabbe adored her bossy spitfire spark-plug femme fatale personality. Women in her line of work felt they had to come off as a hard ass, to make up for their male dominated profession. He spotted a man getting treated by paramedics.

"What's his deal?" Crabbe asked.

"Him." Silva turned up her lip. "The farmer, he called us after investigating the foul smell coming from his grain container."

Crabbe slipped the hazmat suit. The stench of plasma and feces clogged his senses. "And why am I here again?"

"Because this is some freaky shit I think only you can explain."

Crabbe inhaled and exhaled. "This isn't one of your Jason, Michael Myers, and Freddy Kruger?"

"Don't I wish." Silva remarked.

Crabbe met Silva when she came to the shop looking for answers after she thought she had too much to drink or gone crazy after seeing her boyfriend asleep on the couch transforming into a serpent before her eyes.

She said she snuck out of his apartment before he finished his metamorphosis. Crabbe saw something in her, preventing him from erasing her memory. He asked for his address and told her to stay put.

A demon not the usual suspect for evil, but made the mistake letting his guard down. Rules Crabbe made with such demons were protective sex, and not reveal your true self. Demons had too much to drink and associating with humans he made a fatal mistake. He didn't put up a fight since he signed a contract in demon blood stating what would happen if a human saw a demon in its natural form. He made a joke saying "To err is human." When the contract dissolved in holy water so did he, since his blood made the contract a part of him and demons and holy water are like oil and water. They don't mix.

Crabbe put on his costume to blend in and followed Silva to the crime scene. The grain storage container built back in the day when farming was popular, the grain storage now says not built from the ground up, but on stilts with a funnel cone on the bottom for easy access.

Silva handed him tinted goggles to protect his eyes from the glare of the lamps. Crabbe didn't ponder why he saw some officers losing their lunches, but understood why. The stench of blood, feces, and urine was strong enough to peel paint off a wall though the container was rusted inside and out caused by age. Body parts, lintels, and clothing littered the floor of what Crabbe realized was not an ordinary murder. He inhaled to keep his composure.

Silva gave him a look. "You're not trying to get high off the funk are you?"

Crabbe returned the look since everyone inside the container wore a mask to fight the reek. "No, but I know what and who did this and it wasn't natural."

Silva nodded. "That's why I called you for your expertise."

"I know hazmat will clean everything up, but I work better at night and less of an audience."

"It's a date then," Silva replied. "You remember where I live?"

Crabbe understood despite her police training, it still sent chills down her spine knowing things that go bump in the night existed in the actual world. He didn't want her meeting him here alone, thinking the demon that did this would wait for another victim. "I'll call you when I'm on my way."

Crabbe and Silva dressed in their science fiction get-ups and strolled the inside of the container.

"Spotless," said Silva.

The hazmat did their job making sure they took care of any trace of residue left from the victims.

"Let me guess, you don't have any ID's?" Crabbe asked.

"No criminals, but forensics are doing their best. Wallets missing... strange." Silva replied.

"A human was in cahoots with a demon and the victims were..."

"Sacrificed," said Silva, holding herself not from the frosty night air, but the thought of demonic activity. "You know we don't have a task force for such a thing."

"You have me," said Crabbe. He despised demons who escaped hell and preyed on humans.

"How did it get here?" Silva asked. "A fool conjured it." said Crabbe.

"Need I ask why?" Silva questioned.

"Too scared to make a deal with the devil." Silva inhaled. "You are scaring me."

"I got you." said Crabbe.

He was used to hearing those words because Lilac and his sister had demon blood in her veins, but still cringed when they gathered to talk about the fallen angel. Crabbe didn't want one of the few friends like him, who knew monsters existed to feel uncomfortable.

What frightened them, angered him.

"I'll take you home. I got all I need." He said.

"You're spending the night," said Silva.

"See? That's why I hate talking to you about..."

Silva shook her head. "It's not that. Yes I get the creeps and I don't watch movies with demons anymore, but you look like hell. No pun intended."

Crabbe laughed. He hadn't slept since he got back from seeing his family and he took care of business at Shaw Heights, so he agreed with the detective.

"You need to tell me everything. I'm still a cop and those men need closure and when we find out who they were I need to inform their families." said Silva.

"When we get to your place, put on a pot of coffee," said Crabbe.

"You know you're taking the couch." Silva remarked.

The Java was strong, despite the French vanilla and that was fine with Crabbe. He didn't worry about it keeping him awake. The perks of being his own boss. Silva got comfortable sitting across from him, dressed in a seductive black gown with slits showing off her thunder thighs. She sat curled up holding her coffee with both hands. Crabbe didn't know if she had anything underneath, but this was business and not pleasure.

"So tell me," She said, sipping her mocha. "What's this fascination conjuring demons and what you think happened to those men?"

"I thought talking about the occult gave you the creeps?" Crabbe remarked.

"I'm home and with you." She said.

"Fair enough," Crabbe smiled. "When people go to the dark side, they want something fast and without working for it. They make a bargain, sacrificing their humanity or a loved one."

Silva frowned. "Are they that desperate?"

"Very," said Crabbe. "They are conjuring a demon. Going to the dark side."

"Selling their soul?" She questioned as her body shivered. Crabbe shook his head. "Yes and no."

Silva shrugged."What do you mean?"

"You sell your soul to the devil, but not to demons." Crabbe took a long sip of java." When you meet with the devil, there's a clearing where no plants grow in North Carolina called the devil's tramping ground. A crossroads of sorts to make your deal with him. A demon is summoned by building a pentagram to trap it and force it to do your bidding."

"If that's true and I'm not doubting you, then how did it get to that grain storage?" Crabbe inhaled. "Amateur and I am human."

Silva shrugged. "So?"

"I don't know everything."

Silva gave a dubious look. "If they brought it here?"

"You can read a book, go online, and still not know what the hell you are doing. No pun intended." said Crabbe. "The fool who conjured this demon didn't trap it and most likely didn't get what he wanted, so to keep the demon happy or from killing him, he does the demon's bidding."

"Such as?" Silva questioned.

"Feeding it humans." Crabbe replied.

"My God!" Silva exclaimed. "Then that means it can roam through this city and..."

"No." Crabbe shook his head. "The connection to the human is like an ankle bracelet."

"I don't understand." Silva replied.

"The demon still works with its conjurer, but in a friends with benefits compromise. It's not trapped and happy about it and free from purgatory. He got something out of it, but not exactly what he wanted and in return, he has to keep it happy..."

"By feeding it innocent people?"

Crabbe inhaled. "They weren't pristine."

"What are you saying?" Silva inquired.

"Those men tried to bash my head in."

"Say what?" Silva cried.

"Yeah, I led them to the woods and gave them some bumps and bruises to take home." Crabbe swallowed hard. "Might be the reason they ended up demon food for failing."

Silva sat up straight. "It's not your fault what happened to them. You're the most unusual man I ever met, but you're a good person and those men made a poor decision and it cost them." Silva sat back exhaling. "They still deserve justice."

"They weren't bad guys, I think it was a club, or cult thing they were doing and not very good at it. I want the leader."

"You and me both." said Silva.

"When this goes down, you know you have to put a spin on this." Crabbe replied.

Silva twisted her neck. She knew what Crabbe meant and she'd have to go against her police training to keep the truth to herself.

"A club initiation that went bad. Was that the reason they came after you?"

"I'm getting close to something and they were trying to keep me from digging deeper."

"An occult detective?" Silva joked.

"Let's keep that between us," said Crabbe. "I've added two cases and more to my plate."

"Such as?" She questioned.

Crabbe swallowed hard. "I had a friend manipulate a man to turn himself in for a hit and run."

Silva got moon-eyed. "Strong magic?"

Crabbe shook his head. "Hocus pocus, but I don't take pride in doing it. Guy's name was Miller... Alan Miller."

Silva frowned. "Where have I heard that name..." She bit her lower lip thinking. "Oh well it'll come to me. But those victims in the grain storage."

Crabbe nodded. "I'll do the heavy lifting and when it's over, that's how we or you will paint the picture."

A few people can cope with the fact things go bump in the night and it's not a fairy tale. Crabbe wanted to keep the horrors to a minimum, knowing it would cause chaos if the world knew the truth, that their next door neighbor or coworker escaped the netherworld, and was making a home among them. Silva, others beside him, his family the exception and he could tell Silva still had a hard time grasping the concept. He played her therapist helping her cope with a snake headed ex-boyfriend.

Silva yawned, despite being full of coffee. "It's getting late." She said.

"I'll leave in the morning," said Crabbe.

CHAPTER 20

Crabbe arrived early at his abode/business. He got his much needed sleep, building enough strength to reset the wards. Motor's customers were a wake up call for him to always keep his guard up.

He parked the S-10 around the back of his house, then got out surveying. Crabbe owned a spacious yard surrounded by a large tall oak fence for privacy and painted it black because the color is for banishing, binding, and protection against negativity.

The Banger sisters loved the color he selected for his fence, he didn't know if they knew the reason he chose it. Crabbe stood in the middle of his yard near the tentacles of his rose bush, without the roses since it was not spring for them to bloom.

He already set the parameters of the area and the wards needed a recharge. The thing about wards is they are energetic barriers erected once and relied upon to protect a person or place. Parts Unknown community needed it to protect humans unaware of the actual world they lived in.

Crabbe could use the wards to keep the demon bounty hunters at bay and it did, but Crabbe wanted the exercise and the wards were like a ring for the fight he had with the goblins and ghouls.

The wards entrap and keep the demons out of his house even though Morocco and Mister Kit would make them wish they never entered his casa. Crabbe stood tall and straight showing good posture to channel his energy. He closed his eyes, breathing slow and deep. Crabbe aimed his palms to the ground pulling his arms up, turning his palms upward, raising them above his head. The sun hung over his head and he drew energy from the burning star. He anchored the golden bars into the earth, the bars naked to his eyes.

"AAAAAH!" he shouted and the bars thickened and vibrated. Crabbe then exhaled. The wards were back in business. The magician entered his house ready to relax when his cell sounded off.

Silva.

He wondered what was wrong. He got up early, putting wards around her house, which he didn't tell her fearing she'd be paranoid, thinking demons would come after her, for associating with him. Crabbe's family and a few circles of friends knew about the bounty. He pressed the phone to his ear and sat at his butcher board rectangle kitchen table.

"Everything all right?" He asked.

"I'm fine," She replied. "But now I remember the man's name... the one from that tragic hit and run on the interstate."

Crabbe frowned. "Alan Miller?"

"Yeah, he got murdered in his cell by one of our own."

Crabbe felt like someone grabbed him by the collar, yanking him up from his chair. He inhaled, closing his eyes. "You mind repeating that?"

"Corporal Ian Lorne gunned down Miller in his cell," said Silva.

Crabbe leaned forward pressing one hand on the table supporting his weight. "Did he give a reason?"

"That's what's so strange. He doesn't recall doing it, even when he sees himself on video pulling the trigger. It's like he had an out of body experience. Like a puppet, with someone pulling his strings."

"Stout." Crabbe whispered.

"Did you say something, Crabbe?"

"Where is the officer now?"

"He's in the hospital psych ward. They declared him not sane enough to be put in a regular cell."

Crabbe swallowed hard. "Thanks Gwyn, I'll be in touch." He put his cell back in his hip pocket then pounded the table. Crabbe raced to his den where he did his seance and tarot card reading.

He grabbed a handful of incense, sorting what scent he wanted to burn. Crabbed chose vanilla and Egyptian musk. He sat on his lavender mid-size sofa, leaning back with his eyes closed, inhaling the fragrances to help him meditate.

"Are you okay, friend?" Morocco asked.

Crabbe opened one eye peering at the far corner to Morocco's booth, which he called home, then exhaled, closing his eye again.

"Stout is at large doing harm and it's my fault." Crabbe replied.

The luminous crystal ball flickered. "How so?" Morocco questioned. "He possessed a policeman's body, making him murder Alan Miller."

The crystal ball beamed and vibrated. "I too am to blame, my friend."

"No!" said Crabbe. "I should have sent him to purgatory. When I get a hold of him, he'd wish I had."

"How do you think he learned such a skill in such a short time?"

"Remember when I said I felt a presence? I believe it was him studying you when possessing Jason Fuller."

"See, I too am to blame. I should have sensed his vile presence."

Crabbe shook his head. "Stout is my responsibility."

The crystal ball blinked. "Are you trying to trace his whereabouts?"

"I'm relaxing to keep from blowing my top."

"So you need me to... "

"No." Crabbe swallowed hard. "Don't take this the wrong way, but enough for at least now. Bad enough Stout is out there like it's a game, now there's a man thinking he's insane and with no proof he had an evil spirit make him commit a hideous crime and lose his career."

"I'm not offended, I understand."

Morocco was not a fan of infiltrating bodies unless for a good cause. The servitor, proud of being called upon, compelled to perform a specific action. He knew his purpose being an entity serving the needs of the magic worker.

Crabbe would be one he'd serve with honor, but comprehended why he felt he'd keep the living clean of being manipulated in doing something they were not aware of.

"How would you go about finding Stout?" Moe asked.

Crabbe stretched, switching to a relaxed position. He got up from the sofa making his way to the mantel. Crabbe picked up a small wooden box. He carried it to a window pulling up the Venetian blinds, allowing the sun to enter his home. Crabbe opened the box taking out two small rose quartz crystals that fit between his thumb and forefinger.

"Excellent choice." Morocco echoed.

"Time for Frick and Frack to go to work," said Crabbe.

Frick and Frack are thought-forms. Entices created by the imagination, power, and intention of a magic worker with a specific goal or mission in mind. Crabbe created his thought-forms his own way, some mages do it with a sketch pad, drawing a vision on how they'd look.

He didn't care whether they were male or female, he just wanted them to be effective. Some have one thought-form, but he wanted two to keep each other company and have each other's back in case of trouble. He gave them each a special power, nothing specific, just giving them a mind of their own to develop their own talent.

Crabbe needed light to give them life. He preferred natural light over artificial light. The sun shone bright so he placed them on the base of the window sill. Crabbe didn't go completely outlaw, he followed most of the rules creating his thought forms. He had to recite words giving them their purpose:

"I NAME YOU FRICK AND FRACK.

BE A BEING OF THOUGHT AND FORM, YOUR WILL IS MINE AND UNTO ME.

WITHIN THE CRYSTAL, NOW BE BORN AND I A PARENT UNTO THEE.

BE MY AGENT IN THE SKIES, BE ATTENTIVE TO MY CRIES

OH SERVANT OF MY INNER LIGHTENING. BE RESOUND, CROSS EVERY PLAIN,

BODY, FORCE, AND FORM, TAKE FLIGHT AND ANSWER TO YOUR GIVEN NAME!

FRICK AND FRACK! FRICK AND FRACK! FRICK AND FRACK!

Crabbe took deep breaths, breathing life force into his crystals. He picked them up one at a time, tapping them on a hard surface till they glowed blinding light telling him they were ready for their mission. He placed them side by side in the palm of his hand.

"Frick," said Crabbe as the crystal on his right glowed. "Frack," he said and the crystal on his left did the same as its sibling. "I order the two of you to seek the evil spirit Stout. Use whatever talent and gifts you have, to mark him once you find him, but be discrete and quick, not allowing him time to figure out what's going on." Crabbe looked around for something to give his bloodhounds a scent to track Stout.

"Bring them to me, my friend," said Morocco. "I believe I have enough essence of the parasite for them to use."

Crabbe took Frick and Frack to Morocco's booth. The crystal ball shone bright on the crystals in Crabbe's palm and then turned into miniature comets rising from his hand then shot through the window in the beam of the sunlight.

"They will make you proud." said Morocco.

"No hard feelings?" Crabbe inquired.

"You did the right thing, my friend." The servitor replied.

He felt Crabbe's anguish at the thought of having another spirit he knew, out there body hopping, manipulating even a friendly spirit gave him a nasty taste in his mouth. Morocco felt proud being Crabbe's servitor. When the two met he didn't want to go into the light, but felt he still had a purpose to fulfill despite being in spirit form and Crabbe understood, making him his partner.

Morocco was glad Crabbe didn't make him feel like a servant of the spirit world, but like family having each other's back.

Crabbe inhaled, "There will be plenty of adventures for you and I."

"It's nice to take a break," said Morocco. "The thought-forms were happy to get out of that box and take flight."

Crabbe chuckled. "They told you that?"

"Not in so many words, but how long has it been since you used them?"

"You and Mister Kit be ready, I will be taking a nightly stroll to clear my head," said Crabbe.

CHAPTER 21

Hiram opened the door, stepping aside to let Larry waltz inside.

"Imagine my surprise when you told me to meet you at the club, leaving my car so I could ride with you to your house," said Larry.

"I don't understand?" Hiram remarked.

"I could have met you here at your place." Larry replied.

"I wanted to show the guys solidarity, you know? I mean to me that's how you build trust and a brotherhood."

Larry shrugged. "If you say so. Where are the guys?"

"In my basement and before you ask, they are completing their task before we all ride back together to the club house."

Larry gave a dubious look. He followed Hiram down the dark hallway. They stood in front of the door to the basement.

"Few homes have basements anymore," said Larry.

"Well," said Hiram looking up and down. "Built in 1926 and the bathrooms have windows instead of the ventilation system. That's overrated if you know what I mean."

Larry cocked his eyebrows. "Trust me I do." They laughed.

"Now before you go downstairs, it's going to be dark so just grab the rail and it will guide you down to the bottom. Be quiet because I told the guys to meditate."

"Okay," Larry shook his head. "I just want to see my cousin Drew."

Hiram opened the door. "You go on ahead and I'll come as soon as I use the bathroom. I've been holding it since we left the club."

Larry stepped inside. "Whoa! What's that smell… and why is it so dark?" He turned to look back at Hiram.

A clenched fist connected with his jaw, sending him tumbling down the stairs. Larry ended up on his hands and knees, as he shook out the cobwebs. He looked upstairs and saw the door slammed shut.

"What the hell is going on here Hiram?" He asked getting to his feet. "Why did you hit me? Where are the guys? Why is that odor getting stronger?" He looked around the pitch black room.

"Hiram! Answer me! What the hell is going on?"

Larry was headed back upstairs when he felt a strong vice grip grab his arm. He couldn't see what had a hold of him but threw up from the stench of feces and decayed flesh. He heard a growl that sent a chill down his spin. Larry got slammed against a wall. His head banged hard against it making his thoughts cloudy. The confused man felt sharp needles penetrating his heart. Larry screamed.

"It's getting late," said Morocco. Now riding inside the snake eye pentacle chain around Crabbe's neck.

"What do you care? You're dead." Crabbe remarked.

"I know you're upset, but you don't have to be short with me," the servitor replied.

"Now you know why I take these night strolls alone."

"Because you're lousy company?"

Crabbe laughed. "Touche. That makes us even."

Mister Kit brought up the rear. "Meow."

"You too, huh? Despite my abilities guys, I'm still human," said Crabbe. "You didn't have to come along." He looked down at the ebony emerald eyed feline.

"We value you, my friend." said Morocco.

"Company on my walks?" Crabbe pondered. "No complaints, but let's head home to our thoughts."

Crabbe took the night walks alone to think, relieve stress, clear his head. The nocuer and nyctophilia magician loved staying up late at night finding relaxation, and comfort in the darkness. Crabbe got what he wanted, quiet time on the way home along with the crisp night air tingling his face.

Bad thoughts danced inside his head. Stout an evil spirit doing evil things, not the first time Crabbe got wind of evil spirits wrecking havoc among the living. He read books and heard stories about serial killers being possessed by disgruntled spirits who died too young or felt they got cheated out of life.

They took their frustrations out on those who they saw living the American dream. Their dream was taken from them. Crabbe never bought into the evil spirit causing people to go around killing as a sport, but a sickness within the person themselves.

A syndrome he called crazy. Stout got his attention that maybe serial killers like Ted Bundy, John Wayne Gacy, the son of Sam, and Jeffrey Dahmer may have had an energumen inside them and then again just crazy.

Stout didn't possess one person, he was body snatching and destroying lives in the process and needed to be stopped. He hoped Frick and Frack would find him soon. He knew Morocco would have found him by now, but he felt sick about spirits inhabiting the living making them do bad things, not that Morocco did.

The servitor is a wonderful spirit and he possesses for the common good. Crabbe dealt with those who had the power to summon demons or dark angels who are all too eager for mischief and mayhem. He thought back to the 1890's about a man named H.H. Holmes, the notorious multitude of Murder Castle.

Whether he became a vengeful evil spirit, nothing was proven, but he did hurl curses upon everyone who played a part in his conviction. Not long after Holmes' execution, his attorney died and the superintendent at Holmes' prison committed suicide.

The coroner who testified against him met a gruesome death, so did the priest and foreman of his jury. Crabbe thought about the crew Stout worked with. He observed the spirit and saw how distraught he was when he found out they made jokes about his demise and not attending his funeral.

Crabbe wondered if he would stoop low enough to take revenge, seeing them living and enjoying their criminal lifestyle while his came to an abrupt end. Morocco came to mind knowing the servitor didn't like Stout and was right about not trusting him since he used an officer of the law to kill Alan Miller and ruin his career. Morocco would have turned over every stone in finding Stout and this was another reason Crabbe settled for the thought-forms, Frick and Frack.

"Rroaw!" Mister Kit growled.

Crabbe spotted what he hoped to find to work out the stress that took over his body after Silva informed him about Stout. Five demons in human form, waiting for him.

"It appears we have company, my friend." said Morocco.

Mister Kit took off blending into the night. Crabbe didn't take his usual nonchalant attitude, instead he engaged the first demon close to him.

The demon decided not to keep his human disguise and the others followed suit revealing their authentic form. The pentacle chain around Crabbe's neck shone bright, releasing a burst of blinding light. Okay thought Crabbe, time for some exercise.

He sized up his adversaries; five muscles on top of muscles, thick as blocks of cube salt if they still make those out of a Hell Boy flick. Netherworld sent some heavy hitters hoping to force Crabbe to unleash his power. The problem he faced, he knew he needed to use it.

The creatures; blood soulless eyes, ape faced, the reddish blue color of a Baboon, tusked teeth shaped like a Sabre tooth, fur resembling a woman's mink draped around a dense neck, broad shoulders, prickly pointy twigs on the spine, arms with the wingspan to make an NBA center envious, hips, thighs, and legs like an NFL linebacker, paws, and hooves with talons. They all stood in an ape squat position and the paws dragged on the ground.

Crabbe summoned power for the right side of his body. His eyes were fiery red and he stood sideways like a gunfighter giving his opponent a slight target. A ram-ape five stepped forward. Crabbe assumed him the leader despite all being the same height and size, standing close to seven feet.

The monster's nostrils flared, blowing steam. It lowered its head and charged. Crabbe stood his ground, his left side human, but his right... Superman would be proud. The ram-ape bounced off him like a tennis ball thrown against a brick wall.

Crabbe charged up one side of his body, fearing if he went supernova he'd lose his humanity so he had to play it safe.

The expression on the ram head's face was hard to read, but Crabbe could tell it surprised him. The creature rose staring at Crabbe as if studying him.

Before he could attack again, the demon-spawn got distracted when he saw one of his comrades attack another. Crabbe smiled. Morocco.

He had often wondered if the servitor could ever possess a demon and he got his answer.

The other two monster assassins had problems of their own. In the moonlight standing well over six feet, a panther faced, luminous emerald eyed, lean muscular werecat with a Greek-God sculpted body, human hands and feet, razor sharp claws, no tail and hidden genitals making Crabbe happy.

He would try to figure out a pair of speedos for Mister Kit later on, but for now was glad for the help. The werecat looked like the Watchman's Doctor Manhattan. Morocco's puppet relentlessly pounded his fellow demon who despite his hideous face, had the look of shock, then while on its back brought his knees to his chest then with a thunderous piledrive, thrust talon hooves into Morocco's pawn's chest, sending him crashing into the forest uprooting a thick rooted tree.

Mister Kit went to work taking on two at a time. The werecat, graceful, quick, and strong, thrust his talons into one of the ram-ape's chest, yanking out a still beating heart. Crabbe frowned seeing Kit devour the heart.

The ram-ape fell with a thud to the ground causing a slight rumble. Kit got to his and Morocco's adversary. The twosome looked like true apes, pounding their chests sounding like bass drums and stamping their feet up and down making the ground tremble. The reinforced wards should hide all activity away from any naked eye that might drive by.

Crabbe flew backwards in slow motion, but in pain. He flew twenty feet landing hard. He got three cracked ribs for being sloppy taking his eye off his combatant. Watching Morocco manipulating his pawn and mesmerized by Kit's werecat figure he got careless and realized these demon thugs were too powerful to overlook and built for total annihilation. Crabbe stood studying this monstrosity, intelligent enough to attack Crabbe's left side and not his charged up right. Crabbe knew he needed to take a page from Kit's book. No fooling around, no time to dance, end this before he or his comrades get hurt.

Crabbe wolverined his ribs, kicking in his healing factor then took the chance charging up all the way. Before he charged forward to engage the lead ram-ape, he saw a form coming down hooves first, landing on top of the ram-ape who used his hooves to kick a long distance field goal.

Morocco didn't let up. He trampolined the grounded ram-ape till everything from intestines to liver and whatever squiggling organ it had inside, met the same fate of getting squished.

A ram-ape laid on the ground, eyes rolled back and pink flesh oozing from its nose and mouth. Morocco made his possessed ram-ape grab his own horns twisting counter clockwise to a sickening crack. He dropped heavily to his knees, falling face first.

Kit got into a test of strength with his ram-ape. The demon delivered a thunderous headbutt stunning the werecat, forcing him to drop to a knee while still locked together. Kit yanked the creature to him, sinking his fangs into its neck the size of a tree branch. The feline snapped his head back with a ram-ape's larynx inside his mouth.

Crabbe went supernova, powering his body to withstand the ram-ape's attack. He caught the creature by the horns halting his charge despite his feet sliding back a few yards. Crabbe lifted the demon by the horns slamming him to the ground on his belly several times. The ram-ape winded giving Crabbe the advantage to inflict more damage. He ripped off the demon's horns making it look like an actual ape.

Blood gushed out of both sides of his head making him shriek in pain. Crabbe took both horns, placing them back inside the ram-ape's head by the points of its antlers. The creature's eyes rolled to the back of his head and he fell face first to the ground motionless.

Crabbe stood above the dead goblin triumphant, heaving and gloating with his eyes glowing. Visions of world dominance danced inside Crabbe's head. Cities on fire, people running around terrified screaming, crying, on their knees begging to live and worshiping him brought a gruesome smile to his face. The devil standing with him with a hand on his shoulder laughing and saying "My son." Crabbe frowned when he saw his family; nephews and nieces crying and hiding, Tomas comforting Trudy telling him, "You're no brother of mine."

Clover and Blossom crying and shaking their heads disappointed, and Lilac screaming. "Get away from me you monster." Crabbe saw fear in Mister Kit who stepped back toward a wooded area looking for cover, "Your humanity, my friend." said Morocco. Crabbe took a deep breath dashing inside his house.

He came back outside with a jug of holy water glued to his mouth, downing every drop while carrying his cane and touching the demon corpse with the engraved pentacle disintegrating them.

The holy water was gone and so was Crabbe's glowing red eyes as they turned back to brown.

"Welcome back," said Morocco.

Mister Kit rushed up to Crabbe rubbing against his leg in the form of a black emerald eyed cat.

"It's late," said Crabbe. "Time to go to bed."

Mister Kit went to his bed basket, Morocco fazed into his crystal ball, and Crabbe strolled up the spiral stairs stopping half way after hearing a knock at the door. A song by the retro music group 'WHO CAN IT BE NOW', sounded off inside his head. Crabbe sighed, hoping it wasn't more demon bounty hunters. At least not like the muscle bound brutes they already dispatched. He opened the door and it was his clients, the couple monsters in the closet and under the bed, Hilda and Elmo.

"We know it's late, but we haven't heard from you," said Hilda.

"I tried to stop her," said Elmo.

"Could have waited...!" Morocco shouted.

"Take the night off, Morocco." said Crabbe stepping aside allowing the children's imaginations to come in.

Crabbe would have preferred a daytime talk, but the monsters in the closet and under the bed came out at night during a child's bedtime.

"Don't mean to be rude," said Crabbe. "Jenny is fine and I will give you an update on my progress, but I am dealing with a lot right now."

"Told you it wasn't a good time to bother him," said Elmo. "I told her we should leave when we saw your fight."

Crabbe saw the somber look on Hilda's face. Like a mother worried about her teenager staying out too long past curfew. He turned to Hilda.

"I know she is fine and I know you want her back, but she is better off where she is now, than back with the Fosters," said Crabbe.

"We know they are bad people." Hilda replied. "Sorry to drop by so late, but..."

"It's okay and I understand," said Crabbe.

"I need you two to..." He exhaled holding up a hand.

"Not bother you again and you'll be in touch with us." Elmo remarked.

"I have a lot going on." Crabbe replied. "Unless they've got another kid." Hilda and Elmo shook their heads.

Crabbe smiled. "Good and if you two don't mind."

"Say no more." said Elmo, taking Hilda by the arm leading her to the door.

"Good night." said Hilda and the imagination fazed through the door.

Crabbe climbed the stairs, got undressed and fell face first on the bed.

CHAPTER 22

She didn't glow because of the sunlight. Her radiance was pure angelic and goodness despite living a tortured life.

Ruthie's soul was free of the turbulence caused by a devil worshiping father, who was too dumb to know a deal with the devil is fool's gold. He sacrificed his family and all he got was eternity in hell. The funeral ended hours ago and Crabbe waited for the crowd to clear so he could stand at the grave alone feeling a peace of mind.

"Thank you." said an angelic voice.

Crabbe smiled. "For what?" He stared at her luminous floating form. "I scared you to death."

"It was my time and you were what I needed to get home." Ruthie replied.

Crabbe nodded. "You're not the only one at peace."

Ruthie smiled."You saw it too, huh?"

Crabbe watched Motor sitting at the grave site and in church. His face was drenched in tears, but not for sorrow. Tears of joy flowed from his eyes because his tormented cousin found peace.

"Motor is a good man," said Crabbe.

"Best big brother I never had." Ruthie replied.

"He told me you two were close."

"Motor came to see me more... the only family member." She said.

"Well you had a packed house today." Crabbe remarked. "Some people aren't strong."

"Don't hold it against them. Didn't want them to see me that way. Hated putting Motor through it."

"You shouldn't be hard on yourself." said Crabbe. "You couldn't help it."

"How did he know you could help me?" Ruthie asked.

"Intuition can be a powerful thing," answered Crabbe.

"He doesn't know everything about you does he?"

Crabbe inhaled. "I plan to keep it that way, but I think he knows enough." He looked toward the sky squinting, paying heed to the bright sunlight.

"Don't worry it's coming," she said.

"Can it wait till I get home?"

Ruthie giggled. "I'll make an exception."

Crabbe felt another presence. He looked at Ruthie flashing a blinding smile. She no longer had the blood red eyes enhanced by dark circles from lack of sleep. Her eyes engaging; iris bright white, her hair brown and braided in cornrows. The entity Crabbe got wind of, a woman almost the same age as Ruthie, but Crabbe knew was much older, but didn't age since she died young.

"I want you to meet someone." said Ruthie.

Crabbe blushed. "Your mother."

"Thank you," she said, nodding her head. "I'm Natalie."

"Pleased to meet you," said Crabbe.

"Who better to greet and escort me through the pearly gates?" Ruthie asked.

"So you don't plan on roaming the earth?" Crabbe asked.

"Ruthie got moon-eyed. "Do you need me to?"

"No." said Crabbe. "I was making small talk." Go straight to heaven he thought. You deserve a peaceful rest and don't owe me a thing.

"I owe you a lot." said Ruthie with a beaming smile.

"You and your mother have a lot of catching up to do." He replied.

"You better hurry to your car." Natalie remarked.

Crabbe inhaled, nodded and then strolled to his Geo Metro. He thought about taking the car no longer manufactured to Bob for maybe a rebuilt engine like the S-10.

He made it inside his car the same time the sky turned gray. The flood gates of heaven opened. Tears of joy welcoming a new angel into the fold. R.I.P Ruthie, R.I.P. You deserve it. Crabbe headed for home thinking good thoughts about one friendly spirit then anger took over his face thinking about Jeff Stout.

San Remo is an Italian bistro on Central Avenue. The eatery's not a large establishment but acceptable to those who preferred small compact crowds. The food was nothing to write home about, the Veal Parmesan overwhelmed, hidden in the river of tomato sauce with the burnt cheese looking more like an island in an ocean of red.

Sal Dana, the lucky man fishing for the meat in the sauce didn't mind. He enjoyed the hole in the wall Italian cuisine diner because it sat outside the city which meant he didn't have to worry about law enforcement making guest appearances and he could hold his poor man's version of a board meeting with his boys to give him reports on the shake down of local businesses.

"So boys?" Sal eyed his three associates, sitting with him at the back of the restaurant in a booth, watching him sticking a fork into what looked like over cooked veal drowning in its sauce.

He shoved it into his mouth chewing like it was the best he'd ever had. His guys knew too well there was no food he didn't show that reaction to.

"What's the good news?" said Sal, taking a sip of cola to wash his food down.

Murray called Lurch for resembling the Addams Family butler took center stage. "The north side business came through which should be no surprise." He looked at Ralph and Pitt to gloat. "My boys always bring their A game for collecting."

None of the lieutenants brought the day's haul to the meeting, not that it was any secret to the employees of San Remo as they catered to lower tier gangsters.

Ralph cleared his throat. "May come up short, but my guys say tomorrow will make up for what they didn't get down today. Heads will roll if they do not meet payment."

Sal swallowed hard. "When you say roll...?"

"You know..." Ralph made a body language gesture. "You know, break something. Ain't nobody gonna die." He gave Murray a look.

"Hey!" Murray pointed. "That was a one time thing. Water under the bridge."

"Where they found the body." Ralph muttered.

Murray stood giving an icy glare.

"Enough already," said Sal motioning for Murray to sit down. "We're family and shit happens but we got results. None of us went to jail, the flat foots got some cash and all is good. So you two kiss and make up, but not here in front of me while I'm eating."

Pitt snickered.

"Well..." Sal gestured.

"You're up." said Murray.

Pitt inhaled. Ever since his man Stout went down he's been the least productive of the three and feeling the heat. To make up for his lack of production, he took matters in his own hands, but liked it better when he sat back like a boss getting reports from the minions.

"Things ain't like it was since my key man went down, but his replacements are catching on to how it's done. When we get back to home base you'll be pleased."

"Stop beating around the bush," said Ralph.

Pitt nodded. "Like these two clowns I got the job done."

Sal gave Pitt a stern look. "You know why we don't do the muscling ourselves?" He frowned at Pitt. "It's because we don't want the cops on our ass. The hired help are expendable. I appreciate you going above the call of duty, but you better find somebody who's desperate and stupid like Stout, because if you don't and the fuzz come sniffing your way…"

Pitt pursed his lips. "You have my word it won't come to that."

"It's funny," said Ralph. "You used to talk all that shit about your boy Stout and now that he's gone… well like they say, you never know how much they mean to you until they're gone or something like that."

Murray frowned. "Yeah, I don't think that's how the saying goes, but I know what you mean."

Pitt turned toward Ralph. "You know I always said you should talk less because when you talk too much, you always end up proving brains ain't your best friend."

Ralph rose from his seat. "Outside. You want to talk shit to me then do it outside where I show you who's smart."

"You just prove where your brains are at," said Pitt.

"I'll wipe the floor with you."

"Ralph," said Sal. "Sit your ass down and you both shut the hell up." He looked at them. "Your stupidity is upsetting my digestion. I think we all realize that Stout was a valuable asset to us all and he is a missing link in your chain P, but he's dead and gone. So instead of us getting on each other's nerves talking about the dead, let's toast him and like the world keep on going. Is everybody good with that?"

The guys all nodded and toasted to Stout's memory. Pitt and Ralph shared a glare but they threw no punches.

"Maria!" Sal shouted.

A short portly woman with hair the color of snow in a bun, exposing her trench face came out of the kitchen.

"Bring me and my boys more food and drinks will you." The woman nodded, heading back into the kitchen.

Pitt wrapped his arms around his body, shivering. Like a domino effect the other three did the same. "You guys feel that?"

Sal nodded. "Like a goddamn iceberg in here. Maria turn up the heat too."

"Feels like death," said Ralph.

Murray gave a stern look. "P's right, you shut your damn mouth. You talk too much."

"What did I do? What did I do?" Ralph replied. "I was referring to the change in temperature."

"Then that's what you should have said." Pitt remarked.

"Okay, okay, sorry, but it's cold enough to get frostbite." said Ralph.

"Ralph, shut the fuck up." said Sal. "Maria! Food and heat please."

The old woman came out with a tray carrying lasagna, spaghetti and meatballs, Veal Parmesan, Fettuccine, a bottle of red wine and incense. She placed the food on the table then walked around the dining area carrying the incense and chanting.

"What the hell are you doing?" Sal asked.

"I sense an evil spirit in here." she replied.

"Maria," Sal grumbled. "This ain't the time or place for your superstitious shit. It's fucking daylight for Pete's sake."

The old woman continued her chanting and spreading the incense around the room. The four men unwrapped their arms from around their bodies shaking off the chill they once felt.

"Whatever the old gal did worked," said Murray. Pitt nodded. "Yeah, nice and warm again."

Ralph did as he was told, keeping quiet, but scanning the room nodding his approval things were getting back to normal.

"Dig in," said Sal. "Don't let this food go to waste."

Stout stood on the street corner giving the eatery an icy stare. Whatever the old woman did, it worked. But now was not the time. His former comrades when it suited him needed to suffer before he dished revenge.

Let them have their last supper in peace. Stout had plans and the bistro was not the place. Salute to the old board for dismissing him from the premises. Well played, he thought and he would do her no harm because he respected she had a right to protect her eatery. As for those morons, he'd hit them where it hurts.

CHAPTER 23

Hiram stood at the door waiting to enter the house. He wanted a cigarette but didn't smoke, afraid if he did, it would act like an ignite and he'd catch fire.

Hiram shook his head knowing he's hell-bound for his sins, so he might as well wait until judgment day.

He yearned for a drink and would hit the nearest watering hole when his conjunction ended. Hiram wondered what was taking them so long to answer the door. A trap, he thought.

After all, it was almost midnight and he hadn't seen the Longs after getting Jenny from them.

He paid them good money and they didn't mention any need for more, but the heartless couple had played foster parents before and treated the children before Jenny the same, pretending to be parents of the year, only to act like the witch out of Hansel and Gretel, except they didn't eat them, but traded their foster kids for money.

Hiram helped cover up their disappearance to where they went; overseas to be slaves to perverted powerful people in the Middle East. He shook his head feeling guilt thinking about what became of the children; dead, perverts violating them, and then his situation.

He would sacrifice Jenny to his demon lover. Hiram almost threw up calling the goblin from Hades his lover, since he had sex with the foul creature. He conjured her and all she gave him was power of a soon to be defunct club where he was now sacrificing his members to her for breakfast, lunch, and dinner. Hiram leaned over to the side about to upchuck whatever his dinner was, when the door opened. He gathered himself after seeing Robert standing in the doorway.

"You okay there, fella?" Robert asked. You look like you've seen a ghost."

"This is the time they come out." Hiram replied.

"Come inside where it's safe, me and the misses want to have a word with you." said Robert.

Hiram walked with his hand over his right pant pocket making sure his pocket knife was handy, in case he needed it. He knew it was too late to rethink meeting the couple tonight. If they planned anything sinister against him he could take them.

Robert, short with a body afraid of a treadmill, walking sideways and taking deep breaths even when he took a seat and got up from it. Joan, tall and slender, always looking around as if something was waiting to grab her. Her own shadow scared her, thought Hiram.

"Can I get you anything?" Joan asked.

She always played a good host offering refreshments when he came over which he stopped and picked now of all nights to pay them a visit at their request.

Hiram sat down hoping what they had to say tonight wouldn't take long. He snorted. "Let's get this over with."

"Wow!" said Robert. "We haven't seen you in a while and you want to leave already?"

"Those visits were business." Hiram replied.

Robert and Joan looked at each other. "Yeah," Robert nodded. "That's the problem."

Hiram shrugged. "What are we best buds?"

"Business." said Robert. "We are business partners."

Hiram laughed. "Sorry, You didn't get the memo."

Robert and Joan gave each other a look. Hiram wanted to sever ties with the creepy parents of the year. He made some calls along with passing out some cash so they could no longer adopt children.

Hiram paid to keep his name in the dark in case the Longs asked questions that would lead back to him. He knew it was too late to turn over a new leaf, nevertheless at least he could go to hell with a less weight of sins on his guilty conscience.

Robert held hands with Joan. "The little woman and I were talking."

A dubious look came across Hiram's face. She's three inches taller, the top of his head doesn't reach her shoulder, and she's the little woman? Must be a pet name. He thought.

Hiram sat crossing his legs with his hands folded on his lap.

"Indulge me," said Hiram.

"We save our money and you know we have our jobs, but we miss the instant cash if you know what I mean?" Robert stated.

Hiram inhaled, exhaled, and nodded. In his business it is important to work with like minded people. The quick cash circuit is a popular thing among folks like himself. He couldn't explain his new found feelings of compunction for his past transgressions.

Hiram pursed his lips. "What's that saying... good times don't last forever, but bad times linger longer."

Robert shook his head. "Can't recall."

"Well now you have and you said, you still have jobs so be thankful," said Hiram.

Robert frowned. "You know it's like a smoker can't give up cigarettes, or an alcoholic keeps falling off the wagon."

Hiram snorted. "Your point?"

"I can't break the habit." Robert stated.

"Well," Hiram threw up his arms. "I ain't no group counselor so..."

"But you know how to make things move and shake," said Robert.

Hiram inhaled. "If you want a lap dance, you know where to go if the little woman don't mind."

"Since when did this become a joke?" Robert questioned.

"You're right." Hiram stood and stretched. "It's getting late and I don't want to hear from you again. Time to move on."

Robert shook his head. "We can't let you go."

"You don't want to go there." Hiram retorted.

Robert hunched over looking down toward the floor. "Bet you never even had a nine to five job."

"Billions of people do it every day." Hiram remarked.

"It's a bitch," said Robert. "I know you did or said something about me and Joan that we can't hold an infant."

"This is getting boring." Hiram turned to leave.

"Your sister and nieces." said Robert.

Hiram felt like his feet got stuck in cement. His body went numb. He exhaled, replaying in his head, what he thought sounded like a threat.

"Now you're getting nasty," said Hiram, wondering if they knew where Lisa and the girls lived and if so, then they knew Jenny now lived there too.

Robert didn't mention Jenny so Hiram took a deep breath, controlling his anger, deciding to see how the rest of the conversation would go.

"What do you propose?" Hiram turned back to the parents of the year.

Robert gave a gruesome grin. While Joan looked on the verge of a nervous breakdown. She rubbed her hands together, looking around the room, twitching where she sat trying to get comfortable, breathing like she was having a panic attack, and being the silent partner. Hiram realized she wanted no part of this, that this was all Robert.

"Give us another kid and..." Robert held up a finger. "Your contacts and you sit your ass out of our way."

Hiram laughed, confirming they had no clue Jenny would become his niece. "This sounds like blackmail, but you have nothing to make me shit in my pants. So I guess this is goodbye and good riddance."

"You're not the only one who has resources," said Robert looking at Joan forcing her to nod in agreement. Hiram put his hands on his hips counting to ten inside his head. Why was he entertaining these losers in a conversation knowing they were not a threat to him? He observed Joan sitting constipated and maybe she was, while her husband danced like a desperate lap dancer trying to get a dollar in her G-string.

Hiram touched his pocket containing his lock blade. He murdered no one, though he'd witnessed brutal deaths by his demon lover. Grabbing his stomach then covering his mouth to keep from throwing up. He should always remember to stop referring to the hell spawn as his lover because it made him sick.

A weak link in Robert's chain, not that the cretin imposed a threat, nevertheless he thought he'd gotten to him with his threat. The fool sat next to his wife straight and chest out, believing he had the advantage.

"Okay, okay... I have an older girl, and she is being run through the system. I feel sorry for her. She deserves to have a stable home."

"Hey," said Robert pointing at himself and Joan. "We are what you need."

Hiram snapped his finger. "Right under my nose."

"How long would we have to keep her till you erase her out of the system and get rid of social services?" Robert asked.

Hiram smiled. "What can I say, money talks."

"How long would we have to keep the brat?" Robert questioned.

Hiram shook his head. "Not long at all. In fact there's a guy I know in Europe willing to pay five hundred thousand."

Robert got moon-eyed. "Now you're talking. Now you're talking."

Hiram clapped his hands together. "Then we have a deal. After this we don't see each other ever again?"

"Fine by me, but what's your cut?" Robert asked. "You can have the whole thing as long as you never bother me again." Hiram replied.

"You have my word." Robert retorted. "When do we do this?"

Hiram unlocked the door standing half way out. "I'll call you."

"Can you tell me anything about the girl?" Robert asked.

Hiram rubbed the back of his head observing, he saw a woman biting her lower lip, breathing in and out fiercely, looking at him and her husband, like he was watching a tennis match. A woman on the verge of a nervous breakdown. Her husband wide eyed, drooling about how he would spend the money.

"Well she's big for her age, not good on the eyes, and shy, so one of you..."

"Me!" Robert blurted like a student trying to get the teacher's attention. "The little woman is my support, she won't mind sitting this one out."

Hiram nodded. "I'll call you then."

Robert walked over standing close to him. "If you don't, I will call you."

Hiram smiled. "No doubt."

The vengeful spirit bothered Crabbe more than he wanted to admit. He traveled back to the grain holder where the fateful five met their demise. The men who died here tried to do him harm, still they didn't deserve to be a meal for a demon.

He wanted to make sure they would not feel they got the wrong end of the stick and take their frustration out on innocents like Jeff Stout, who thought this was a game, making Crabbe grind his teeth. The room of death was now clean. A job well by the city's hazmat team.

The human debris if left to rot would cause health issues for the living, by contaminating the atmosphere. Crabbe stood in the center, he didn't come empty handed. His cane was handy, in case he ran into his friendly neighborhood demonic bounty hunters, and a backpack. He took out a white chalk and drew on the surface a large pentacle symbol. The triangle star inside a circle used by any good magic wielder.

It represents the elements: SPIRITS (Love & Birth), AIR (Power & Death), WATER (Maiden, Initiation, & Wisdom) EARTH (Law, Repose, Crone) FIRE (Knowledge, Consummation, & Mother). He didn't know Mages argued over the names. The spellcaster put it with religion and you don't argue religion, at least by his rules.

Crabbe was born a Baptist and proud of it. He considered it the outlaw of all religions because it was not bound by strict rules like the others. Crabbe shook his head over the argument about the Pentacle versus the Pentagram: A Pentacle is a five pointed upright star encased inside a circle. The Pentagram is a five pointed upright star without a circle. According to occult, pentacles represent white magic and good, and man's intellect and reason. It uses the symbol as a talisman for objects starting psychic powers.

The pentagram signifies dominating the mind over elements and demons, spirits, phantoms, and ghosts are enchanted by this sign. A soul's eye and you will minister unto legions of angels and hosts of fiends. The Pentacle suited him for the task at hand. He wanted an innocent conversation that they will not roam free harming the living to exact their revenge, if on their minds. The purity of the sign should mellow their souls.

Crabbe put white candles at the points of the star lighting them. He placed a round metal cylinder with pincushion holes placing incense sticks inside each hole. Crabbe grabbed his lighter, lighting the sticks that brought their own fragrance.

He started the ceremony: "REMOVE THE CHAINS OF TIME AND SPACE. RELEASING THE SOULS CONDEMNED TO THIS PLACE. I ADJURE AND COMMAND THEE, SPIRITS, TO APPEAR BEFORE ME. SO MAY IT BE."

The flames of the five lit candles rose strong. Faint faces of the fated five appeared at the star points of the pentacle.

"Glad you all could make it." said Crabbe. "Before we begin I'd like you all to introduce yourselves."

Crabbe stood in the middle of the pentacle. "Drew." said the spirit at the top of the pentacle. "Stan." said the spirit on the right.

"Wally." said the spirit on the left. "Levi." said the spirit below Stan. "Ellis." said the one below Wally.

All five souls sounded somber and lost. "So is this your new home?" Crabbe asked.

"You mocking us in death?" Stan asked.

"There is nothing funny about dying and the way you all left this earth is tragic and not just for you, but those you left behind wondering where you are." Crabbe retorted. "I don't want the name of the person who caused your demise because I am not here to help you get revenge on him or her, judgment day awaits the perpetrator if that's any consolation for you."

"As long as he gets his." said Stan with his flame flaring with anger.

Crabbe had an idea of the person in question, a man, though his concern now was controlling potential vengeful spirits.

"What do you want from us?" Levi asked. His spirit attached to the lower left of the pentacle point.

"There is one vengeful spirit roaming around wreaking havoc among the living and I want to make sure you guys don't do the same," said Crabbe.

He studied the flames and the fainted faces of the doomed spirits. The upper three of the pentacle carried frustrated looks, the left spirit named Wally seemed to accept his fate. The right lower spirit had the look of self pity, his name Ellis. Crabbe held off on questioning, he used his clairvoyance to read the tortured souls.

Drew, the one spirit who had yet to voice his opinion.

Stock broker, married with three children. Reading his vibes about how dumb and big a mistake he made, joining what he now realized in his afterlife was not a club at all, but a pile of shit that still hadn't flushed.

He didn't know whether Drew knew his cousin Larry had suffered the same fate as he or if it would make him feel better that he too found out how unpleasant it was to get devoured and digested by a demon. The magician decided not to tell, he believed the cousins would have their family reunion soon. He focused on Stan, the fellow with a career in finance. He too was stressed about the mistake he made and his family having sleepless nights, thinking of what might have happened to him.

A flash of light flickered before his eyes, his wife is unfaithful, seeing another man, and hope to find his remains, to cash in on the insurance policy.

Wow! What a bitch, thought Crabbe.

Wally the bookworm looking spirit. An expecting father, who wondered what sex his firstborn would be, boy or girl. His wife would now be a single parent. She talked about having more kids and not wanting their first born to be an only child.

If she were to marry again, their first born would never have a full blood sibling and if it is a boy he'd never play catch with him and if a girl he'd never walk her down the aisle on her wedding day. Crabbe heard a sigh that said boy did I screw up.

Levi, a construction worker and divorced with two boys. A sports fanatic who looked forward to watching his boys play football on Friday nights. He critiqued their games giving pointers on how they could play better in the next game and they enjoyed his coaching.

They didn't see much of him unless it was football season, loving the time they spent together, though now Levi knew that was over.

Ellis, who some might consider a flunky security guard. He had no wife, children, no social life except alcohol and internet porn. Crabbe shook his head since it explained why he was the first to get in, being desperate for companionship.

"Was your intention to kill me?" Crabbe asked.

"Maybe," said Stan.

"I guess?" Levi replied.

"We were told to scare you." Wally retorted.

"I just wanted to belong." Ellis commented.

Crabbe waited to hear from Drew still sulking in self pity.

"You carried lead pipes and baseball bats. Didn't look like a scare job to me."

"You're alive aren't you?" Stan mocked.

"Not for your lack of trying and after seeing and talking to you guys, walking among the living is a good thing," said Crabbe.

"You think this is funny?" Drew questioned

Crabbe nodded.

The head of the fateful five spoke, completing the circle of truths. "Nothing funny about dying. It's so final and more so to those who believe they had more to live for and some, if not all did."

Crabbe snorted. "If you weren't trying to kill me, then what was your purpose?"

"What difference does it make? You want the name of the guy who told us to go after you?" asked Drew.

"I told you I'm not here to help you get revenge. You need to trust karma. I'm here to give you some closure and grasp of things. To accept what has happened so you can make a peaceful crossover."

"Are we going to hell?" Wally asked.

"You didn't kill me or anyone else have you?" Crabbe questioned.

"No." said Ellis.

"You're still here because you want justice meted out to the person who set you up. I can promise his time is coming." Crabbe stated.

"Why does he get to keep walking among the living and we, languish here?" Drew questioned.

"The universe has its own way of dealing with people who have done wrong. It doesn't do what you want it to do, as for how fast you want swift justice, it may be a day, week, month, a year or more, nevertheless, wrongdoers get what's coming to them." said Crabbe.

"You said universe." Drew replied. "What about God?"

"Did He make you join this front club? Did He make you come after me? Were you thinking about Him when you chose this path?" Crabbe questioned.

"What do you mean front club?" Levi asked.

"Human trafficking, young girls." said Crabbe.

Dead silence, no pun intended and flames started flickering. The spirits were aware of cryptic things going on and though Crabbe couldn't tell, he felt they got sick and disgusted about joining something they thought was unique and adventurous. Crabbe believed he got his point across.

"If some hard headed teenagers or college kids come by, ignoring the yellow tape. Let them be and figure it out for themselves they shouldn't be here, okay?" Crabbe glanced at the dimming candles. "You know when to move on when a light appears and you can walk through it. You who have children may be reincarnated in your generational timeline. That will be your chance at redemption through generations, to live a fulfilling life so keep your chin up, until then do nothing to piss me off or I will send your souls to hell."

Outside of the feed container a cool breeze swept by carrying a chill, embracing Crabbe's face.

Arctic air helped clear his thoughts and heighten his senses while relieving stress. Discussion with the spirits didn't anger him nor did he feel sorry for the restless souls. He thought about Morocco, a spirit who wanted to remain among the living not to hurt, but to help and not because he had done wrong while alive, he figured he could do more good as if the afterlife gave him powers.

Crabbe didn't interview Morocco to be his servitor. He did not need one, nevertheless, with the spirit world being so unpredictable, Morocco proved to be a valuable asset and valued his friendship; the servitor became family, a brother from another mother and father keeping him grounded, reminding him who he is helping keep his humanity intact.

One servitor was enough, the fateful five were not candidates. Crabbe got what he wanted, easing his mind that they wouldn't try to follow the same path as Jeff Stout, an evil avenging apparition, still, he knew the genies dwelling inside the feed container wanted revenge.

Though not out of envy of those walking around, their distraught focused on the man who sealed their doom. The laws of payback come in different circles. They say God doesn't like ugly, meaning He will punish you for your deeds. It may not happen right away, but the person who committed the wrong will get punished.

Crabbe thought about the Wicca religion. The Wicca do not have any demons or Devils and they are all about the earth and nature. Crabbe was living proof since Satan's blood coursed through his veins and he dealt with demons after his night walks. He doubted if any of the fateful five were Wicca. Wicca believed in a law that decrees 'HARM NONE' translation being that they believe in karma, that any bad we give out will come back on us. Crabbe would not play God for the souls of sorrow taking care of the person who caused their demise.

They'd have to wait for karma. The walk to the S-10 wasn't long; it seemed that way because Crabbe was into his own thoughts. He stopped when a foul odor attacked his nostrils.

He looked at his truck then shook his head. Crabbe saw a small statue of an old man with his back to him sitting on the tail of the S-10 and Crabbe realized the odor came from the man's ass. He spotted a second man, middle aged, a good distance from his partner and Crabbe didn't blame him for giving the little gassy man his space. Crabbe observed the bigger man's head.

Shaped like a torpedo, Crabbe tagged them as demons. Human heads come in many shape and sizes, but with his history working and walking at night, meeting strange men, women who then transformed into scaly, furry, skinless, serpent, and spider eyes, depending on what type of goblins were crawling out of hell to collect the bounty to retrieve the devil's plasma, or ignite the fire within him to lose his humanity and become the devil's vassal.

So far no such luck, yet they kept coming, each hoping to be the one to get the job done. Crabbe studied the old man wearing a jacket, toboggan, jeans, work boots; he sat with his back turned to the tail of the S-10. Crabbe saw it as disrespectful to him, his property. He sniffed, rubbing his hand over his face. A toxic smell snuck in his nostrils burning his nose hairs. Crabbe stared, wondering if this was the ghoul's power, releasing gas from his ass. If so, it was lame he thought, nevertheless effective at making him spit.

The fart found its way into Crabbe's mouth. He frowned thinking bad enough to smell, but to taste someone's fart... disgusting. Crabbe punched the little old demon in the small of his back knocking him off the truck. The demon acted like an old man with back problems. It served him right for thinking he could collect on the bounty, instead of staying retired in hell.

Torpedo head took off his wool cap revealing to Crabbe what he thought an incubus and not human. Torpedo had seemed upset, at seeing his partner rolling around on the ground rubbing the small of his back. He lowered his head charging at Crabbe like a bull.

The magician wanted to go home and two desperate losers from the underworld were cutting into his sleep time. He whirled like a matador slapping Torpedo on the side of his head. The ogre, now more agitated for being toyed with in addition to seeing his partner on the ground sprawling holding the small of his back.

He charged again, getting the same result. Torpedo stood up straight rubbing his head with a smile on his face. Crabbe observed, confused that neither goblin changed to their true nature. The air was foul again, Crabbe glanced over his shoulder and saw the little ghoul on all four aiming his ass at point blank range. He released his potent toxin deadly and silent. He who smelt is the one who dealt with it.

Crabbe shook his head, not his brand and having demon powers, his defense mechanism kicked in like a sinus problem blocking out the horrific odor. Crabbe whirled around grabbing the diminutive troll tossing him like a wiffle ball into his partner. The look on Torpedo's face told Crabbe the toxic gas worked better on him. Crabbe stretched and yawned, strolling over to the would-be assassins who were more dangerous to themselves than to anyone else.

They must have been a pain in the ass annoying Satan for him to send these losers. He wanted to get rid of them, sending this duo on a mission they were not qualified to complete. Crabbe ignited the pentacle carved on the bottom of his cane.

He raised it like a branding iron placing a luminous circle star on the pointy top of Torpedo who looked as if he wanted this ending to rescue him from the old bag of ass gas. He got his wish, yet he didn't turn to dust.

Crabbe wanted him to continue his annoyance to the devil and did the same to the old fart. Let the devil take out his own damn trash, thought Crabbe. He hopped in the S-10 heading back to Parts Unknown, a unique street name that suited him and what he did.

Crabbe entered his abode stretching and yawning. He took off his coat and placed it in the coat closet with his cane. Mister Kit greeted him, circling and rubbing up against his leg. Crabbe bent down scratching under the feline's neck.

Kit's sandpaper tongue licked his hand. Crabbe headed upstairs with Kit trailing behind. He loved his sleep attire, loose fitting oversize black T-shirt and matching baggy black shorts. He checked his email. Silva sent him a message regarding voodoo murders. Crabbe shook his head thinking what the hell; too much going on now to worry about voodoo. The magician turned off his computer then flopped down on the bed joined by Mister Kit.

CHAPTER 24

The liquor store on Fremont avenue was owing for protection.

"Come on old man. You know the drill, open up that safe and we'll get out of your hair." said Leech.

"You heard the man. Pay up and we will see you next week." Jones replied.

Leech and Jones are part of the Sal Dana tree branch working under Pitt. They replaced the deceased Jeff Stout. Stout worked alone, but since Pitt was under fire, he decided two would be better to get their protection payment back on track, since the demise of his former enforcer.

Wordsworth the store keeper carried a different attitude this time. He walked past the two goons, locking the door and changing the open sign to closed. Leech and Jones gave each other a bewildered look. They haven't been shaking down Wordsworth long, but he never did that before, closing up shop and he usually had his protection money ready for the taking until today.

"What's going on old man?" Leech asked.

They were used to Wordsworth being quiet. He gave them their money and they heard him exhale on their way out.

Jones and Leech continued to dwell in the land of confusion.

"Look old man," said Jones. "Don't know what's going on here, but we got other rounds to make see?"

"What are you, a prohibition gangster?" Leech inquired.

Jones went wide-eyed.

"What's the matter with you?" Leech asked. He turned with his mouth dropping open.

A shotgun aimed, then opened fire, blowing the upper half of Leech's head off leaving his tongue and lower teeth intact.

Jones, speechless, moved backwards like a snail, wearing gore from Leech all over his face and chest.

His back pressed against the wall, Jones couldn't take his eye off the standing corpse of his partner whose upper region kept spurting blood into the air, till the body found the urge to fall forward allowing the floor a new paint job in crimson. The shopkeeper stepped around the counter holding the shotgun to his shoulder.

He stood at close range over the cowering Jones who drew his knees up to his chest and head ducked down between them like a turtle in its shell. The alcohol store owner pressed the barrel against Jones's skull. He looked worse than Leech.

Crabbe stood in his kitchen shaking his head. He slept longer than usual. Sleep, the spellcaster smiled, was never his friend. Crabbe couldn't remember the last time he slept eight hours. Coffee made, but forgot the cream. A look inside the freezer and he was taking out vanilla ice cream. Crabbe put two scoops inside the SNOOPY mug that said "NOT BEFORE MY COFFEE." He poured Chicory on Cassata, turning the combination into a snowball in hell. He laughed thinking who came up with the name. His cell set on vibration did just that on the counter. He picked it up. Silva.

"What can I do you for?" Crabbe asked.

"Got some freaky shit for you to check out, so get your ass down here." said Silva.

"Okay," Crabbe replied. "Where are you?"

Silva's way with words fit her personality and looks.

Crabbe took no exception doing as she asked. He arrived at the scene of the crime, the liquor store murders. Crabbe used a shadow spell helping him tag along with Silva.

The usual faces were there doing their jobs. Sergeant supervising patrol officers and leading the efforts of the homicide unit. Detectives like Silva getting facts and statements from potential witnesses and complainants.

Patrol officers maintaining the integrity of the crime scene keeping bystanders out with the help of the yellow tape.

Forensic Science Technicians collecting, classifying, and analyzing physical evidence from the victims and crime scene. Medical Examiner/Forensic Pathologist recording the position and condition of the victim and related evidence to determine cause of death. From what Crabbe could tell both men took close range shotgun blasts leaving nothing to the imagination.

He saw the City/County Attorney working with investigators to expedite any necessary search warrants, but Crabbe doubted that would be vital since it seemed to be a store robbery and he saw a man blubbering sitting down in handcuffs. Forensic Photographer using high-tech cameras, lenses and filters to photograph any materials or impressions, evidence in a trial.

Silva worked alone, convincing the powers that be a partner would get in her way. Crabbe followed her wherever she went, stopping and observing the first victim or culprit.

"The top half of his head exploded and this is what's left." Silva murmured, trying not to look crazy talking to herself.

Crabbe inhaled thinking though the deceased was human, it reminded him of a demon he fought years back with lower case teeth, serpents used their forked tongue to sense where you were since it didn't have eyes to see, ears to hear, or a nose to smell. Crabbe shadowed Silva to the next victim with his head wedged down between his legs like he was going to give himself a blow job.

The back of his neck and shoulder were blown off by the weapon Crabbe predicted after seeing an officer holding a shotgun. Silva decided they'd seen enough, making a beeline to the exit.

"Where are you going, detective?" A gruff voice inquired.

Silva rolling her eyes whirled toward the voice. Captain Rupert Melville. He annoyed her because she refused to have a partner and went over his head to get her wish.

"I'm... feeling queasy." She grabbed her stomach as if to vomit.

Melville threw up his hands. "Okay, okay, take it outside." He frowned.

"Got enough gore in here, don't need you adding to it."

"Thank you sir, don't want to contaminate the crime scene."

Silva waltzed six blocks from the crime scene ducking in an alley checking behind dumpsters for privacy. Crabbe appeared, dumping his shadow spell.

"What do you think?" Silva asked.

Crabbe swallowed hard before answering. He told his family there was no one special in his life which wasn't true since Silva knew enough about his world being more than black and white.

She didn't know his complete origin and what she knew came out because her demon boyfriend forgot to hide his true nature. She needed rescue from him and therapy.

Crabbe studied the confident athletic woman. Her hair cut pressed tighter to her head shaved on the sides and back giving a masculine yet sexy feminine appeal to Silva's powerful girlish face.

Snug fit white blouse tucked inside painted on blue jeans, but her breasts and personal business hidden, because of her fitness physique fit the clothing like a glove and her trench cloaked her body withholding Silva's backside. She wore cream colored sneakers making the magician exhale because wearing black pumps would've dropped him to his knees.

"The spirit who smoked Alan Miller using one of your men in blue. How's the officer doing?"

Silva inhaled and nodded. "Happy he got in Shaw Heights instead of the penitentiary. I don't keep tabs, but have heard nothing bad since we committed him."

Crabbe leaned back on the ridged faded red brick alley wall. Margo Parker didn't hesitate saying he owed her a favor. He was two in the hole for her. Crabbe told her enough to convince the head honcho to admit the man in her care was by an evil spirit, possessed.

Parker surprised Crabbe with how open minded she was, about a world some people considered to be make believe. He didn't tell her everything, nevertheless she made room for another patient and now there will be a sit down to discuss an unwanted partnership.

Silva pursed her lips. "We got us another one don't we?"

Crabbe nodded. "But these guys were asking for it and it was only a matter of time before they got what was coming to them."

He exhaled. "You ever heard of a man named Sal Dana?"

Silva nodded. "Small time hoodlum shaking down small shop owners. The way he likes it, no rush for the big time, but this is the first time somebody fought back."

"Wait a minute..." Crabbe gave a dubious look. "You know what's going on?"

"Hold on." Silva retorted, pointing her finger. "Nobody's been killed until today. A few broken bones, bloody lips, and noses and that's all. The shop owners didn't press charges, these goons were never there and it ties our hands when we don't get cooperation. So back off."

"I'm not jumping on you." said Crabbe. "These shake downs are done with mean looking guys with harsh language and baseball bats?"

"Baseball bats?" Silva questioned.

"Not important." Crabbe replied. "The store owner had a shotgun?"

"Just for show." Silva shrugged. "He said in case someone came with a gun and they never have and he'd paid them before." She exhaled.

"He said he was about to give them the usual payment and something took over his mind, but he doesn't remember shooting anybody."

Crabbe banged the back of his head against the wall. A vengeful spirit at large and he was tormenting his former crew. Stout knew where they got their money and he'd be lying in wait, using the shop owner's bodies as temporary hosts, traumatizing their minds after committing murders they'd know nothing about. Stout would have to get restrained or Shaw Heights will have no vacancy.

"I assume the shop proprietors are old, which is why no actual violence has taken place." said Silva. "Maybe I should stake out shops where the Sal Dana gang make their money?"

"This is beyond police business." Crabbe remarked.

"And yet here we are." Silva replied.

Crabbe pursed his lips. "I'm not trying to be funny, but you better roll up your sleeves."

Silva gave a look. "What's that supposed to mean?"

"Supernatural trouble is what I do," said Crabbe. "If you don't want to end up a casualty you let me handle things."

Silva got moon-eye. "You're doing a bang of a job so far."

Crabbe smirked. "You're drawn into my world now and I hate that. The feed container murders by a demon summoned by a fool. A revengeful spirit causing deaths, wrecking lives because he is in misery and wants company. Two evil supernaturals wreaking havoc in this city. A horrific story and yes Gwyn Silva you're in it."

"What can I or my fellow officers do?" She asked.

"Pray," said Crabbe.

"Sometimes it feels like begging," Silva replied.

"To those who don't help themselves." said Crabbe. "I have help... they're taking longer than I expected but they'll get the job done."

"Made from your world?"

Crabbe snorted. "From my heart and soul."

Footsteps were heard coming down toward the alley.

Crabbe started chanting: "WHEN YOU FIND YOUR PATH IS BLOCKED. ALL I HAVE TO DO IS KNOCK."

Crabbe opened an invisible door disappearing behind it.

"There you are." said an officer. "Captain got worried and sent me to look for you."

Silva waved. "Think I got it all out of me. Go tell him I'm on my way."

The officer nodded, walking back to where he came from.

Crabbe became visible again. "Teach me that trick," said Silva.

"You have the power to know now when something unusual is happening and that binds you to me. But it's to inform, not engage. I'll do the heavy lifting." said Crabbe.

"Do I have a choice?" Silva questioned.

"Be safe lady, be safe." Crabbe retorted.

CHAPTER 25

Crabbe walked into his place as if he came from a nine to five job. He never worked a real job and didn't care to have one. The magician continued down his dark dim lit hallway. He loved his home business atmosphere which would give most people the creeps except maybe, his next door neighbors the tattoo queens, the Banger sisters. Crabbe grabbed a couple of incense sticks, Frankincense and Myrrh brands known for protection, health and spirituality. The word spirituality danced in his head. He lit them with a lighter then proceeded to his velvet tan lounge chair and sank into it with a long sigh.

"Why so glum chum?" asked Morocco in one of his five crystal balls around the compound. This one sat on a bookshelf in the corner of the library. Crabbe didn't want his servitor friend to get bored settling in one place like his booth with life-size mannequin.

"Stout struck again." Crabbe replied.

"A penny for your thought-forms?" Morocco remarked.

Crabbe gave a slight smile to Morocco's comment. The servitor wanted to venture out to find Stout, but because of Stout leaving innocent patrons traumatized from committing acts of violence they wouldn't partake in, Crabbe forbade his servitor to go body jumping. "You go out, find a host to pursue Stout who has his host, then what?"

"I will catch and retrieve him and you can send him straight to the netherworld." said Morocco.

Crabbe snorted, nodded, and rose from the comfort of his chair. He went to the kitchen then came back with a small glass of Bailey's Irish cream on the rocks. The drink contained a hint of Irish whiskey.

Crabbe, not a heavy drinker, felt he needed a strong drink for a serious conversation with his servitor. He went back to his seat nursing his carouse. "Morocco you have a hard on for Stout."

The crystal ball harnessing the servitor flickered. "Pardon?"

"You engage in a fight... both using your host and it ends badly. You killing his host or him eliminating yours. You're already in the afterlife so no harm, no foul, to you or Stout. But your hosts got involved and not by their own will."

"Crystal clear my friend. The thought-forms don't seem to be faring so well." Morocco replied.

"Frick and Frack can't do what you do and I don't want them to. Their job is to monitor then mark him and I will step in."

"You lie in wait while he continues his killing spree? Is it because the people he's doing in are bad?" Morocco questioned.

Crabbe took a longer swig, swallowing hard. Stout's previous casualties were bad men yet they didn't deserve the long goodbye as the prohibitions would say. He pondered for a moment if his servitor's comment hit home. Was he sitting around waiting for Stout to take the Sal Dana gang? Was he going to let the vengeful spirit get his revenge because he found out they didn't give a damn about him dying? Either way it's wrong and he knew Stout had to be stopped.

The thought-forms will do the job he intended for them and he admitted he would like it to be soon, rather than later. Crabbe's intuition told him to wait. He had a demon on the loose and two birds with one stone came to mind. The blueprint to his plan wasn't clear, but it was coming together. So patience is a virtue would be his battle cry for now, no matter the damage.

He knew Stout's intentions and his focus, he wanted to punish and eliminate his former circle.

"Not true," said Crabbe.

"So the thought-forms are your extension of a branding iron... tag you're it, hmm?"

Crabbe downed his Irish cream, rose from his chair making his way back to the kitchen. He came back with a mason jar and a shot glass. Crabbe put them down on a small round mahogany table. He grabbed the jar, twisting the lid, pouring the liquid in the shot glass. Crabbe threw it down his throat, swallowing hard.

"Is our conversation upsetting you, my friend?" Morocco inquired.

"Enlightening," said Crabbe. "This drink is one of my canning ventures, no tomatoes, pears, or peaches." He lifted the half empty jar." Sliced Jalapeno peppers, 2 cinnamon sticks, cubed watermelon, three tablespoons of honey, and two cups of red wine. Store for up to six months in a cupboard or fridge."

"What does a drink such as that do?" Morocco asked.

"Organic is a pharmacist's worst nightmare. Mind over medicine. Plant life can be harmful, but vegetables and petals from plants can be what the body needs. When I look at nature in full bloom, I see health and beauty regenerating.

Not saying that's what happens when I drink petals mixed with alcohol and spices. But I feel confident the properties are at work, doing something good inside me rather than mammals giving birth, believing they are extending their bloodlines. A catch 22."

"Very insightful friend," said Morocco.

"I'm not Harry Dresden or an X-man sending a burst of energy to take out a foe. The thoughtforms are meant to keep tabs on him and when they tag Stout I'll be able to keep the loop on him, nevertheless, I'll have to play two birds with one stone."

"Before your ingenious plan works, there will be more body counts." Morocco replied.

Crabbe took a swig from the jar. "When I come across a nature channel and see a scaly devouring a furry animal it bothers me. I don't get too upset seeing a furry on furry or scales on scales food chain.

Watching rodents getting fed to serpents bothers me but as they say, different strokes for different folks. I guess because fur looks more comfortable to snuggle than scales."

"Some women wear the snake skins well my friend," said Morocco.

Crabbe didn't know what year or when his servitor died or his experience with women with snake skin garments.

Crabbe chuckled, thinking a lot better than him since most of the women wearing scales were demons, attempting to squeeze and drain life from him.

"What I'm trying to say is there's a cause and effect for everything and you have to let the cycle of life play out," said Crabbe. "You know I can't afford to exert myself."

"Your humanity is important, however I just hope you know what you're doing." Morocco retorted.

Crabbe toasted then finished his cordial swig.

Java, The Hut Coffee House located on North Graham street was surrounded by condos, taverns, an industrial plant, and a Circle K convenience store. Crabbe parked the Metro on 9th street, behind a row of cars outside a gate, encasing condos. He killed the engine, got out, and walked down the sidewalk.

He noticed a man wearing a black toboggan, below average height making him short, black, facial hair, brown jacket and jeans, holding back as if waiting to follow. He tracked Crabbe till he saw him enter the coffee house.

Crabbe thought about demons harassing him at night, but never during the day. A first time for everything, but did they want a brawl for it all during twilight? Crabbe erased the thought from his mind when he saw Margo Parker, the director of the Shaw Heights facility stand up near the back of the drip house.

Crabbe embraced the establishment; much like his store/house dim lit, with the smell of espresso like incense to make it authentic, varnished wooden walls, floor, and countertop.

The employees wore uniforms dark brown and light tan khaki pants. Parker wore a black velvet jacket, white knitted crew neck helping her jacket fight off the chill, jeans and sneakers. She looked different, her body didn't remind him of a female wrestler, her face more chiseled than full and her hair drifted down to her shoulders, the front silver and back raven black.

She wasn't wearing glasses and Crabbe assumed contacts; he gestured he wanted to sit facing the door. Parker gave him what he wanted.

They got comfortable giving the waitress their order; Parker ordered an espresso and banana nut muffin, Crabbe ordered a cappuccino and blueberry muffin.

The door opened with a tall thick young man, wearing an orange street worker vest with his cell phone glued to his ear strutted in. No big deal till he walked toward their table and kept acting like one of those clocks where a soldier kept marching back and forth.

Crabbe got annoyed pondering why the man didn't park his carcass. He did after Crabbe and Parker gave him the evil eye. A demon thought Crabbe and if so why in daylight?

"Guess you know why I invited you here?" Parker inquired.

"The men admitted to your facility don't deserve to do jail time." Crabbe replied.

Parker pursed her lips. "There's crazy and there's crazy. The two men I am doing you a favor for are out of touch with reality and are not faking it. That's why after talking to them they are under my care." Parker remarked. "But I need to know if this is going to be a continuing theme?"

Crabbe studied the woman's transformation. She was at least late forties or early fifties. Parker held up well enough to be under the arm of a younger man. If she offered, Crabbe would not turn her down.

"What's wrong? Why are you looking at me that way?" Parker asked.

"Sorry." Crabbe blushed. "You look different than the first time I saw you."

"I wanted to make you feel at home," she smiled.

Crabbed nodded. The lady has a sense of humor.

"To answer your question," he swallowed. "I hope not."

The waitress brought back their orders.

"You need to come clean," said Parker.

Crabbe sighed. He could count on one hand how many people knew about his special powers and Gwyn Silva still didn't know the full extent.

"The world isn't black and white."

"There's Asians, Latinos..." Parker smirked.

Crabbe smiled. The woman definitely has a sense of humor. This is good he thought, because it helps.

He respected the woman for taking in as he put it, his patients with no questions asked until now.

"If I bring you into my world, well there is the chance of going back if you choose, but if you stay then your life will change forever."

Parker took a sip of her coffee. "My grandparents, all four of them told us tales that made your hair stand up and skin crawl. What disturbed me sincere.... they were sincere."

"There's make believe and make believe." Crabbe retorted.

Parker leaned in. "Make me believe."

Crabbe took a bite of his muffin then washed it down with his mocha. "I take it you didn't buy that light show?"

"I know it wasn't cheap parlor tricks," she replied.

"I have a special skill set that allows me to perform unique..." Crabbe got distracted watching the man who came in after him watching them. Hope this fool isn't a demon he thought.

"What's wrong?" Parker asked. "Is it that asshole who couldn't find a seat?"

Asshole was right and Crabbe's patience was wearing thin.

Why won't these fools leave him alone knowing what he can do to them?

Parker turned and stared, forcing the man to avert his eyes.

"Why did you do that?" Crabbe asked.

"We're not bothering anybody and people should respect other people's privacy. You want me to confront him?"

"No. He's turning his back to us. Think you scared him." Crabbe hoped it wasn't a demon because he might put Parker on his list. A bold woman like this would go good with Silva, but he'd have to protect them both if push comes to shove.

"I've helped priests with exorcisms and no, Ruthie wasn't possessed if you believe that."

"I studied those tapes and saw she had her fits around 1 am. I know the world is full of questions that are best not answered. The look on her face was peaceful," said Parker "But I still don't know what you do or who you are."

Crabbe snorted. "I don't think we're in the right surroundings to discuss this."

"I'm staying at the Weston. Thought I deserve a retreat from the abnormal."

The hotel sat on 500 South College and 100 Stonewall.

Parker's voice smoothed, her body language swerved indicating an invite. He'd oblige her allure because he suspected with Stout on the loose seeking revenge against his clique, meant more innocents might get possessed to committing murder. Crabbe glared at the man glancing over his shoulder instead of minding his own business.

"Our friend don't seem to know where to put his nose," said Crabbe.

Parker rose. "I'll lead the way."

"Where did you park?" Crabbe asked.

"Around back."

"You go on. I want to see what our friend does," said Crabbe.

Parker walked past the man who kept the phone glued to his ear. She left and the man glanced back toward Crabbe. The magician inhaled then got up to leave. He made it outside, stepping to the side. He texted Parker. She replied, giving him her room number.

Safe and sound, he thought and now for the matter at hand. Crabbe parked across the street so he waited and less than five seconds later the man came with the cell attached to his ear. A stare down from Crabbe made them strangers. He disappeared around the corner. Crabbe crossed the street to his Metro. He spotted an old man with facial hair the color of snow, staring at him with a cell phone attached to his ear. What the hell, he thought. Crabbe hopped inside the Metro, driving off, shaking his head.

CHAPTER 26

Exercise is the best way to handle stress. You get a partner and the two of you motivate each other to do that extra rep and set, pushing your bodies to the limit.

Crabbe compared his escapades to an old beer commercial; he didn't have it too often, but when he did he made the most of it. The magician stressed over demons eating humans and a vengeful evil spirit on a killing spree while leaving the people he possessed comatose after being told they committed a murder they knew nothing about.

Parker needed a relief too. She ran an institution full of people no longer connected to reality. Crabbe imagined Parker checking on patients everyday to see if they got the proper care and if the results were positive. She talked to their families assuring them their loved one was in excellent hands. Parker had to be confident her staff were qualified to do what she paid them to do; helping patients get better. The spellcaster was glad to oblige in relieving her tension. They sat up in bed, snuggled together for quiet time.

Crabbe pondered on Parker's transformation from when they first met. The woman had a thick solid body. She looked older sitting behind that desk at Shaw Heights. Her body was now toned, slender, strong, and sexy. Crabbe got wide eyed, thinking she could be a demon. He shook his head thinking that he'd know. Dealing with them up close and personal, being seduced, then vanquishing them for trying to collect the bounty. Crabbe laughed.

"What?" Parker inquired.

Crabbe shook his head, keeping his thoughts to himself.

His mind traveled back to the foreplay, he teased her hot box area slithering his tongue on Parker's inner thighs. When he was about to pull away she grabbed a handful of his bushy Afro hair and clasped her hams squeezing his head, forcing his tongue between her pleasure walls. She moaned ecstasy as his tongue covered every nook and cranny of her sugar walls. Here's to you Mrs. Robinson.

"Any reason that man was eyeing you?" Parker asked.

"Story of my life." Crabbe replied.

"Is it a good read?"

"If you like horror, supernatural, and paranormal." Crabbe remarked.

"You an occult detective?"

Crabbe grinned. "Trouble is what I do. If it's eerie."

Parker sat up. "That wasn't cheap parlor tricks."

Crabbe got a text from Father Leary. The one man who knew more about him than his own family. Any time the Padre contacted him he answered. Crabbe hopped out of bed in the buff returning the text. Parker turned on the lamp light. She supported herself against the brown bed board, purring like a kitten, surveying Crabbe's body.

His body definition was not built by lifting heavy weights, but lean as a jogger or someone who spent a lot of time on a rowing machine, yet strong and symmetrical. She approved of his junctions.

"I had a friend once say if it couldn't touch his navel then he couldn't talk to her," said Parker.

"She didn't hurt his pride after he took off his clothes?" Crabbe questioned.

"I didn't bother to ask. I was too busy laughing." She winked. "You have nothing to worry about."

Crabbe did his own observation after finishing his text. A Rod Stewart song came to mind about an older woman named Maggie May. He said when the sunlight hit your face, it showed your age and the same could be said about Parker in the chandelier light. Stewart also said that it didn't matter none, because in his eyes she was everything. Crabbe's eyes were pleased with what he saw.

The woman was a beauty with enough juice to have any twenty something man, but he knew she had too much class to go on the prowl for younger men. She wanted answers to what happened that night, when he turned out the lights in her compound in order to do his work.

Parker didn't want him to think she was naive to something strange going on and he respected her enough to not insult her intelligence.

Crabbe smiled. He would do her as Silva, but not bring her too far into his world like Silva.

Silva got this far because she dated a demon and he felt she might have ended up at Shaw Heights if he didn't take her under his wing giving her the 411. He'd give Parker baby steps because he needed her, in case Stout were to violate other innocents to do his bidding for revenge.

Crabbe wondered if this would be a recurring thing between them. He didn't want it to be and not because of their age difference, he wanted a relationship similar to what he and Silva have, even though they fought the chemistry building between them. Sex with Parker, a stress relief and he knew she felt the same, building a strong friendship, yet not strong enough to tell her about demons and evil spirits wreaking havoc in the city.

"Is it important?" She asked.

Crabbe continued getting dressed. "It's all business when he calls." He nodded.

"So..." Parker got out of bed possessing the body of a twenty year old woman. Crabbe swallowed hard, amazed by the transformation from when he last saw her. He exhaled hoping she wasn't a demon. She smiled while getting dressed when she caught his gaze.

"I took advice from my Pinterest board." She sat on the bed putting on cream sneakers. "Cut out sugar, fast foods, eat more organic food, add spices to my coffee, drink organic water before going to bed and exercise."

Discipline and strict diet plus exercise, no she is no demon, thought Crabbe.

Parker stood adjusting her jeans. "Do I need to make sure I have a vacancy?"

Crabbe shrugged. "Not for me I hope, but let's play it safe."

"Noted." said Parker.

Crabbe grabbed his head, closed his eyes, gritted his teeth then dropped to his knees.

"My God!" screamed Parker, rushing over and holding him in her arms.

Visions clouded his head. He saw the three men he encountered earlier. The man who followed him to the Java The Hut Coffee House, another one hovered around him and Parker inside the joint, and the old man staking out his car.

All three according to his vision were in the woods at night, standing in a circular hard plantless ground area, talking to a man wearing mime make-up and a black top hat.

Crabbe got to his feet when the visions and his migraine cleared his head.

"Are you all right?" Parker asked.

Crabbe breathed deeply. "Like nothing ever happened"

Parker gave him a concerned look. "Seen a doctor?"

"Not since I was an infant." Crabbe remarked. Parker's mouth dropped as she stared at him.

"You wouldn't understand." Crabbe replied.

"Do I want to?"

"Thought you had this room for another day or so?" Crabbe inquired.

Parker flashed a brilliant smile. "Got what the doctor ordered," she winked.

"Time to get back to the salt mine. You have my number... you know, in case you have more patients."

Crabbe nodded. "Yeah... sure,"

Their lips became magnetic, finding it hard to pull apart. Parker pressed his nipple like a button pushing him out of the room. They both had their own worlds that needed them.

Hers, helping people come back to reality and his, playing his own brand of superhero.

Crabbe got the intel from Father Leary. One of his elderly church members needed her prescription and the pharmacy told her to come around midnight. Crabbe felt the same as Leary did; what pharmacy stays open around or after midnight? Leary didn't want to go in blazing away with his holy shotgun, making a mistake if the perpetrators were not demons.

So who you going to call... GHOSTBUSTERS the original... maybe? Certainly not the girl team. No, you call Crabbe H. Appleton.

Leary informed the woman to wait for Crabbe before going inside. The magician hoped she followed Leary's advice. Nashville, a small country county with farm animals, crops, tractors, a chicken plant out in the bluegrass district.

The name itself Nashville and not Tennessee, but southern and didn't sound like trouble. Where Crabbe lived, Parts Unknown Road... yeah. The Metro made it in good time yet Crabbe wished he had the S-10. He preferred the truck for drives out in the country and he'd see if Bob can juice up the Metro like his truck, though he may have to pay him. No problem, thought Crabbe.

He had more on his mind than saving an old woman walking into danger.

Crabbe thought about the vision that gave him his migraine. He knew of the place where plant life feared to grow.

THE DEVIL'S TRAMPING GROUND.

In the rolling hills of southern Chatham county, North Carolina, there's a mysterious, barren circle that has become one of the state's most enduring legends. It lies off an old dirt path near the Harper's Crossroads area in Bear Creek, and it's known as: THE DEVIL'S TRAMPING GROUND.

According to legend, the Devil himself visits the site to stomp around inside the circle, contemplating evil and thinking about ways to win souls for his fiery pits. The sparks created by his cloven hooves have destroyed the very earth in the circle, and nothing, not a tree, plant, or weed will grow on the spot.

Objects left in the circle before dusk often disappear, or are found later, tossed far out of the boundaries of the Devil's space. Thrown so they say, by the Devil himself, angry that a mortal would dare to leave something in his circle.

Animals act up at the site. Dogs whimper and cower and refuse to enter the circle, wild animal tracks were never found on the soil, and legend says that even birds won't fly over the spot.

The circle itself is about forty feet in diameter and barren. Scientists have occasionally studied the strange patch of land, but they have presented no satisfactory reason to explain the conditions there. In years past, there were those who attempted to plant seeds in the desolate circle, but each time the plants refused to grow. Others have tried to transplant vegetation into the area, but it all withers and dies.

Chatham County was founded just before the American Revolution, and from its earliest days, the legend of the trampling ground grew. The early Scotch-Irish settlers gave the spot its name, believing that the Devil, like a man, aided his thoughts by pacing around in a circle. The Tramping Ground, they believed, was his private spot.

Over the years, people have attempted to spend the night in the circle, hoping to catch a glimpse of the old scratch, but no one has reported success in either staying the entire night or dealing with the Devil. Some stories say those who have attempted to stay in the circle, have run out in a wild state bordering on insanity, after a quick glimpse at the Devil's true face.

An old rural state road leads to the infamous spot and folks have spotted a shadowy figure in the woods, near the road leading to the circle. Perhaps it is the Devil himself, or one of his many minions, watching the circle and waiting to claim any helpless souls who dare to step on the Devil's tramping ground.

CHAPTER 27

There were many legends, and Crabbe knew a good number of them. He knew also, that his visions don't lie. Those three men were like blind mice, if they were meeting Satan to make a deal, which would most certainly mean selling their souls. Crabbe shook his head. Everyone can't be saved.

A sign welcoming him to Nashville greeted him and the pharmacy was up ahead on the right. A hole in the wall dealership with a lot, full of old cars across the street from an abandoned auto shop, an insurance company sat on the right side of the street. Crabbe spotted a late model two door beige Impala.

He pulled up beside it, a thick elderly woman with short snow color hair sat in the driver's seat. Crabbe was glad the woman did what Father Leary told her; to sit and wait. The magician eased up to her driver side window, placing his hand on it hoping not to startle her. She turned smiling, rolling the window down.

"You must be Mister Appleton?" She inquired.

"Yes, ma'am." Crabbe replied. "But please call me Crabbe."

"You can call me Laura," she said.

"Next time," said Crabbe. "For now, I call you grandma."

She looked over her glasses hanging on her nose. "He sounded so serious when I told him I had to drive out here to get my prescription around midnight. But this is my pharmacy."

"Have you ever heard of a pharmacy staying open around or past midnight?" Crabbe asked.

Laura shook her head. "But they knew I needed my medicine."

"What time did you call them?" The magician asked.

She shrugged. "Before noon, I guess."

Crabbe cocked his head, his eyes widening. "And they are just getting it ready at this hour? Don't you think that's odd?"

Laura pursed her lips. "I need my medicine."

Crabbe nodded. "Okay let's go get that medicine." He stepped back allowing her to get out of the car.

"You're my grandson, right?"

Crabbe smirked.

"What, I can't have a black grandson?" She questioned.

"No... I mean..." He opened the door.

"Shall we?"

Laura led the way inside the pharmacy. It had canned foods, snacks: cookies, chips, and candy bars. Other aisles had detergent, soap, bathroom cleaners, paper towels, and toilet paper. The proprietor, a young woman clothed in a dress that looked like it was made from red drapes. Her face was pale and full, long black hair and two large lumps of flesh down below her waist.

Her partner was a native of India as far as Crabbe could tell. What part, he did not know, but the man was average height, stocky and bowlegged. Neither of the two look pleased seeing him accompany Laura. Their name tags read Milan and Rita.

"Mrs. Brown," said Milan in a strong accent. "Here is your prescription."

She took it and smiled.

"That will be thirty-five, ninety-five." said Milan.

"Does it take this long to prepare a prescription?" Crabbe asked.

Milan smiled. "We were busy today."

"A first time for everything." Crabbe remarked.

Milan handed Laura her receipt.

"And who are you?" Rita asked.

"I'm her grandson,"Crabbe retorted.

Milan and Rita gave each other a look.

"What?" Crabbe questioned.

"A white woman can't have a black grandson?"

"Oh no... sure... yeah it can happen." They both said with words stumbling out of their mouths.

Laura giggled and Crabbe walked her out to her car making sure she got off safe, before returning inside the pharmacy.

His intuition told him something was wrong in Denmark and it wasn't because a pharmacy was open past midnight. Crabbe learned to trust his instincts, because of his years of experience, protecting the topside from what lurks below.

You don't have to look hideous, furry, scaly, or disfigured to be a monster.

If these two were guilty of doing sinister things, Crabbe would apprehend them and contact the local authorities. If monsters, then they'd get the monster bash.

Crabbe leaned on the counter. "So this is not the norm?"

"Unless you need a prescription we're about to close," said Rita.

Crabbe studied the young woman. Attractive face, nice hair, and if she joined weight watchers who knows.

"I'm mind over medicine."

Crabbe observed the pharmacist; fidgeting hands, sideways glances, rapid inhaling and exhaling.

Crabbe focused on Milan. "What part of India are you from?

Bangalore or New Delhi ?" Crabbe laughed.

"You know I always laugh when I say New Delhi, coz it makes me want to ask for a sandwich, but in your case, you'd make the hoagie and eat it at the same time." Crabbe joked, eyeing his enormous belly.

Milan glared at him. "Your grandmother's gone and you need to do the same."

"I second that," said Rita.

Crabbe nodded then gave both a stern look. "In time you'll learn that monsters have nightmares too."

"We're not afraid of you." said Rita.

Bingo! Crabbe thought. "All you had to do was behave." he retorted.

"I admire you for not letting the bounty entice you."

"We just want to live in peace," said Rita.

Minions often escape Hades unnoticed and some ask for permission, making Satan believe they want to collect the bounty, not realizing some just want to get the hell out of hell, because it's quite obviously, an awful place to live.

Some of those who leave the white picket fence do so, taking human forms and following the creed of not being evil. They even find a human to make a life partner and later reveal who they are and the human accepts them because after all, love conquers all. Crabbe shook his head thinking, more power to them.

However, some goblins stick to their true nefarious nature, like these two.

Crabbe pursed his lips eyeing the back of the store. "Mind if I have a look around?"

"You're not a cop and you don't have a warrant." Milan blurted.

"New Delhi." Crabbe smirked. "Again I'd ask you to make me a canape, but you'd eat it and yes, I am the law when you got something to hide."

Milan dropped to all four limbs looking natural, and explaining why he was standing bow legged. A crab-spider, keeping his human features, ran up the wall positioning himself on the ceiling. Rita surprised Crabbe with her agility, leaping flat footed on top of the counter.

She lifted her dress to Crabbe's chagrin firing a baseball sized web at his face. He eluded, but his Afro was not so lucky.

Crabbe knew he'd have a devil of a time washing that out. Crabbe dashed through the aisles, staying low and dodging what he considered large spit-web balls.

They splattered, dripping and oozing down the walls. Disgusting.

He squatted behind a shelf for cover, but had to move quickly, evading a Milan dropping down from the ceiling, who got hit with a spit-web ball. Milan glared at the counter as if to say what the hell.

The crab-spider glanced at Rita who returned a glare of her own, like she was saying, you should have watched where you were falling. The substance spread over Milan's body like wildfire encasing him in a cocoon.

Crabbe shaking his head upon observing Milan thought to himself, serves you right for trying to ambush me.

Rita kept firing away despite immobilizing her partner.

Crabbe figured she thought he couldn't sit still forever and she'd hit her target once he was on the move again. She was part right, but ignorant to not know he could have ended them by blinking his eyes. Crabbe however, didn't want to kill them.

He thought of the duo as a comedy team, except they must have murdered for them to be on the offensive. He would send them back to hell to get punished by an upset Satan, who'd be furious with them for not leaving Hades to do his bidding.

Crabbe reached inside his trench taking out his trusty cane.

After his almost ill-fated battle with the jackals he decided to never leave home without it. Rita fired from both barrels as the balls came from both sides of the aisle.

Crabbe gripped his cane tapping the engraved pentacle with his index finger making it glow.

The magician leaped up over the top of the shelf tossing the cane like a javelin, aiming for the web sacks. Crabbe ducked down behind the shelf in the blink of an eye avoiding a web ball splattering against the wall. A gasp then a whoop on the floor.

Crabbe rose once the barrage of webbing came to a halt. He walked up to the counter picking up his cane along the way, looking over the counter at the fallen Rita, lying on the floor overwhelmed by her own web. The cane jammed her web sacks forcing them to explode within her body shooting up through her nostrils, mouth, and ears covering her body. Crabbe saw the web threads over her mouth and nose moving. She lives, he nodded, as he didn't want any casualties. Crabbe went to the back of the pharmacy.

Three cocooned bodies lay across three wooden tables with tubes sticking out of them. Using the glowing pentacle tip of his cane, he cut through the webbing. All three victims had been mummified and used as plasma shakes.

Before their mummification they were elderly and the goblins figured they didn't have relatives to miss them or they'd be far and wide or nonexistent. Crabbe sent the twosome back to purgatory, letting Lucifer deal with them. He got on the pharmacy phone making an anonymous call, reporting what he found and mentioned the dealership should be investigated.

Crabbe left before the local police arrived to avoid being questioned. He was sure they'd heard complaints about the pharmacy, but were too Mayberry to look into the matter. They'd put out an alert for the two pharmacists now dwelling back in the netherworld, never to be seen again. They'll eventually list the case under a miscellaneous file of unsolved mystery, though Crabbe had closed the case.

He contacted Father Leary letting him know he was right about his assumption. Crabbe cruised down the countryside heading back to Parts Unknown Road, expecting a long, deep deserved sleep.

CHAPTER 28

Stout smiled contemplating his afterlife, not so bad. He considered the pros: you get to die once, you never go hungry, and sex is no longer a need... desire, yeah.

Body hopping inside a man with a beautiful wife or hot girlfriend became his hobby since while alive he settled or spent good money on cheap women. The cons: he wanted to eat, drink, and have sex.

He missed busting heads with his bat. Stout enjoyed watching people cower. The money was good and better than a nine to five job, with an asshole boss watching your every move. You get instructions, go out on your own using your own discretion as long as you get the job done and he did.

Stout shook his head thinking, he could still be busting heads if he had not gotten bit by the road rage bug. The guy cut him off, he drove up side by side, they exchanged words, gave each other the finger then pulled over to confront each other. The man got to use his fist and he brought a Louisville slugger to a fist fight and he won, till he headed back to his car and Alan Miller in his red hot-rod sent him to his maker. Stout smirked, feeling proud he paid back Miller in his jail cell.

He found it amusing being a spiritual serial killer, on a revenge killing spree against the Sal Dana gang.

He already put another dent in his old boss Pitt, making him a joke around his overseer and brother's in arms. The next crew he eyed worked under Ralph Malph, better known as Ralph the mouth. The king of wisecracks, always making jokes that he laughed at himself. He needed a kick in the ass and his boys; Mills, and Rivers will be added to the list of casualties of small business owners fighting back, with the help of an evil servitor.

Ralph's paid for a protection spot, an old Chinese dry-cleaners run by a husband and wife in their mid to late forties. Stout arrived on time watching Mills and Rivers looking confident of an easy pay day. The two bag-men strolled inside and Stout floated through the glass doors.

Jon and Lei Po stood behind the counter. His wife, three inches taller, was mouthing off in their native tongue. Rivers and Mills didn't understand a syllable, but they knew she wasn't being hospitable. Jon tried calming his frau down.

He didn't understand her new found attitude. She never liked throwing away money, but Lei cooperated like her husband to keep the peace. Jon lifted the brown leather bag of money and Lei grabbed it, racing to the back of the cleaners. Mills gave Rivers a look and he hightailed after her.

"You Mr. Po!" said Mills rushing behind the counter. He grabbed Jon then punched him, dropping him to the floor. "Stay right where you are."

Rivers shoved aside clothes on hangers inside plastic bags, searching for Lei. He swore, pushing and yanking his way through the maze of clothes blocking his vision. Rivers turned the corner coming to a complete halt. His body froze in a stance of shock. Mouth open, but no sound, eyes wide and in confusion. Rivers' body went limp, collapsing to the floor. Mills recognized the sound of a body hitting the floor. He'd sent four men down in bar room brawls and alley fights. One permanently.

"Rivers... Rivers! Everything okay?" Mills asked. His focus went back to Mr. Po who started to rise. A downward right hook to the jaw floored him.

"Don't you move," said Mills. "Stay put." Mills headed to the back of the cleaners. He spotted the soles of Rivers' brown loafers face up and the bloated man flat on his back with an unwound clothes hanger sticking straight up toward the ceiling through his left eyeball. The thin metal went into his eye connecting to his brain. It is said that this type of death causes no pain, it's instant.

Mills, taken aback by what happened to his fellow bag-man, didn't notice a wet noose tied sheet looping over his head and tightening around his neck. A mechanical sound and the carousel conveyor with clothes on hangers in plastic started rotating. The wet sheet tied to the conveyor constricted Mills who fought to loosen it from around his larynx, but the more he tried, the more it got difficult to breathe as he succumbed to darkness.

San Remo Italian eatery was not the meeting place for the Sal Dana gang today. They didn't admit it, but they were still shaken up with all the weirdness that took place there, and getting rescued by an old superstitious woman. Sal went to her after his boys went on about their business, he asked the woman what incense she used to bring sanity back to her bistro.

She gave him frankincense. The woman didn't explain why or what evil spirits hate about frankincense, but told him to burn it to keep them away.

The meeting place today was at an old pool hall off of old Statesville road. Cheap booze and cigarette smoke the fragrance along with the incense. The pool hall was out front where most of the drinking, cursing, and smoking took place.

They sat in the back, at a round table that wobbled and chairs on their last legs. Burgers, fries, and soda in styrofoam cups, instead of made from scratch Italian cuisine. Pitt foot the bill for the food, trying to make up for his boys not bringing in the loot of protection money, nevertheless, it's hard to do when you're dead.

"Burgers and fries, huh?" Ralph questioned. "Guess it's the best you can do under the circumstances."

"Fuck you," said Pitt chomping down on his burger, he glared at him then grinned, watching Ralph taking a bite of his patty.

Ralph chewed, then frowned, grabbing a napkin to spit in.

"Hey!" Murray blurted. "Show some manners."

Ralph inhaled. "Sorry." He glared at Pitt. "This flunky put mayonnaise on mine and he knows I hate mayo!"

Pitt shrugged. "Don't blame me, I told them to hold the mayo and to put mustard on your burger. Guess they didn't listen."

"You ass-hole," said Ralph.

"Bring it." Pitt retorted.

Both men rose from their chairs, ready to rumble. Sal looked at both men while dipping his fries in ketchup and Murray leaned back, folding his arms waiting for the action to start.

"So, youse guys going to bop or kiss and make-up?" Sal questioned. "If not, sit your asses down so we can figure out what the hell is going on around here." He looked at Ralph. "Take a damn napkin and wipe the shit off."

"That's tacky, you still taste it." He lifted the bun frowning using the napkin then added mustard and ketchup hoping to cover up the residue left by the mayo.

"What are you, Mr. Etiquette all of a sudden?" Sal asked. Ralph bit into his burger looking satisfied with the new taste.

"Alright already now, let's get down to business or what's left of it." Sal looked at Pitt. "Youse cursed, bad luck, bad mojo or what?"

"Yeah." Ralph laughed. "Three strikes and you're out."

"Ralph put a sock in it." said Sal. "I'm talking to Pitt here."

Pitt shrugged. "What can I say? Shit happens."

"Must be lactose intolerant or taking too many laxatives?" Ralph remarked.

Pitt inhaled. "You're pushing it. You're pushing it!"

"Hey!" Sal blurted. "We're family and we support each other."

Ralph pressed his index finger to his thumb running them across his lips like a zipper.

"I lost my main man," said Pitt. "These two I had were getting the hang of it... don't know what else I can tell you."

Ralph snorted, shaking his head. "Let me show you how it's done." He took out his cell.

"Hey, are we good?" Ralph hung up turning pale and wide eyed.

Murray frowned. "Ralph? Why you acting like you've seen a ghost?"

"That was the police." Ralph replied. "Hope you used a burner," said Sal.

"Always." Ralph replied, still looking shaken.

"What did they say?" Pitt asked.

"Hello, how are ya," answered Ralph, giving Pitt a stern look. "Of course I hung up as soon as I heard it was the police."

Murray grabbed the remote. He turned on the TV, an old fashioned box model hanging on the wall on top of a platform. The reporter announced two men dead at the Po Dry Cleaners. Murray turned off the tube.

Ralph sat back bewildered.

"Tag you're it." said Pitt.

Ralph rose from the table getting furious. He grabbed Pitt by his shirt, yanking him to his feet. "You Fucking jinx! You motherfucking jinx!" Ralph shrieked.

"Get your damn hands off me!" Pitt retorted.

Sal stood up for the first time. "I'll end youse both if you don't sit your asses down!"

The general spoke and the men obeyed. Sal gave Murray a look. The tall man got on his phone.

He nodded giving a thumbs up. Then left the table heading for the door.

"Where youse going?" Sal asked.

"I told my guys to stay put till I get there," said Murray. "The situation calls for a hands on."

"Smart." Sal nodded, motioning to Murray to go on.

Ralph meanwhile, started praying.

"What do you think you're doing?" Pitt asked.

"I go to church." Ralph replied.

"Yeah, and I'm the next Pope." Pit remarked. The two men stood face to face again.

"Ralph," said Sal. "Go to the bar and bring back something strong to drink."

Ralph sighed, stomping off to the front of the pool hall. Sal got up and set up incense. He lit them then sat back down.

"What you do that for?" Pitt inquired.

Sal exhaled. "We need all the help we can get."

Crabbe sat in his study after closing shop from selling some herbs and spell candles. He used one of his jarred botany nectar to sooth his soul, after getting a text from Silva that Stout left another victim hollow and soulless, about committing murder to two more goons of the Sal Dana gang. Another patient for Shaw Heights and he'd be expecting to hear from Margo Parker any day now to explain.

The spellcaster had no explanation except doubt about his thought-forms Frick and Frack, but the waiting game was getting close to the two minute warning and he'd be more than ready to pounce on the evil spirit wrecking this havoc. He didn't want to hear Morocco give his two cents of I told you so regarding how he should also be body snatching to stop Stout.

Crabbe had a plan for his servitor, but not right now. It bothered him playing the waiting game, letting Stout get his revenge not caring who got hurt in the process. He was glad Silva didn't ask him to come to the crime scene and relieved she figured it out that Stout the evil spirit perpetrator did not care who he hurt as long as he gets retribution. Crabbe shook his head thinking it's not like Sal and his guys planned Stout's demise.

What happened to him was his own fault getting involved in a road rage. Stout lied, didn't take his death well, and felt disrespected by his former employers for not attending his funeral. Crabbe sipped his drink. He trusted his thought-forms despite Morocco trying to mend his wounded ego. Crabbe exhaled hoping they were doing more than sunbathing.

Murray returned to the fort, dumping a bag of loot on the table. Sal nodded his approval at the size of greenbacks his mountain of a man brought back. The smile on Sal's face beamed more than a preacher looking over his collection plate.

"This is why you my right hand man," said Sal. "You went out to see the problem and got productive at the same time."

"How's your boys?" Pitt asked. "They still standing?"

The giant sat down, poured himself a shot of bourbon then swallowed it in one gulp. "Sent them home until further notice."

Sal gave him a look. His smile vanished, replaced by a stern expression with furrowed brows.

Murray caught his glance. "Until we find out what the hell is going on, no need to see if my crew is scheduled for some bad luck."

Ralph slapped the stable. "See, I knew it."

Pitt frowned. "Knew what?"

"Sitting next to you is the reason my guys are taking the long goodbye." Ralph retorted.

"You're crazy," said Pitt.

"Call me crazy again, I dare you." Ralph replied.

Sal cleared his throat. "I got a better idea." He took the bag of money off the table. "You guys are going to follow the big man's lead."

Ralph gave a dubious look. "No disrespect, but just because the mountain here brought back a bag full of doe and his guys are safe and sound don't mean we won't be so lucky."

Pit nodded. "Yeah", to what Ralph said.

Sal guzzled two shots back to back, allowing the rye to settle, raising an eyebrow. "What youse two brothers all of a sudden?"

"In here we are family." said Pitt. "I'm no fan of the mouth here, but he got a point and I've lost three guys and now he lost the same way my boys did and now they living in the boneyard."

"So how are we supposed to make money?" Sal looked at his lieutenants. "We hit these places weekly and now we short of help, that means youse two need to do what Murray did and he did it despite his boys still in tow."

Pit looked at Ralph. He felt the vibe that the mouth wanted to say something smart like him, though they both knew their place not to step out of line against Sal. The lard belly was not known to be a rough house, but he put this operation together and up until now, things were running smooth like a well oiled engine.

Murray cleared his throat. "I say we relax for a week."

Sal got moon-eyed, as he wasn't sure he heard right. "What the hell you say?"

"Till we figure out what's going on." added Murray.

"We been doing good gathering the lettuce unless you want to tell us something?" Sal quizzed him.

Murray turned facing Sal. Ralph and Pit breathed a quiet sigh of relief because of the three of them, Murray was the man Sal listened to when it came to reason.

"Hey!" Sal sounded off. "Youse guys know me. I'm a penny pinched. I don't waste no doe."

"That's why you're the big cheese." said Murray buttering up Sal's ego. "We need to figure this out because people are dying, our people. Now I don't believe in jinx or hoax, but something ain't right boss."

"So we take a week off and see what happens?" Sal asked.

"You're as rattled as we are." Murray continued. "Since when do you burn incense?"

"Okay, already," Sal inhaled. "We're all jumpy, but we ain't going to waste time looking at each other afraid to breathe. We going to talk and figure this thing out before it ruins my business, understood?"

Sal filled the four shot glasses to the rim. They lifted their drinks in unison reaching an agreement throwing their shots down the hatch.

CHAPTER 29

Hiram shook his head, breathing heavily. Another rough night of disgusting putrid sex with a demon.

He had to take her mind off Jenny. The demon didn't know Jenny's name yet demanded Hiram find a young girl for her to devour. He did not know what eating a child would do for the monstrosity, he already sacrificed people to her and the goblin looked bloated and smelled foul as before, when conjured. Hiram never got anything more than the demon's name and at this point he didn't care to know. He wanted to send her back to the bowels of hell where she belonged. Hiram read books, in fact periodicals became his new read.

He wasn't going to college or the military after dealing with an abusive father; he didn't need a drill sergeant breathing down his neck. Hiram needed to make money without the daily grind. Maybe he watched too much television about guys going to dive bars, meeting men who didn't look like much, but rolling in doe and that's what he wanted.

Hiram went to water holes, buying drinks and eavesdropping on conversations, getting the crap beat out of him then begging for his life, asking to get involved in cryptic business, earning more than the average poor soul pulling a nine to five to make a living.

He met the right people and when given his assignments, he dotted his I's and crossed his T's. The racketeer beamed once the money touched his hand, he lived a stress free life ignoring the fact people were getting hurt along the way.

Hiram didn't care about them as long as he got his money, no worries who got stepped on.

His benefits helped his baby sister Lisa and her girls when her man turned out to be a shit ass. Hiram bought her a pleasant house, put her and the girls in a nice neighborhood, something they didn't have when they were kids. Big brother smiled now that Lisa is a mother of three.

The adoption went fast and stress free when you know people who know people, influenced by the almighty dollar. Hiram's good feeling didn't last, Robert Long and his demon lover took up space inside his head. Robert wanted a meeting with the powers that be, who were above Hiram.

Hiram wanted to get rid of a pest. His pest control worked out of netherworld. He swallowed hard, pledging it would be his last sacrifice for her to ravage. Hiram wondered if the little woman would tag along. A part of him hoped not, he wished once the conclave with her husband ended, she'd get the hint after a few days he won't be back and be packing up to get out of town.

Hiram stared at a book, the literature about witchcraft intrigued him.

He read about movies and TV shows dealing with exorcists and poltergeists based on actual events. So he bought the literature thumbing through it till he got to the chapter about conjuring demons. Hiram wanted more than being a huckster, a go-between. The liaison business was profitable, nevertheless, why shouldn't he sit on his own throne. Hiram shook his head at the thought of selling his soul to the devil, a definite no no.

He believed Satan existed and to trust him to keep his word, well from what he read from other books and seen in movies, the man in the red suit and not Santa Claus, didn't let you enjoy yourself before coming to claim your soul.

Hiram bought a used car or went second hand getting what he thought was a low rent demon. He'd get what he wanted, in addition to keeping his soul. He got to be head of a club catering to men looking for adventure, but now things had gone south and the best thing to do with his order was to dispatch it. Hiram exhaled thinking of all he went through, to end up getting nothing in return, he had to cut his losses.

Robert and the Demon. He opened the book turning to the page titled conjurations by day. Hiram skipped Monday when he saw the name Lucifer, again no deal with the devil. He went all the days of the week and the one day that seemed harmless was Tuesday.

He saw the word lust ignoring it and instead he paid attention to finding riches and did exactly what it said to do, to conjure his demon now his lover, making him realize he should have not disregarded lust. The demon loved sex and he had to deliver and she did her part, but made no promises if and what success he would have and how long it would last.

With the title, leader of the pack disappearing and the lust remaining, with the pending question of when he would deliver her a little girl. Hiram slammed the book shut. He would see Robert soon and introduce him to his higher ups.

"With all that power it doesn't make it any easier sitting back while evil has its way." said Leary. "You are a man with extraordinary skills, but it's okay to ask for help when you need it."

"I hope that never happens again." Crabbe retorted.

"Lavender for the eyes... honey for the throat." said Father Leary preparing Crabbe's tea.

"Lavender for the eyes?" Crabbe frowned while taking his tea. "That's a first."

"Learn something new every day." said Leary, his brother Tomas' college football teammate.

Crabbe grew up admiring the mantel of trophies owned by his big brother. Crabbe believed he too could have been a football star, though not as big as Tomas, he would have been a good running back, wide receiver, or a defensive back. He didn't play sports of any kind because of the curse his family convinced him to accept as a gift instead.

Crabbe sipped. "I have herbs in my shop. I tell my customers to burn or dress their candles."

"I read." Leary retorted.

"Not just the bible." Crabbe remarked.

They laughed, getting comfortable in Leary's spacious study inside his grand ranch abode.

Leary lived in the suburbs three miles from his church. His home modest, was painted white for purity.

A large varnish wooden fence gave the clergyman privacy in the two bedroom attic home, built back in seventies when size mattered unlike the modern day homes you don't get anymore for the buck. He sat in his lazy boy recliner while Crabbe got comfortable on the couch.

"Thanks for taking care of that business in Nashville," said Leary. "Was it as sinister as I thought?"

"Gruesome." Crabbe exhaled. "Bloodsuckers taking advantage of the elderly and last I heard, the car lot next door got shut down for taking the victims' vehicles."

"Should've joined you." Leary gritted his teeth. "It's been a while since Stella and I did the Lord's work."

Crabbe snorted. "Thanks, but no thanks. Didn't need any guns ablazing. The twosome are back sitting in the bowels of hell."

"I'm grateful for your help putting your own problems on hold." Leary pulled out a folder. "This can wait... the little girl is doing better."

Crabbe replied, "I'm listening."

"Six years old, fell down a flight of stairs running from a monster in the closet. Parents complain seeing a hideous silhouette through the shower curtain when they take their showers, they think they are dreaming waking up in the middle of the night face to face with light bulb sized eyes staring at them."

He handed Crabbe the file. "Location and everything you need to know when you have the time."

Crabbe gripped the file. It got his ire when demons harassed children. "You had me at little girl."

Leary took a sip of his tea relaxing in his lazy boy. "Talk to me."

Crabbe focused on his tea in deep thought. With his family miles away, safe from his activities, leaving him no one but his servitor to open up to, but Morocco's ego took a hit since he got bottled up because of an evil spirit wreaking havoc in the city, body snatching innocents taking out his revenge against those who mocked him, making him feel worthless and without dignity while alive.

No excuse thought Crabbe to go around ruining the lives of the living.

Crabbe nursed his tea looking at Father Leary.

The priest stood at six-two, weighing two-thirty looking like Mister clean deck in black with a cue ball smooth face. No facial hair including eyebrows. His skin like porcelain, no wrinkles though Crabbe knew the man to be like Tomas, mid to late forties. "Do you give your servitor the same treatment?" Leary asked. "He's upset with me for grounding him," said Crabbe. "Now I'm..."

"Don't second guess yourself." Leary intervened. "Despite your gifts you're still human and don't forget it." He snorted. "Pardon my manners, how's the family?"

Crabbe straightened with a smile. "They're great. Sage, Tomas' oldest, is off to college and law, Clover is doing the same. The rest of the nieces and nephews... they're being raised the right way. Blossom and Lilac are doing fine. They are all safe as long they are miles away from my activities."

"You're not in this alone." said Leary. "Your family don't have as much as you, but I think they're capable of taking care of themselves."

"As long as I'm around they won't be on the front line." Crabbe remarked, as Leary nodded. "Plus, I'm kinda rusty myself."

"The same goes for you though." Crabbe laughed, teasing Leary.

"You're calling me old?" Leary retorted, feigning annoyance.

Crabbe shook his head laughing. "Not a chance."

Leary was no stranger to the supernatural paranormal game, joining the party when one of his own got lost in a bad exorcism. He felt distraught and called his best friend to lend him a listening ear. Tomas gave him a shoulder to cry on, as well as opening up to his fellow clergy man about their family's history with the devil.

Leary impressed his old teammate when he didn't bat an eye of disbelief and even got intrigued when listening to Tomas mention he had a kid brother, who took the bulk of the demonic powers, and wound up using it for good against the forces of evil. Tomas made sure to tell Crabbe that Leary was the next best thing if he ever needed support.

The Appleton family knew nothing of Morocco, Mister Kit, the dragons, Silva, and now Parker. Family should not know everything and Leary, an adoptive brother, gave Crabbe a confidant to talk to among the living.

"You good on holy water?" Leary questioned.

"I could swim in it." Crabbe remarked. "And Clover, she still got the goods?"

Crabbe raised his eyes, "I don't look at my sisters that way and you..."

"...Are human, but dedicated to the church." said Leary.

Crabbe sighed. "Strong and thick boned." He shook his head. "There. You happy now?"

Leary closed his eyes with a smile. "Just like I remember her. If she were not bound by marriage, I might leave the church."

"Till death do her part." Crabbe remarked. It caught him off guard, Leary's infatuation with his big sister.

Leary laughed. "Like Superman we all have a kryptonite."

"I'm glad to hear your family is doing fine," said Leary.

"Thank you and yes, they are." Crabbe responded.

Leary sipped his last drop of tea placing the cup on the table then clasping his hands together gave Crabbe his undivided attention.

"So how are you doing with those two birds?" Leary asked.

"With one stone." Crabbe muttered, snapping his finger. "You should have known there was a reason I came to talk to you."

Leary shuddered. "And here I thought it was because we haven't seen each other in a while."

Crabbe smirked. "Yeah, long time no see." He snorted. "I didn't come here for therapy or just to catch up."

Leary nodded. "Though I qualify in both." He folded his bulging biceps in his black T-shirt. "Any new people in your life?"

Crabbe nodded. "Two women..."

Leary gave him the eyes. "A love life?"

"Let's not get ahead of ourselves." Crabbe cleared his throat. "One is a cop and the other runs a mental institution that's coming in handy thanks to the evil spirit running amok."

Leary gave him a stern look. "So it's professional then?"

Crabbe gave a wavering look. "Why wouldn't it be? Being who I am, I can't involve anyone in my world and be worrying about their well being."

"You got some, didn't you?" Leary questioned.

"To relieve stress, nothing more." Crabbe replied.

"I can imagine both professions, law enforcement and running a facility with so many patients to be responsible for. Good for you."

"Things are getting awkward," said Crabbe.

"How much do they know?" Leary asked.

"One dated a demon ending in an unpleasant experience so she knows more than the other and the other knows the civil service I performed qualified me for being more than a miracle worker."

"You don't deserve to have a life?" Leary asked.

Crabbe gave a funny look. "They will never go on a hunt or war. I need allies not complications."

"Speaking of..." Leary retorted.

"A human is feeding other humans to his conjured demon, to go along with the evil vengeful spirit." Crabbe exhaled. "I'm doing a lousy job as a protector."

Leary leaned in. "You can't save everyone." He straightened in his chair. "Serial killers have gone on killing sprees for two years or more."

"These are not serial killers. They're of the occult." Crabbe stated.

"Which makes it more difficult for you to do alone."

Crabbe sighed. "I have help going about, but slower than I'd want them to."

"Would your servitor speed things up?" Leary asked.

Crabbe shook his head. "He has pure hatred for Stout and would make matters worse. I fear they'd go body hopping to any available, adding to the body count."

"What you're saying is, if one gladiator goes down he'd look for another champion."

Crabbe nodded.

"Right, how nice," Leary whispered.

"Now that you mention it, we can't have that, but you can't keep beating yourself up over it."

Crabbe gave him a puzzled look. "Can't I? Should've sent him straight to purgatory and when I am through with him, he'd wish he had gone because now something far worse awaits him."

"Just listening to you gives me an adrenaline rush."

"You've got to stay under control," said Crabbe.

"You likewise, nevertheless the adrenaline rush...... it's intoxicating." Leary replied.

"You know you could've died." Crabbe stated.

"Just like football, keep your head on a swivel, watching out for your blindside." Leary remarked clenching his fist making his biceps bulge.

Crabbe took Leary's invitation to go on a venture to a biker bar that acted as a last stop gas station. Leary got word that when people stopped at the watering hole for a restroom break or to quench their thirst after a long trip, they seemed to take up residence.

The clergy man, always intrigued when supernatural activities reared its ugly head since his up close and personal encounter with the paranormal hitting close to home. He saw it as his calling, though Crabbe disagreed. He wanted to tell Leary he wasn't the first, nor would he be the last to lose someone close to things that go bump in the night and he shouldn't dedicate himself to a crusade against the occult.

Since chrome dome refused to listen, Crabbe played liaison keeping Leary out of harm's way, knowing what

Stella the holy water shotgun can do, but so much for a muscular former linebacker now a man of the cloth. He took on assignments investigating them for Leary, protecting Tomas's best friend.

"Something else troubling you?" Leary asked.

"Visions.... Spidey senses are tingling, telling me trouble is on the way." said Crabbe.

Leary shook his head. "No rest for the weary my wayward son. I miss that show."

"You can catch it in reruns." said Crabbe.

"I didn't like the way they questioned the morals of the Lord." Leary remarked.

"When a show goes on for fifteen years, the writers have to manipulate new ideas to keep viewers interested." Crabbe stated.

Leary sneered. "Still you gotta have faith."

Crabbe pursed his lips. "Those who believe know the difference between fact and fiction."

Leary gritted his teeth. "It makes my blood boil."

Crabbe rose from the sofa clutching the file. "I don't argue religion."

Leary stood, walking Crabbe to the door and giving him a hug. "May God be with you."

Don't let your eyes get bigger than your stomach. Robert thought of his mother's words when he was a boy asking for seconds. His dad never said much, he'd look, shake his head and go to the living room with his paper to watch the evening news.

Robert pondered on what she said because was his eyes bigger than his stomach? He wanted Hiram erased as his liaison so he could have personal contact with the people or persons who had children for trafficking. Robert sat inside his car waiting to get a text from Hiram.

He didn't like the location, parking on a dirt trail inside a wooded area. He sighed thinking, sometimes you gotta do what you gotta do to make it. The cryptic lifestyle he chose made him comfortable, but the greedy bug bit him to think bigger and solidify his future.

Robert thought to do what he needed, to cut out the middle-man. He checked his cell then shook his head. The broker he's supposed to meet with, he'd tell her or him to pick a building, a bar, anywhere they agree was discreet. Why the forest he wondered? To test his bravery? Robert wasn't a nature guy.

He could care less about the birds, bees, squirrels, rabbits, and deer during the day, let alone at night. When he made rounds to the store or leaving a strip club at night, he'd cringe driving down a road sandwiched between the forest.

This get together had better be productive, not that he was some bad ass to make whoever he was meeting with feel any pain, but why the fucking woods?

No full moon shone on the forestry, just his headlights and he turned them off to preserve the battery. Robert made sure his doors were locked. He felt nervous not hearing a frog croak, owl hoot, or crickets chirping. Robert gritted his teeth, was this some sick joke payback from Hiram to put a scare in him for the way he was approached..... well it worked.

He got jittery sitting alone in pitch blackness. Robert left Joan behind feeling regret since she would at least have kept him company. He didn't bring her because she was doubtful. Joan said they had enough money that they should pack up and leave for a fresh start. He convinced her they needed one more score and then vamoose.

Robert inhaled and again negative thoughts clouded his head. He wondered what else he could do besides think of being by himself in the heart of a dark eerie forest. He jumped when the light of his cell got his attention. Hiram's text telling him his person of interest arrived and waiting for him deep in the woods. Robert didn't like the sound of that, nevertheless he'd come too far to let this macabre night go to waste.

He vowed to have a talk with Hiram when this get-together was done. Robert wasn't an expert in distance, but felt he drove far enough into the woods, fearing he might hit a soft spot of dirt bogging down his car and he didn't want that.

Robert reached inside his glove compartment taking out his Glock. It held fifteen bullets and Robert relaxed a bit, with the comfort of having a friend to call upon in case he needed help on this bizarre night.

The text from Hiram instructed him to look for a forked path inside the woods. Robert turned on his cell phone flashlight. A luminous box appeared on his cell LOW BATTERY. Great thought Robert, easing out his gun. A thump behind a thick tree got his attention.

"Who's there?" Robert questioned. "Are you the one I'm supposed to meet?"

The cell light went out.

"Shit!!" He raised the Glock and why not, since he stood in the abyss of tar, not being able to see his hand in front of his face. Robert didn't see a figure, but recognized footsteps breaking branches, crunching dry leaves underfoot.

"Before you get any closer can you give me a name?" Robert asked. "Look I came out here to talk, to work out an arrangement without Hiram."

The footsteps got closer, louder, and heavy. Robert threw up. The stench of rot, decay, and whatever other smell combo not just forced him to lose his dinner, but backed him up with a hard bump into a thick tree trunk. Robert's recovery breath returned until the foul stench got worse than before and the cell phone light returned.

It revealed a horror beyond Robert's wildest nightmares. He dropped his gun.

He bought it in case he got deep into the trafficking game and planned to go to the firing range to get accustomed to using it. Robert came back to reality realizing this was not a Stephen King novel, but a nightmare. He and this monstrosity were the chief characters and his character the victim. Robert thought about his mother. His eyes got too big for his stomach.

CHAPTER 30

Crabbe arrived at his home on Parts Unknown Avenue. Parking in the rear next to the S-10. He entered through the front door where his business dwelt not to do inventory, but he saw the tattoo parlor lights on and thought it weird seeing the sisters open for business, this early in the morning.

They told him about clients paying big money for their talents at sometimes odd hours. He started to ignore his intuition, nevertheless his gut feeling told him different.

Crabbe stood at his door pretending to go inside and in unison a customer appeared from the parlor looking as though the sisters had satisfied his need so he was leaving.

The man stood facing Crabbe, making him swallow hard. He recognized the man as one of the three hounding him at Java The Hut Coffee House. Mister cell phone who found his seat after Crabbe gave him the look, the asshole. He gave a mocking look as if to say I know where you live.

He grinned, nodded then got inside his heap giving a stare down that ended when he was out of sight.

Crabbe entered his house from the back. He'd talk to the sisters once the sun climbed high in the sky. He stood inside his kitchen debating whether or not to have a drink and not from his botany jars, a strong rot-gut. Crabbe grabbed bourbon made by the Glenlivet distillery. It did the trick.

"Why so glum, chum?" Morocco asked.

"Smell you later," said Crabbe. "Time for bed."

9 am and Crabbe wasted no time making a beeline to the Banger sisters tattoo parlor. He rang the doorbell.

Precious greeted wearing a black thigh high T-Shirt carrying a Jimi Hendrix picture holding a large cup of cappuccino .

He smelled fresh baked cinnamon rolls, and saw scrambled eggs and bacon. He gave a glance to Motor's place open for business serving breakfast. Crabbe had visited the parlor before, the ladies didn't have a stove though, he wondered who made the trek to retrieve early morning grub.

"Who's that at the door, Precious?" Peaches called out.

"A visitor you'd be happy to see." Precious replied, hiding her smile behind her chicory. Peaches came to the front sporting a black Iron Maiden T-shirt to match her black leggings.

Crabbe realized she made the run instead of baby sister, but the leggings didn't hide much of big sister's person to the imaginative mind. Peaches beamed glimpsing at Crabbe. "Don't be so rude, invite him in," said Peaches.

Precious stepped aside, eyeing Crabbe up and down as he waltzed inside, yet his intuition told him to look over his shoulder. He saw Bob Graham envying him. The family was all here, getting ready to start their day. The key word family.

Crabbe considered the bistro owner, car dealer, and the tattoo sisters his family which was why it concerned him to see the man from the coffee house leaving the sisters' commerce.

"Had breakfast yet?" Peaches asked.

Crabbe devoured two slices of thick bacon then grabbed a grand cinnamon bun, a trade mark of Motor who believes in large Danish and a cup of espresso with cream. He sat with the sisters in their customer lounge. The lounging area contained unfolded sheets and pillows telling him the sisters slept here instead of going to their flats. Peaches and Precious gave each other a look. Crabbe had visited before, but never broke bread until now, he noticed their observation, but he was hungry.

"Got back late from visiting a friend and noticed a customer," said Crabbe. "None of my business, but I didn't know you take customers that early in the morning."

"He paid very well and had to have it." said Precious.

Crabbe gave a dubious look. "A tattoo?"

"A trilogy." Peaches remarked wolfing down her scrambled eggs.

Crabbe took a swill of his coffee, clearing his throat. "Trilogy?"

"Yeah, and she's trying to impress you," said Precious, exchanging facial expressions with her sister. "Three guys wanted the exact same tattoo."

Crabbe straightened inhaling deep then releasing a slow exhale. "The others came together during the day?"

Precious and Peaches gave dubious looks.

Crabbe snorted. "I'm curious to know if it's a faze or club thing."

Precious shook her head. "The other two came at reasonable times, but we charged the third extra because he said it was an emergency.'

"And we don't take customers before sunrise." Peaches stated.

Crabbe pondered. He didn't want to or like prying into other people's business unless it dealt with the occult. His uneasy feeling being the reason he played the nosy neighbor and the man leaving the parlor giving him a mocking look disturbed him. The small business community he shared with the Bangers, Motor, and Graham made them his tribe and he was sworn to protect them from harm.

Crabbe shrugged."Do you have a picture of the tattoo?"

"We do." Precious replied. Uncurling off the couch to retrieve it. She hustled back, giving the white sheet of paper with the ink illustration to Crabbe. Precious smiled blinking her eyes curling back on the couch. Crabbe examined the drawing.

Thick pointed lines like horns curving outward then the same design coming across making a smiley face and upside down frown with a line straight down the middle. All ends pointed. Crabbe didn't know if the sisters knew what they were doing when they performed their craft on the men.

"Where did you put the design?" Crabbe asked. "Below the neck to the chest," said Peaches. "Not a big design, but small." Precious retorted.

Crabbe finished his cinnamon bun and lukewarm coffee. The sisters had a Gothic presence about them. The pale skin, dark lipstick and eye shadow yet nothing carbon or sinister in a disturbing nature.

Crabbe rose. "Ladies, it's been a blast." "Leaving so soon?" Precious questioned.

"We don't have a client until noon," said Peaches.

Crabbe smiled. "I have a business to run and you both need to get ready I'm sure." He looked at Precious wearing her T-shirt. "We'll get together again."

"Promise?" asked Precious.

Crabbe stood half-way out the door balling the paper inside his pocket.

"Scouts honor."

"Thank you and come back again," said Crabbe putting up an out to lunch sign after shutting the door watching a customer exit. He sold herbs, incense, and spell candles.

Crabbe looked out the window; the dealership sold some cars, Burgers, Brew, and Pizza 2 was crowded and customers were aplenty for the Banger sisters.

Crabbe took a break to study the tattoo design. He sat at his fortune telling table. Morocco traveled to one of his crystal balls. "Is it important my friend?"

"A sigil." Crabbe replied.

"Sounds like the bad kind." The crystal ball beamed bright.

"Selling your soul to the devil." Crabbe retorted. "Without making a deal."

"What are you saying my friend?" Morocco asked.

"Three fools getting served up like instant mocha." Crabbe sat back staring into space.

"A black cloaked man wearing a top hat sold them on the idea they could have powers too after seeing him pulling a rabbit out of his hat."

"They are blind to what the sigil means?" Morocco questioned.

"Clueless." Crabbe snorted.

"What are you going to do about it?"

"I can't save everybody," said Crabbe.

"And what does the man manipulating them get out of it?" Morocco asked.

"A fool too, thinking he can trust Satan."

"How do you know all of this, my friend?" "Just my spidey senses tingling."

"I don't see the humor in this, my friend." Morocco replied.

The devil is taking a vacation from down below lurking in the bushes and Crabbe didn't know why.

"My wit keeps my head clear," said Crabbe. "You should know that by now."

"Accept my apology."

Crabbe inhaled. "None required and my visions displayed the trailer to this awful movie."

"So you know what's going on?" Morocco quizzed.

"Still a jigsaw puzzle, Moe." Crabbe replied. "The devil will get three souls without cutting a quick deal."

Outside, a car was getting cranked up, with its engine revving.

Crabbe's phone rang, intruding on his thoughts.

"What's up?" Crabbe sighed. "No rest for the weary. I'll be there."

"Is it not one thing then there's another, my friend?" Morocco asked him.

Crabbe was already standing and heading out. "Duty calls."

A slight breeze made the leaves ruffle. Silva stood beside Crabbe observing the crime scene. He stood silent deep in thought.

"Park Ranger called it in and when I heard how weird, I thought about you," said Silva.

Crabbe smirked. "What? Me being weird or my neck of the woods?"

"Both." said Silva

Crabbe snorted. "You did right. It's not my vengeful spirit. It's the demon on a feeding frenzy."

"Great." Silva muttered looking around making sure she and Crabbe had some privacy. "Found no ID, a man who drove out here by the clothing left behind and tire tracks, but car's gone, meaning someone planned his murder then took out his car doing a detailed clean up job. Well, except for the remains. Thank God for forensics." She pointed out the tracks coming and going. Silva squinted looking at Crabbe. "You know who the victim is don't you?"

"I'll catch you later Gwyn." said Crabbe.

Silva knew she should be going by the book asking Crabbe who he was off to see, but her world was not ready for the bizarre and unexplainable. She still didn't have a handle on it yet, so she thought it best to leave it up to the man she labeled born to handle the situation.

Crabbe arrived at the Long's house at 9 pm. He waited inside the Metro till 9:30 before walking up to the door to announce himself. Joan answered wearing a green pajama top and nothing else. She was about to call Crabbe by his stage name, but he waved her off entering her home.

"Crabbe H. Appleton, at your service."

Joan stepped back doing what most women do, when thinking a man is checking out her breasts. She grabbed her pink robe covering up. Crabbe allowed the gangling woman to have her moment, though he felt insulted since she had nothing physical that would interest him.

He looked around; boxes of all shapes and sizes littered the house.

"Going somewhere?" Crabbe asked.

"You're not the police and not who you said you were when we first met so..." Joan replied, shrugging and rocking her head side to side.

Crabbe stepped closer. "It's none of my business, nevertheless when grown-ups mistreat children I make it my business. You and your husband were making money off of children the wrong way. I'm not going to ask how many came through that door and got sent off to never, never land.

Wherever you're going, I hope you find peace." He studied Joan, noticing she showed no sign of concern about her significant other. Time for a curve ball, he thought.

"By the way, where's the man of the house?" Crabbe questioned.

"Why do you care?" Joan replied.

"I have friends in law enforcement that will dig deep and hard if I mention a certain couple taking in young girls and not raising them to go off to college. If I do that, then the only trip you'd be taking is to the calaboose."

Joan took a seat on her sheet covered couch. Her body slumped and head hung low as she looked toward the floor. She didn't know much about the man sporting the 1970's Afro and sideburns. Joan did know she wasn't going to see Robert ever again.

She loved her husband, but felt them building distance as he wanted more and she became a shadow to him. Joan knew he didn't run off with another woman and she tried to convince him they should leave town to try and clean up their act. He put up an umbrella making her words raindrops.

They were in a dangerous business and if you push the wrong people, it could be fatal. Robert would either come back boasting or he'd call telling her to put on a fancy dress so they could go out and eat to celebrate. No phone call and no walking through that door, meant he bit off more than he could chew.

Joan exhaled. "How did you find out about us?"

"Monsters," said Crabbe. "In the closet and under the bed."

Joan frowned. "Excuse me?"

"When were you planning to leave?" Crabbe asked.

Joan laughed.

"It's none of my business, but we probably won't see each other again."

Joan exhaled. "Had more than I thought to pack." She stretched and yawned. "Wore me out."

"May you have a safe stress free early morning start," said Crabbe.

Joan frowned. "What was that remark about monsters?"

Crabbe smiled. He didn't want to scare or hurt Joan, notwithstanding she was no saint. She was involved with Robert in trafficking young girls and deserved to have a disturbing sleep.

"Let's just say I have sources that are outside of the normal," Crabbe replied.

"What are these sources, some sort of otherworldly figures?" Joan asked.

"Yes, sort of, and seen through the eyes of a few, mostly children." Crabbe pointed out. "Most people can't see them, which is quite normal, since they're only seen by those they wish to be seen by."

Joan brushed her hair back over her ear.

"I was a child once."

"Obviously." Crabbe remarked.

"I believed in such things, and my parents often came into my room at night, staying until I went to sleep. I got older and knew better. Besides, I never saw any such things."

Crabbe shrugged. "What can I say? Still, they told me about Jenny. They knew and liked her."

"How else could I have known about any of it?" He added.

Joan leaned forward drawing her knees together holding herself. She'd sleep alone tonight and many more, without the comfort of Robert ever again, if he ever did make her feel safe. Joan may find someone else to fill that need, however tonight she'd hear things, feel eyes on her and once morning comes she'll make a hasty exit. Lucky for her the monsters are harmless. Not that she knew anyway.

"You have a talent for making people feel uneasy." Joan stated. "I know Robert's not coming back and I've prepared myself."

"Give me a name." Crabbed insisted.

Joan wasted no time singing like a canary. "Hiram. No last name. He was our liaison."

Crabbe nodded. He had the name of the demon conjurer and now he would lie in wait for this Hiram. "To help you with your trafficking of young girls?"

"Judge, jury, and executioner, are we?" Joan remarked.

Crabbe glared. "You know damn well some if not all those young girls met an undeserving fate."

Joan lowered her head. She knew the blaxploitation man was right. Joan wanted to call it quits, but Robert kept pumping in her head that not all money was made by hard work and luck. Spilled blood fattened a lot of pockets and he felt why not them, despite the circumstances of others.

"I already feel guilty. Did you come here tonight disturbing my rest to rub it in?" She questioned.

"No," said Crabbe, shaking his head. "I want to know your intentions. Whether or not you plan to continue what you and Robert started, instead of turning a new leaf."

Joan gave him a stern look thinking it's none of your damn business Mister Afro. "What must I do to convince you I no longer have the stomach for it anymore? Not that I ever did."

"Then why did you?" Crabbe asked.

Joan gazed into Crabbe's eyes. "You ever been in love?"

Crabbe swallowed hard. He was aware love could make a person do drastic things. He on the other hand had lustful flings; love them and leave them fast, but in his defense, the women were not all human and he already feared spreading his demonic blood.

"I'm sure you want to get an early start in the morning." Crabbe stated shaking his head. "But if you keep your old habits I will know and I promise, you'll regret seeing me again."

Joan sighed, swallowing hard. The hairs on the back of her neck stood up and a chill ran down the spine. She looked at the man with the long thick sideburns ending with pointy tips at the corners of his mouth and the neat bushy mushroom atop his head. He didn't look imposing yet his words penetrated her soul.

The look in Joan's eyes told Crabbe he got his point across. Crabbe never harmed a human and wasn't going to start now. He dispatched demons because he felt they didn't belong topside and if they did come from down below he would not tolerate them abusing their powers on unsuspecting humans. Crabbe wanted to scare Joan straight. He whirled on his heels, heading to the door taking that as his cue to vamoose. Joan curled up on the couch holding herself, shaking.

Three cups of Java was no help for a restless night. Joan hoped she'd never see Crabbe H. Appleton ever again. He made the monsters thing seem quite real. She felt eyes on her, a presence standing in the room, even right by the bed, but she refused to open her eyes fearing something or someone would be there.

It made for a disturbing night. Joan thought the night would never end, that the sun had forgotten how to rise. When daylight entered her bedroom, Joan made a beeline to the kitchen making a pot of strong black demitasse.

A few hours later she stood outside her home, a now empty house looking like the Amityville Horror.

The movers were all loaded up waiting to move like the Oregon trail. Joan smiled recognizing a familiar face pulling up in the driveway, onto the curb in a blue Ranger. Her nephew. She called her sister asking to stay at her place till she got settled in her own digs. No questions were asked about Robert since the family never did warm up to him.

Joan knew she'd have to explain later, so that should give her enough time to come up with a good lie. For now, she was going to be with family. Joan hopped inside the truck, giving her nephew a kiss on the cheek and they drove off.

CHAPTER 31

Hiram threw down shot after shot, till he grabbed the bottle of bourbon, turning it up toward the ceiling sandwiched between his lips. He squeezed his eyes as the booze scorched his throat. Hiram's resume kept getting more impressive for his entrance to hell.

He had no one else to serve up to his demon bitch. Hiram wasn't drinking out of guilt of his latest victim Robert Long. He was drowning in his sorrows because now, his demon harlot wanted the main course... Jenny. His new niece and no way was he going to serve the goblin family. Lisa and the girls welcomed her with open arms. He felt good, he felt he'd done something right, not that it would make up for all the wrong doing overflowing his cup of misery.

One good deed doesn't erase his sins.

Hiram thought about getting baptized, but envisioned the water boiling once he got lowered into it. Jenny made him feel good. Lisa would be an exemplary mother and give her a home. Hiram grabbed another bottle of.

He now knew why his demon wanted the young girl. He laughed thinking about it. She wanted the child, hoping for eternal youth by devouring her. Hiram got sick thinking how stupid he was conjuring a monster and not getting anything in return. He looked on the bright side if there was one, if he'd made a deal with the devil he would have lost his soul by now. He shuddered, guzzling the whiskey knowing picking a demon instead of Satan himself, was smart nonetheless, but still dumb because what had him hitting the bottle, was he translated a threat from his demon lover.

A threat targeted towards him, Hiram thought of being eaten by his demon lover and that was another thing..... he'd had sex with the monster. He did everything in his power to please her; sex, feeding her human beings who acted like insects.

He was making a personal stand; his last sacrifice Robert Long was his last for the demon. He sent emails to all club members, the club, if it ever was one, was now defunct. Hiram took the coward's way out. A meeting standing at the lectern would have required the surviving members to ask questions he had no answers to, without lying about what happened to the former club members. Emails would have to do and hope he'd never run into any of them ever again. Hiram tightened the circle cage to contain his demon. How long it would hold he didn't know, but he hoped long enough for him to get help and send the creature back to hell.

Pitt didn't enjoy doing his own dirty work, since his bagmen got deep sixed and he feared the same might happen to him. He carried a small caliber revolver with him to make sure he didn't end up like his and Ralph 'the mouth's' crew.

Pitt didn't care much for the changes Sal made, influenced by the suggestions of Murray, his most successful and trusted in doing shake downs, preserving the lives of his own. Pitt didn't stand alone in disliking the new agenda of going around to their selected businesses getting protection money.

He smirked thinking about protection money from whomever. The businesses needed protection from the Sal Dana gang and no one else.

Pitt took a deep breath, entering the back of the bar serving as a bar and pool hall. He exhaled thankful to survive another day of not ending up dead by the hands of people they thought were pushovers.

He'd kept track of the shop owners who went wacko not knowing and believing they could do such a horrendous thing, and last he heard, they were still finding it hard coming to grips they took a life. He approached the table and as usual was the last of the three to make it home with his bag of goodies. Pitt didn't care for the grin on Ralph's face, acting as though this was a contest.

Fool, thought Pitt. They worked as lieutenants with field agents doing the leg-work instead of them. He shook his head sitting down, realizing Ralph and he would never see eye to eye, nor be on the same page.

"Glad you could make it." Sal stated.

"Nothing unusual about me being the last to arrive." Pitt remarked.

"Listen to you," said Ralph. "Getting a silver tongue."

Pitt inhaled thinking he needed a fresh start. The Sal Dana gang had gotten stale. He liked what they were doing since it kept him from a daily grind and if he worked an actual job, it would be in a warehouse where he'd be confident playing a supervisor's role.

He was that in this gig until his men got sent to marble city. Pitt pondered why he, Ralph, and Murray were still alive to do the task their men couldn't finish. Murray put his guys on hiatus and Ralph like him (and it made him sick on the stomach thinking he and this asshole had something in common) wanted to seek new recruits. Sal listened to the giant about doing more of a hands-on job and Pitt hated it.

"Go on and take your pot shots, who gives a shit?"

Ralph got moon-eyed. "What... you ain't going to give me the business? You just going to be a punching bag?"

Sal gave Ralph a wicked look. "Put a sock in it." He glanced at Pitt. "Yo stocky, if youse got something on your mind, now's the time to spill it. That's why we sit here at the round table to discuss what's going on, our next move, or how we can expand."

"I did this shit when we first started and I can't get into it anymore," Pitt snorted. "I enjoyed having guys report back to me and I give you the results."

"Sounds to me like you want to be boss." Ralph remarked.

Pitt gave Ralph a look. "You'd be lying if you said you don't feel the same." Ralph for once had no sassy response.

Sal leaned back nursing his beer. "Look, fellas, I get where you coming from, yet we making up for lost time. I'll be the first to say I'd rather it get back to the old ways and who's to say it won't?" He shrugged. "Remember I was the one keeping tabs on youse guys when you worked your way up to being my lieutenants. Unless you can tell me how and why the deaths of our previous guys took place, this is how it has to be for now."

Pitt looked at Ralph. His annoying coworker felt the same even if he didn't want to admit it. Murray never opened his mouth unless he had something important to say at these junctures and no one ever tried forcing him to speak. They've grown accustomed to letting him sit and observe as if he'd critique the conversation and then correct them. Murray drank, folded his arms, and nodded.

"I'm as clueless as you when this went down," said Ralph. "So far, business has gone back to where we were getting the protection money and no hassles from the cops. It's strange not seeing the other business partners knowing they're in the nut-house, trying to figure out what the hell went wrong and I admit, I too am doing the same."

"Youse guys keep coming back to the fort safe and sound so why complain?" said Sal.

"Pitt swallowed hard. "Because what derailed our racket... it ain't natural." He shook his head. "Sure we're back up and running, but who's to say it won't strike again and most important one of us?"

The room went silent with each racketeer to their own thoughts. Ralph spent more time in church than he ever did, Sal bought incense by the bushel smoking up the room, Pitt recited the Lord's prayer every time he went to bed and got up in the morning. Murray, well the big man kept everything inside.

The current events had left everyone shaken and stirred. A night-lite, protection charms on windows, garlic, and rock salt.

"Okay." Sal blurted. "Before a deadly silent gas sneaks in burning our nose hairs, who has a notion?"

Pitt shook his head. "Can't believe I'm saying this, but shit seemed to escalate when Stout kicked the bucket."

"I hate you as much as agreeing with you," said Ralph. "I can feel that bat swinging loser's presence. Don't ask me how, but with Pitt's boys and mine biting the dust..."

"You saying we're being derailed by a ghost?" asked Sal. "He did excellent work, nevertheless he was trying to kiss ass working alone, just like when youse guys started out, instead of in pairs. Maybe if he had somebody to work with, that other person would have kept his ass inside the car instead of him going on a road rage. He was a butt kissing idiot who got what he deserved."

"Hey Murray... you okay?" Pitt asked.

The giant rose above the table with a face of rage and bulging eyes.

Business was slow so Crabbe thought it'd be nice to take the Metro out for a spin, enjoying the sun playing peek-a-boo with some clouds giving it a temporary eclipse.

Crabbe passed a strip of malls looking on the verge of being a ruin, surrounded by businesses on the nasty side of the economy.

A mom and pops grocery store, ABC for liquor lovers, Family Dollar, and a financial loan office seeking people in need of cash. Crabbe got his attention drawn to someone he thought was a man from his visions. He stood on the sidewalk, looking like a comic book villain with hands on hips, gazing at Crabbe.

The Metro made an abrupt stop and before Crabbe could get out to confront him, the cloaked mystery man vanished, just as a text from Silva told him to get his ass over to Graham street pronto.

Crabbe arrived parking the Metro at one of the broken meters that sat around the city. He didn't know why the city was lazy about fixing them, none the less it meant free parking and he couldn't beat that. He cast a shadow spell, though the skies were colored grey, teasing the chance of rain. Crabbe played shadow instead of his usual crime investigator when joining Silva on her crime scene escapades.

It was less spell work and even though the sun was taking the day off, well better to be safe than sorry. Others would see an illusion and his real self was for Silva's eyes only. She stood in front of the building between it and yellow tape, hands on hips glaring at Crabbe with body language saying what took you so long.

He grinned, shaking his head, thinking if the femme fatale ever heard of traffic. Silva didn't say a word, she pivoted making a beeline inside the building infested with the usual task force doing their jobs. Crabbe knew the drill following the detective instead of the chance of her looking foolish talking to herself.

She led him to the back room where three of the Sal Dana gang met their demise, including the head man himself. The tour started with Pit sitting at the table, taller because his neck extended from his shoulders with his head almost resting on his genitals.

Pitt looked like an unboxed Jack-in-the-box. His eyes bulged from its sockets. A body on the floor belonging to whom Crabbe assumed Ralph the mouth, looked like a Pez dispenser with his jaw line separated. His eyes widened in shock from pain he no doubt felt.

Crabbe shook his head imagining the agonizing pain of having your jaw yanked downward, extending your smile.

Victim three the head honcho, Sal Dana. His face was bludgeoned, a fat lip, broken nose, eye swollen shut, and gash on top of his melon. He died sitting down in his chair holding a handful of what Crabbe recognized as unlit Frankincense.

Not that it would have made any difference. The fourth who Crabbe suspected did the carnage and was nowhere to be found, Murray. Stout must have possessed the big man to help put his old gang out of business.

Crabbe noticed a gun in Sal's other hand, a revolver and it looked like he got off some shots. Silva gave a shoulder to her artificial shadow to follow her outside. They stepped over and around the spilled alcoholic beverages, broken glass, and blood littering the floor. Crabbe gave a sarcastic thought, cleaning up on aisle five. The duo made it outside and Silva found them some privacy.

"What do you think?" Silva asked.

"A homicide" Crabbe replied.

Silva gave a look making a fist wanting to punch Crabbe for his smart ass remark.

"Insensitive, I know," said Crabbe. "Big man of the group Murray put down his mob. He had help."

Silva frowned. "You mean your spirit got his revenge."

Crabbe inhaled, keeping his anger in check. There was nothing for Stout to have revenge against his former crew. They mocked him and the way he died, nevertheless, it was not their fault how he met his end. Crabbe figured while Stout was alive doing the bagman solo, he was trying to impress Sal to get a spot at the table.

Sal maybe led him to believe he could have a seat and when Stout sat in on their meetings he found out he was just an afterthought, motivating him on his quest to take them down.

"Witnesses?" Crabbe inquired

"Private party." Silva replied. "Barkeep said everyone fought to get out the front door when they heard shots."

"He's stuck inside a corpse." Crabbe stated.

"What do you mean?"

Crabbe licked his lips going into his own thoughts. He didn't like the detective getting drawn to these paranormal incidents like a magnet and he wasn't going to give her a supernatural 101 crash course on his thoughtforms, Frick and Frack. He snorted, nodding his head because they made their move, sealing the evil spirit inside his last host, the late Murray.

"Crabbe?!" Silva placing her hands on her hips. "I asked you a question."

"Sal and his boys are hovering around harmless, disoriented, frustrated about what has happened to them, waiting for satisfaction."

Silva gave a dubious look. "Satisfaction?" He shrugged. "When Stout gets his justice then they will find their way to the afterlife."

"Above or down below?" Silva questioned.

Crabbe shrugged. "Not for me to decide, but they didn't murder anybody. A nickel and dime crew with the talent to put fear in people, making them pay protection money. Wrong yet nothing sinister."

"Won't they harm customers that come here to unwind?"

"No." said Crabbe. "You are in my world, and know spirits and demons exist. Spirits around us get upset and angry for dying young or when about to have a life changing experience and have it taken away for some strange reason. Most of them are jealous and envy those who are young, continuing to live life and its cycle, trying to figure out why me and not him or her. But that's why they say life's not fair."

"And the demons?" Silva asked.

"They're just glad to get the hell out of hell and who can blame them."

Silva laughed then caught herself when patrons walked by. "Do you know where Stout is now?"

"Won't belong before I do, but I'm going to let him suffer. He will carry around a dead host for some time." He saw Silva's glaring look. "Trust me I know what I'm doing. Two birds with one stone."

Silva pursed her lips. "So no more havoc?"

"No reason. You have your own work cut out for you."

"What?"

Crabbe swallowed hard. "Make sure your boys don't apprehend Murray since he'll be looking like a zombie from the walking dead." Crabbe nodded, walking away leaving Silva with a bewildered look.

A monsoon downpour however you see it, is the type of rain that puts a damper on things if you plan to have a day with the family, or a night out in the town. Not what I had in mind, thought Stout. He got his revenge, but now he lost the power to body swap.

Murray had served his purpose and now he couldn't get rid of the big lug. He knew it wasn't because Lurch here was dead.

Three bullet holes to the chest and a hole to the forehead now dried, made him look like a native of India or is it the women folk who sport the look? Either way it sucks being stuck inside a corpse.

Stout had plans. He wanted to check out the blonde at the mid-night diner over on South Tryon. He didn't want to take over her body per se, but sample the goods. Sex was no longer an option, yet he learned how to enjoy though hopping out when engaging a man, but staying inside during lesbian encounters. He smiled thinking about two desirable girls getting together. Stout got angry thinking if this was it.

Murray's body was as mobile as the Frankenstein monster, or a robot. His movements were rigid, and he could hardly bend at the knee. Stout tried transferring to another body touching three homeless men, but that almost caused a fight and when they got a load of dead Murray, well no one had to tell them twice to skedaddle.

Stout made the alley and dumpsters his home, till he figured things out. Sal and the gang gone, meant he had no more thirst for retribution. He didn't want to go to purgatory and he didn't want to live in hell while on the topside. Stout exhaled knowing living inside Lurch here, moving around like the walking dead would not cut it.

He thought of the glow within the body. He knew Murray wasn't trying to re-enter, he'd shoved him out, leaving him with a dubious expression of what just happened and by now Murray like the rest of the crew, realized they were dead. The two bookends burst of light making him a sandwich boggled his mind.

When his deed was done, they blasted their way inside the big man's body making him feel like he gained some new powers.

Stout got excited thinking he was going to metamorphose into something incredible, after all he was now a ghost with capabilities he didn't have when alive, so this new experience could be an upgrade right...? Wrong.

Stout's vicissitude felt like a vice holding him in place.

He didn't know why the two lights wanted to share the body with him, but he didn't like it. He had no elbow room so for now he had to make do with his new roommates buying time in the rain to work things out. Being a ghost gave him all the time in the world. What it didn't give him though, was knowledge that these two lights were Frick and Frack, sent by the one person that even as a ghost, he had good reason to be afraid of.

CHAPTER 32

Nightfall and the rain halted to a drizzle. Crabbe didn't mind since his oversized authentic brown Highlander duster made for any occasion kept him dry. His black Converse Chuck Taylor high-top canvas sneakers were dry because he cast a waterproof spell. Crabbe trekked into the dusk trying to clear his head.

He had a lot to ponder on, and wasn't concerned with bounty-hunting demons planning an ambush, something that often happened during his walks on the home front. No visions of Satan plotting, the demon human eater, and the vengeful spirit weren't sugar plums dancing inside his head. One would have to wait for later, the other two he believed, a climax on the way.

He didn't like his thought-forms, Frick and Frack taking their time putting Stout on lockdown and for how long would they be able to hold him without him finding out they need a charge. The magician hoped they stayed energized long enough till his plan was completed.

When their deed was done, he'd discuss their purpose and ask why they took their time getting a hold on Stout and this allowing him to harm others. Crabbe smiled thinking about the plan he had in store for Stout, involving the demon, it made him lick his chops.

Crabbe stepped out to clear the darkness clouding his mind, and to blow off some steam and what better place than a bar full of demons. He thirsted for a fight, to be a bully and though the goblins were innocent, he didn't care because they were demons.

These delinquents cared nothing about Crabbe and his bounty.

They simply wanted out of hell. Tired of the endless darkness lighted by fire and brimstone, smell of feces, decaying flesh, it made them yearn for something new and refreshing. So when they escaped, they understood to remain far from the spellcaster's wrath, they must abide by his rules and leave mankind alone.

The ghouls have a special place they call their own, to unwind. Some go to the watering holes with normal humans in disguise, none the less when they want to be among their kind, they choose the bar with no doors. Invisible to the human eye but not their own. The bar looked like a brick wall, but was a door to an alley passage.

Crabbe spotted one local; a five-six, weighing a buck thirty curvy blonde, though she'd altered her appearance into many women of color, he still knew her as a demon vixen by the name Mercy. Real or nick-name, Crabbe didn't know. Her reputation for sexual escapades, leaving men craving for more and out for weeks from her promiscuous wanton.

She preyed on humans saying they look better than her ogre brood. Whatever man bedded her had better have good cardio. Crabbe saw her authentic form; raven hair shaped like goat horns, tan complexion she got from the incubator down below and hieroglyphic tattoo from the temples of her head down the sides of her neck to her spine that would make the Banger sisters jealous, white short sleeve blouse open to her cleavage with a black leather corset containing her breasts.

Charcoal stripes painted on slacks and ebony heels to match. She puffed a dark cheroot between her pink pouty lips, button nose, dark eyes and brows.

"Not tonight handsome." Mercy retorted with authority.

"You knew of my intentions?" Crabbe replied.

"You left a lot of scars the last time you were here." Mercy stated. "We didn't deserve it then and we don't now."

"In a different frame of mind." Crabbe shrugged. "What can I say?"

Mercy glared, puffing out a circle. "Sorry?"

Crabbe joined Mercy side by side leaning against the wall. He was getting used to the bounty hunting gig put out on him. Night after night, the devil sent his hordes testing the young magician, trying to raise his blood pressure. Crabbed found out about the bars and planned his own ambush.

He was wreaking havoc within the confines, until Mercy used her tail to constrict him. He could have broken free, but her soothing voice harnessed the savage beast. She convinced him some demons didn't give a damn about collecting the bounty and knew Satan was a liar.

They just enjoyed being away from the bowels of Tartinus and had no intention of going back. Crabbe saw the truth in her eyes and words. In return he did her a favor, getting rid of the tail and replacing it with a definitive booty-luscious booty then replaced her demon ears with a pair resembling her favorite Star Trek character Mr. Spock.

"What's bugging you to come down here, looking to start a fight?" Mercy questioned.

"Having a hard time controlling situations."

Mercy snorted. "So...?" She punched his shoulder. "You're human."

They laughed.

"The offer still stands." She said, dragging out a long smoke through her nostrils.

"You're a nympho." Crabbe stated.

"Every girl needs a hobby." Mercy replied. "So how about it?"

The back door visible to supernatural eyes swung open. A seven foot tall burnt to a crisp man, stepped outside for a smoke. Mercy, not frightened, grabbed Crabbe's hand holding it like they were lovers.

"Well, Well, Well.... Come to blow off more steam?" The giant asked.

"Ashes." Crabbe muttered gazing at Mercy.

She wasn't holding his hand for comfort or fear. Ashes wasn't a jealous boyfriend or ex-lover. He was the bar overseer and Mercy's boss. Crabbe didn't know if Ashes ever loved. Ashes wasn't a demon, a spirit, but he reminded Crabbe of a fireplace log that burnt from the inside and if you touch him with a poker, he'd crumble like the log in the fireplace, releasing flames from within.

His person lit up like a Jack-O-Lantern, though his head wasn't shaped like a pumpkin. Ashes face was skeletal with teeth looking like his gums receded if he had flesh. He wore a newsboy cap, buttoned shirt that used to be white, with a bow tie.

A sweater vest, slacks cuffed at the ankles, and penny loafers, all charcoal color. His clothes told Crabbe he was a late century man and when he spoke in his raspy gravelly voice it sounded as smooth as a saxophone. He was a chain smoker and when Crabbe saw him he had a cigarette glued to his lower lip. Ashes resume; a saloon proprietor who acted as a liaison and informant, for occult detectives and the paranormal world. Hanging around demons suited him, because they were the closest thing to family he had.

"You two a thing now?" Ashes asked.

"Long time no see." Crabbe remarked.

"How's your servitor?" Ashes questioned dragging the word. "Tell him I said hello."

Morocco and Ashes had history. The kind that wasn't kiss and tell. Crabbe remembered how a crystal ball his servitor settled it illuminated like a supernova till Crabbe calmed him down.

"What do you know?" Crabbe asked.

"You." Ashes remarked, sampling Mercy holding Crabbe's hand. "And a few other goody two shoes."

The comment, outdated, proved the walking night lite was ancient, with dressing like back in the prohibition era. Crabbe couldn't tell what race he belonged to, though he classified him once as a black man.

He wondered if the man met his fate during a time where a black couldn't scratch his ass in public and was wearing what looked like fancy clothes, making him stick out like a sore thumb and a target to the eyes of racist whites.

"I'm a delightful book to read, but you ain't got time to sit under a lamp light with all you got going on." said Ashes.

"Then answer my question." Crabbe demanded.

"Don't want to make your servitor jealous." Ashes remarked.

"There's no competition, you and he have unique skill sets, however, you're not welcome in my home."

"Ouch.." Ashes replied. "If I didn't have this burning sensation inside me, you might have hurt my feelings."

Mercy smirked.

"Mercy." Ashes crooned her name while eyeing the hand she was holding. "What you up to girl?"

"You too hot for me, big man." Mercy replied. "Makes for an awkward workplace."

"Putting more wood in the fire, baby." said Ashes, his gravelly voice symphonic.

"Ashes." Crabbe swallowed hard. "If you know something..."

The walking inferno gulped down his fag allowing the smoke ooze through his ventilation body. He put another gasper between his teeth. "Your surrogate father don't have enough nails and wood, but he is building something with an amateur carpenter."

Mercy felt a rise in Crabbe. She squeezed his hand bringing him back down to earth.

The bloodline was made by a desperate ancestor who paid the price in the long run. Crabbe never considered Satan anything more than feces dwelling down in the sewer. He took pleasure using his unwanted gift for good, sticking it to Lucifer Morningstar. Crabbe translated Ashes' term carpenter, describing a fool making an ill fated deal with the devil.

"He's human and thinks he can take me down," said Crabbe.

"You catch on quick." Ashes replied.

"Not too many of my kind know about me so..." Crabbe gave Ashes a look.

Ashes grumbled a smirk. "Yeah, I'm the candle that burns both ends." He puffed a cloud of smoke from his body.

"Look at me. Nothing to lose and nothing to gain. Never will be human again and no desire to be a demon. Supervising a supernatural bar and listen if you'd..." He smiled. "Infiltrate me into your brood, my services are free."

In the paranormal world you need allies. Crabbe would not shy away from any eyes and ears that could help him with his battle against the macabre.

"If you have to run this by your servitor, I understand," Ashes remarked.

"You have a real hard on for him." Crabbe replied.

Ashes growled a laugh. "That burned off a long time ago."

"Too much information." Crabbe retorted.

"Right now they are in the stages of building." Ashes inhaled, then exhaled, allowing his body to be a chimney. "So finish your current ordeals."

Mercy sighed in exasperation. "Okay you boys have reminisced enough and the conversion is circling." She pulled Crabbe in her direction.

Crabbe glanced back at the towering smoke stack. "You should try cutting down or that shit will kill you."

Mercy waved. "Early night Boss. You got this?" Ashes nodded.

"Get a haircut!" Ashes shot at Crabbe, then smiling at Mercy. "And Mercy when you get back, kiss and tell."

Mercy gave him the finger. Ashes hummed at the gesture, using it as a symbol of sexual pleasure. As close as he'd ever get.

Rumors have a way of becoming true when you experience it yourself. Mercy a demon and her love 'em and leave 'em fast lovers, human. They never stood a chance against a nympho like her.

Mercy, a bucking bronco that could never be broken, at least not by a mere mortal. Crabbe, unlike his fellow earthlings, possessed the stamina Mercy had been craving since becoming a top-side resident. He allowed her to ride him to her heart's content.

He lost track how many times he exploded between her hungry thighs. Crabbe got moon-eyed when it hit him; they were not using condoms. He did not want to be a father and knew Mercy would never be mother of the year. What would the kid look like? How would he explain to his family they have a half-demon for a nephew or niece?

Clover would have his hide. The riding stopped. Mercy dismounted, falling on her back, letting her hand fall, smacking Crabbe on his nose.

"Hey," said Crabbe.

"What a buzz kill, dude." Mercy replied.

"You know what I was thinking?" Crabbe questioned.

"I have no desire to be a mother." Mercy retorted.

"So you on the pill?" Crabbe asked.

"I am supernatural." Mercy remarked. Crabbe nodded. "I will leave it at that."

They both stretched breathing heavily. Mercy resorted to her smoking habit to Crabbe's chagrin. He said nothing since he was a guest in her house. Crabbe took the time to check out her décor, Casablanca, Raiders of the lost ark, paintings from Jackson Pollock, the overrated Picasso, along with abstract art testing the visual depth of what one sees, when looking at a canvas splattered with a collage of colors, all meshed together.

Mercy's stay above Hades cultured her. Her home was very human which Crabbe had no problem with, but traumatizing men after their escapades was another matter. Her studio apartment meant she was here to stay.

"Change your habit," said Crabbe.

Mercy took a long draw from her fag. "Where are you going with this?"

"Humans don't have the stamina to keep up with your desires."

Mercy snorted. "I have killed nobody."

"Yet." Crabbe stated. "I'm not trying to tell you what to do with your love life…"

"Am I in danger of getting vanquished?"

Crabbe sat up. "Try holding back… let your partner take the lead."

"And if I don't like or cannot be satisfied?"

Crabbe smiled. "Then do like most women. Fake it. It's the human thing to do."

"It beats the hell out of going back to hell." Mercy stated.

"You're not a monster." Crabbe replied. "So there is a difference."

"You would have been back in the confines of fire and brimstone a long time ago."

Mercy pursed her lips. "Admirable demons like me."

Crabbe grabbed her hand kissing it. "I had sex with one." She snatched back her hand folding her arms pouting.

Crabbe sat up straight giving Mercy a bewildered look. "Did I say something wrong?" Crabbe asked.

Mercy snorted. "Why do men have to ruin special moments?"

Crabbe slumped down, realizing he used sex in place of making love. Even demonic femme fatales have feelings. He shook his head.

"We're not lovers." Crabbe said with a shrug. "Unless you trying to tell me something?"

"I can replace Ashes." Mercy retorted.

Crabbe played it off though he wanted to relax from Mercy pulling the kill the headlights and put it in neutral. Conversation was changing and he approved.

"What are you talking about?" Crabbe questioned.

"Wasn't he your informant for keeping tabs on demon activities?" Mercy asked.

"I don't see you as a--"

"Snitch?" Mercy remarked. "You're right, I am not a rat, stoolie, sneak, tattletale, fink, or a mark."

Crabbe smiled. "You want to be my canary, informer, source, and better yet tipster?"

Mercy giggled. "Tipster sounds cool."

"It's not a home." Crabbe replied. "Ashes was none of those. If I drop by and he was out taking his smoke break which is all the time. We'd kick-start a conversation and he'd tell me what was up."

"How did he get his information?" She asked.

Crabbe swallowed hard. Mercy's question proved she's unqualified to be his eyes and ears for the underworld. She possessed super strength and not only for sexual encounters, but he'd seen demons topple others and not being a chauvinist, Crabbe had seen female demons put down their male counterparts with their bare hands, talons, claws, fangs, and tails.

He knew Mercy would meet her maker if a goblin found out she was playing with a double edged sword. Crabbe liked Mercy.

"Ashes is a sore thumb." Crabbe remarked. "He's not a demon, spirit, or a zombie. I call him an undead who fits in nowhere, yet he's more suitable around the paranormal, because he's not normal. Ashes has no place to go. He blends in better with the demon crowd and he's smart enough to mind his business, only honing in on conversations and giving me the gist, whenever I might drop by which is once in a blue moon."

Mercy nodded. "I know it would be leery if the natives saw you coming around seeking me out."

"If you do this...be your true self. You hear something that's important then sing like a canary." He handed her a card.

"Crabbe H. Appleton, at your service."

Mercy observed. "Where were you hiding this?"

"I'm a magician." Crabbe said. "Leave that here."

"Yeah, because I might reach inside your pocket pulling and whoops." Mercy smiled at him.

"You got it." Crabbe replied.

"How do you think he got that way?" Mercy asked.

Crabbe frowned. "I believe they burned him alive and he prayed.'

"To become what he is now?"

Crabbe nodded. "An ancestor responded to his plea, keeping him from making a last minute deal, with his soul giving him his undead presence."

Mercy pursed her lips. "And you know this?"

"Clairvoyance." Crabbe replied, going into a temporary vow of silence thinking about the walking chimney. He saw the tall handsome black man's origin. How he got his name Ashes.

Burned alive at the stake in a remote clearing, screaming out incantations. Crabbe realized the smoke stack had a voodoo background. He used his voodoo to call his ancestors to give him his afterlife presence, to get his revenge on those who thought they had a right to take his life. Ashes' crime was no crime at all, except for being black in a period where dating or whistling at a white woman was a death sentence.

"Penny for your thoughts?" Mercy gave a flirtatious pose.

A demon like her could withstand Ashes origin, but it was none of her business and the more he thought of Ashes' demise it angered him. Ashes got his revenge against his tormentors.

Crabbe couldn't imagine the horror of the men facing the towering cinder, setting them on fire with his Midas touch.

He sought them out at night making it more frightening yet, not that they didn't deserve it.

The magician pondered if the revenge for Ashes had stopped. He knew the victims of his wrath have descendants and it wouldn't be fair for them to pay for their ancestor's crime. He'd have a talk with the human smoke stack if he'd called it quits, though Crabbe had yet to hear about any incidents of deaths caused by being burned alive.

"Time to hit the road." Crabbe yawned.

Mercy spread herself out naked. "Up for round two?"

Crabbe smiled.

CHAPTER 33

At 8 am, the smell of 100% Colombian coffee filled the kitchen air. Crabbe didn't remember what time he left Mercy's apartment or walked through his own door, but his body ached from the workout she gave him. He smiled hoping she paid heed to his words to ease up on the mere mortals she invited to her bed.

Crabbe grabbed his ebony mug, then the ten cup carafe too small for his percolator. He broke his original cleaning it, thinking about Stout and the human devouring demon. He needed a twelve cup despite the box saying it was ten and he didn't want to buy another.

The landline phone rang. Crabbe wasted no time answering since he designated it for family.

"Is everything all right?" Crabbe asked. "You tell me." Clover replied.

Big sister and second mother, Clove had a unique sense of detecting her baby brother's burdens.

"You're up early," said Crabbe.

"As are you. You getting plenty of sleep?"

"I need little." Crabbe exhaled

"Don't care if you got the bulk of it, you need your rest."

"Going back to bed as soon as we're done talking."

"You know I've got to worry." said Clover

Crabbe smiled. "Wouldn't have it any other way. How's the rest of the kindred?"

"You're the one doing the supernatural thing."

"Glad you all are doing good." Crabbe smiled.

"You be careful and take care of yourself," she said.

"Give everyone my love. Counting the days till the holidays."

They hung up and Crabbe added cream to his coffee.

"Good morning my friend."

Crabbe inhaled. "You going to make me regret putting a ball in every room."

"You have my deepest gratitude." said Morocco. "You know you have family here too."

"You making a point?"

"Family helps each other, my friend."

Crabbe stirred then sipped his coffee. "The thoughtforms are like my kids... sort of."

"Have they called home yet?"

"Ha! Ha! Hilarious." retorted Crabbe.

"I'm serious, friend."

Crabbe enjoyed his Java. His plan was to allow his thoughtforms to contain Stout inside the deceased body, until further notice and Morocco would get his chance to go back to work. Crabbe wanted to humble his servitor. He'd doubted him when he insisted on using his little energy lights instead of his turban headed chum.

"The violence is on ice and I'm waiting on a piece to this jig-saw puzzle."

The crystal glowed. "A plan's coming together then?"

"Since our boy Stout likes to body hop, I think I might have a permanent one waiting for him." Crabbe replied.

"Sounds diabolical."

Crabbe snorted. "Would you have it any other way?"

"He deserves far worse, really." Morocco agreed.

Crabbe nodded. "Don't you worry. What I have in store for him should meet your approval."

Crabbe felt a presence rubbing and circling in and out between his legs. Mister Kit, his abyss furry feline, making his good morning known.

Crabbe put down his chicory, and opening a cabinet grabbed a can of sardines.

Kit loved them and Crabbe hated the smell. He twisted then pulled back the tin, placing it on the floor.

"Enjoy." Crabbe smiled, making a beeline to the circling stairs leading to his bedroom.

"You can keep Kit company while he has his breakfast." Crabbe shouted half way up.

The crystal ball went dark.

What was this, a tag team? Stout thought. His captors would one at a time leave, then come back charged, holding him in place in a body he had no desire to remain in its decaying form. His captors weakened when night fell on them like a blanket. They seemed to regain strength from a street light and were reborn, getting super charged from the sun at daybreak.

Stout felt loose as if a chance to escape when one left to do whatever it had to do and he knew it wasn't a bathroom break, then again he still had a lot to learn about the supernatural world. Stout knew once they both came back from taking turns leaving and returning to the dead body he occupied, his spirit form became encased in a vice grip.

School was not a friend or a good fit for Stout, though he graduated with a diploma. A slow learner and now he was gathering what he hoped was his chance to plan his escape, from a threesome that was no fun.

Thanks to walking like a robot or the Frankenstein monster, he could move from alley to alley making a dumpster his home. Stout was fortunate those who came upon his person, saw a homeless man in need of a bath and went on their way, leaving him pondering how to get out of his predicament.

271

She opened the door with a look in her eyes. A loved one had died. Crabbe would not use his clairvoyance. He didn't mind prying, but not on Silva. If she wanted to tell him what had her somber, she'd do it in her own time. Crabbe did however play detective on his friend. Hair close cropped and faded on the sides with the top dressed with gel slicking down her scimitar style sideburns.

Gold earrings, a sunflower colored pearl necklace, to match a comfortable snug fit sleeveless dress, two inches above the knee. Open-toe heels, the same hue as he magnificent Popeye's forearm and legs. Before they sat down, she waltzed to the other side of the living room to light half a dozen incense sticks. He continued to check out the dress.

The design, a U-shape at the top exposed her upper back and shoulder blades. A bridge with a zipper attachment and an open arch showing the smoothness of her lower back. Crabbe recognized scents: Vanilla, Frankincense, Myrrh, and White Sage. He told her how incense purifies the air and relieves stress.

They sat side by side on the couch. A file on the coffee table. Crabbe swallowed hard not wanting another case. His vengeful spirit and human devouring demon, reaching somewhat of a climax. He observed her hem displaying more thigh, her hairstyle made her face more mature than usual, though still beautiful.

Silva's eyes were watery, but not ready to rain yet. They said something wasn't right.

She either came from a bad date or cancellation. Crabbe didn't know and he would not snoop. She gazed at him as if wanting a companion, but not for talking. Silva studied her man with the 1970's look: bushy neat Afro, designer sideburns ending sharp at the corners of his mouth, oversized pull over red shirt, old navy loose fitting blue jeans, and black high-top Converse canvas sneakers. She knew he was in his twenties, maybe early thirties, but looked like he could be in high school.

Silva grabbed the file. "I'm not giving you anything, but this might be up your alley when you do other deeds..." Silva stated.

Crabbe gave a nod of thanks for understanding his current situation. "Lay it on me."

"I'm not on the case yet... I took the file because I overheard a conversation though it's incomplete."

Crabbe pursed his lips. "Won't they know it's missing?"

Silva smirked. "I made copies. My job... okay?"

Crabbe saluted. "Yes, ma'am."

She opened the file.

'VOODOO MURDERS' was on the front page and Crabbe stood up making a beeline to the window staring at the closed blinds instead of looking out into the night.

"Are you all right?" Silva asked.

Crabbe didn't answer. Clenching his fist thinking voodoo murders and that meant human sacrifices. The spellcaster didn't need to read the file, knowing it mentioned hearts in the paragraphs. Crabbe snorted, biting his lower lip, knowing that it goes along with the soul.

Soul being the key word and what does the devil want most in the world but your soul? Crabbe glanced back, getting some relief gazing at Silva's thighs, easing his tension. He sat back down, closing the file.

"Promise me you won't volunteer."

Silva shrugged. "I'm still working with you on these weird cases, but..."

"No." Crabbe shook his head. "When what we're doing now gets done, I don't want you anywhere near this. You hear me Gwyn?"

He called me by my first name she thought, realizing a touchy subject sat on her coffee table. "This is what I do and if it's presented to me, it's my civic duty--"

Crabbe rose above Silva. "If that happens then yeah I understand, but promise me we'll go together." He gave her a stern look. "Don't go cowboy on me. We stand side-by-side in this. No solo act."

Silva nodded. "You have my word."

She grabbed his hand.

Crabbe sat back down. "How are you spinning these cases?" He asked. "Promise you won't get angry?" Silva retorted.

Crabbe shrugged. "I'm already upset so..." "Noted." said Silva. "Cult murders."

Crabbe inhaled. "Smart... I understand."

"You know since these deaths are both in the paranormal region I thought it would be better to classify them together."

"You need not explain yourself to me. I agree. People believe in cults more than demons and spirits roaming the earth, wreaking havoc. You did good."

"One other thing," said Silva.

"Oh shit." Crabbe remarked.

"They want to put me in charge of a cult task force."

"Too late to kill the headlights and put it in neutral." Crabbe remarked. "Let me guess, you said yes."

"Thinking about it." Silva replied. "I feel like I'm a magnet pulled to this thing."

Crabbe nodded."Yeah, you said that already."

"So then you know what I'm going to say if they ask me again?"

Crabbe stood up and Silva did the same. He knew it was time to leave before he blew a gasket.

She walked him to the door.

"Wait until I take care of this first and we will have a long talk about what you are getting into."

She gave a crinkled smile. "That's why I called you."

Crabbe nodded. "You... " He placed a hand on her shoulder. "Wait till my plate is empty and you can spin some more."

Crabbe arrived back at Parts Unknown at the time when his community started shutting down.

Bob's Carvana called it a day, the Banger sisters blew kisses to him on their way home, or whatever domain gave them a reason to explore life's temptations. Crabbe smirked, wondering if his fellow enterprises brooded over how he stayed in business, despite being gone more than he ran his store.

He thought of hiring someone to help run his herbal shop. The applicant would have to have an open mind and a fast learner about herbs and products within the confines of his business.

Crabbe was about to put the Metro around back when he got a glimpse of Motor hanging out, taking a puff. He thought the culinary wizard had quit the habit, but it seemed not.

Motor shut down his bistro around 10 pm Monday through Thursday then 11 pm on Friday and Saturday.

He followed the common protocol of using Sunday as a day of rest.

Crabbe killed the engine and got out, making his way to his back entrance, the kitchen. Before he could put his keys on the hook, his front door bell rang. He was sure he left the closed sign on the door.

Crabbe answered, Motor brought with him a jug of his honey sweet tea and a carry out bag holding three Styrofoams of food.

"Can you eat?" Motor asked.

Crabbe's mouth watered, his stomach growled, and his brain said hell yeah. Crabbe took the food inviting Motor to come inside.

"I'll never get used to that damn ornament eye you keep on your shop's door," said Motor.

"It makes me authentic." Crabbe replied. The serpent eye fends off and warns him of danger from his paranormal enemies. Motor was safe, being a regular human.

"Never seen your shop up close and personal." Motor stated.

The tour was quick and fast. Crabbe wished Motor had come around back to the kitchen door, with his more at home exterior. He set the food down on the table. Crabbe grabbed a glass from the cover.

"Next time come around back." Crabbe retorted. "You joining me?"

"For conversation, if you don't mind."

Crabbe gestured for Motor to take the load off hoping he didn't have another relative in need of his services. He opened the boxes and the food was still hot: bacon wrapped meatloaf, boiled broccoli, carrots, garlic mashed potatoes, and a container of brown gravy. Crabbe wasted no time digging in, he closed his eyes savoring the flavor of the food made from scratch.

"Hope I'm not keeping you from anything?" Crabbe questioned.

"My peeps got it till I get back. I was concerned you weren't eating."

Crabbe smiled knowing Motor right on cue. His diet of granola bars, Belvita breakfast biscuits, coffee, water, and diet drinks made him yearn for a home cooked meal.

"Thanks for looking out," said Crabbe.

"No problem." Motor replied, holding back more words.

Crabbe was glad the culinary king said no more. He didn't want to talk about helping relieve her pain. Crabbe didn't know how Motor would react, telling him he scared her to death after realizing she no longer wanted to live. Crabbe hoped he'd never be put in position to play God again. Motor looked around the kitchen.

"I was going to suggest you find a good woman, but your place is nice and tidy." said Motor.

Crabbe smiled and kept eating. He could tell by the way Motor sat his shop creeped him out. His body tensed, knees locked together, the rooms dim lighted, corners dark making it look as if something would jump out and grab you. The way Crabbe liked it since he's a fan of the night, never liking daylight.

"You sound like my sister Clover."

Motor pursed his lips. "Oh no... your personal life is your business. I was--"

Crabbe waved him off. "No worries."

"Ruthie left you some money."

Crabbe almost choked on his morsel of meatloaf. "Say what?!"

"Ten thousand." Motor exhaled.

"Money from the grave?" Crabbe asked.

Motor shrugged. "So it seems."

Crabbe nodded. "I could invest, save for a rainy day--" Motor laughed.

"Did I say something funny?" Crabbe asked.

"We get clouds from time to time, but they don't cry," said Motor.

Crabbe snorted. He looked at Motor, giving him a mental wave off saying he'll be fine getting his rain drops on his home front.

"What made you pick this location?" Crabbe asked.

"Bob's dealership looked forsaken so I gave it company." Motor replied.

Crabbe was the last proprietor to settle on the street named PARTS UNKNOWN. He never asked who was the first to lay down their roots. He wanted a place isolated yet not off the map. The three businesses before him did themselves proud and welcomed his herbal shop as something no more unique than the Banger Sisters Tattoo parlor.

The queens of body paint were living large with the success of winning contests, along with word of mouth and internet advertising, which made them popular. Motor did a great job marketing his eatery, putting it on billboards, freeway signs, and the internet. Bob advertised on the media; camera crews came out to do commercials and he still used the blab sheet taking up a whole page in the ancient periodical that looked to be as extinct as the dinosaur.

Crabbe had a link to all of their websites and he joined Motor on the freeway sign, though his shop wasn't a restaurant.

Motor cleared up a mystery, Crabbe came after the sisters making Bob and Motor founding fathers.

"What brought you here?" Motor questioned.

Crabbe shrugged. "Not a people person, but didn't want to be a last stop gas station before you reach civilization."

The response brought a smile to Motor's face. Crabbe figured with his situation he needed a discrete location. Parts Unknown gave him what he looked for, since he wanted to be his own boss and was concerned about the safety of others, if he worked in the city for a corporation.

Crabbe rocked in his chair to the pros of being in charge. The cons, getting harassed on his clear-my-head night walks by the demon hordes who he made sure they regretted crossing his path. He exhaled a mental thanks to Tomas Jr. and Clover, for loaning him the money to start his business and he paid them back in installments. They didn't like him moving so far away, but understood.

Motor reached inside his pants pocket taking out an envelope. He placed it on the table in front of Crabbe. "I acted as representative or whatever they call it when the required person is not present."

"If she didn't work... how did she..."

"My dad said his sister had an open mind about preparing for the future. She invested leaving money for Ruthie." Motor commented.

"Thank you, Motor." Crabbe replied. "In honor of Ruthie, I'll put it to good use."

Motor rose nodding. "I read and heard you often get a glimpse of something that looks like a person standing there, yet when you turn to see... it's an empty chair or the wall and that's it."

"They say it's the spirit of a loved one, letting you know they're watching over you," said Crabbe.

Motor inhaled then swallowed hard. "Her signature looked fresh. The only time you met her was--"

"We can do a seance," Crabbe remarked.

Motor shivered at the thought. "That's your thing. I'm not ignorant to things unexplained, but I prefer to keep it that way. I'll talk to them when my time comes, until then I'll deal with the living."

"Nothing wrong with that."

"I'll mossy on back to the grease, pots, and pans." Motor pointed toward the back. "Easy way out, right?"

"Back door through the kitchen," said Crabbe. "Motor, is it difficult to advertise on Indeed, and Monster?" Crabbe asked.

"Zip recruiter is good, too." Motor replied. "You thinking about getting some help?"

"Thought has crossed my mind."

Motor nodded. "My customers do ask when you're open."

"Thanks for the food," said Crabbe.

He picked up the envelope as Motor made his exit.

CHAPTER 34

A table covered with books of the occult, two bottles of rot gut, and one running on empty.

Things calmed down now that morning had arrived, relieving the night. Hiram sat clueless, flipping through old and new books about the paranormal, trying to send his demon lover back from whence she came.

He found nothing susceptible to counter his spell and wondered if these periodicals were legit. Books placed before were brand new with the smell to prove it and others dusty, stained, with missing pages that may have had what he was looking for. Hiram felt his pentacle circle was weakening.

The house trembled all night keeping him from getting any sleep. He rested during the day, waking up dreading darkness because it's when the fireworks began. He checked the neighborhood watching for any signs of earthquake, sighing a relief when he saw lights outside and nothing stirring.

Hiram wanted to escape his home, yet his conscience made him stay, feeling responsible for what he had down below. He didn't want to hear or read about some monstrosity on the news hitting homes at night leaving a bloodbath in its wake.

The demon was not built for daylight making him thankful it contained vampire qualities.

Hiram shoved the books away with some falling off the table. He needed professional help.

Not headshrinkers who'd have muscle bound men dressed in white wrapping a jacket around his upper body built for hugging yourself. Hiram ditched the literature for his laptop. A device on the verge of helping to save the trees, without knowing it.

He Googled psychics, voodoo doctors, and mystics. Some of them lived far out, were they for real, powerful, or too dangerous to live around the corner? Hiram saw star ratings from two with half stars to four and no fives. Browsing on, he studied the names of the so-called occult specialists.

Hiram didn't trust the ones sporting names like Sister Rose, Mama Dee, Papa Bongo, Doctor Miracle, and Brother Soul. A name he came across looked sincere with no commercials: CRABBE H. APPLETON: At Your Service.

He even owned an herbal store. Hiram figured this guy must be legit, to have his own business while the others used home addresses. Mister Appleton used his business and not a home residence making him valid. He had something in common with the other root workers living out in the boonies.

The interviews were comical. Nothing brutal, as Crabbe thought it might have felt like an expecting father, waiting for his first born. Being a boss and having an employee would be a whole new experience for him. He felt the need with his fellow merchants concerned about how he keeps his business open, while absent from it so often.

Crabbe smirked thinking about the word business. They should mind their own, but he shared a street with them so nosy neighbors were a part of life.

He thought he found hires, they were too normal to survive in his neck of the woods and would say adios after the first day. The candidates came in all shapes, sizes, and race. Potential employees dressed in hippie attire almost got the job.

They asked if they could use some herbs in his shop as a replacement for cannabis to make blunt when they took breaks or lunch. Crabbe pondered how that might come in handy, getting a buzz in case something weird happened.

He continued to amuse himself at the thought of telling them you better lay off that stuff. Crabbe wasn't looking for anyone with a degree, yet having one in the study of herbs and what not like himself, would be helpful. He wanted someone he could mold into an ally in case chaos raised its head. Who'd understand the world is not as it seems and it is littered with mystery for the open minded. Crabbe threw brain teasers on purpose and when he got dubious looks, he knew they were not qualified. He needed someone who saw the world as himself.

Crabbe sat at the table in the room between his home and business life. Where he did his tarot, palm reading and seance.

"Not going well, I take it huh?" Morocco commented. He played the silent partner of the hiring process.

"I throw questions about the unknown without tipping my hat and you witness their response." Crabbe snorted,

"You'll be sending more to Shaw Heights, my friend."

"I think not." Crabbe laughed. "Now that Stout's on ice things have calmed down."

"In my experience ice melts."

Crabbe pursed his lips. "And that should make you happy."

"Is there something I should know, my friend?"

"Stay tuned, mon ami." Crabbe retorted.

The sound of high heels came down the hallway. Crabbe put up a sign by the door that read 'Now Hiring'. It went away once a candidate entered his abode.

"My friend!" Morocco exclaimed. The crystal ball giving a rapid on and off blink.

"Relax," said Crabbe leaning back. "I got this."

"But we have a --"

"Kill the headlights and put it in neutral, Moe." said Crabbe.

The interviewee stood in front of the table decked in black leather jacket, sports bra, leggings, and heels. Fair skin, peach gloss on her lips, and hair two jumbo braids looking like ram horns on her head.

"Have a seat," said Crabbe. "Tell me why I should hire you?"

"Wow." She replied. "Shoot from the hip... okay." She sat up straight. "Jayne Mills and I am a quick learner."

"Meaning you don't have experience?" Crabbe asked.

Mills shielded her eyes from the bright blinking crystal ball. "I learned on the fly while attending a bar." Mills giggled. "Let me tell you, there are drinks you never even heard of, but you better remember the recipe to keep the locals happy."

You don't have a degree do you?"

Mills shrugged. "Didn't think I needed one... do I?"

Crabbe shook his head. "The position doesn't require one."

"I know it looks better, but why lie?"

"Are you still bartending and if so do you plan to quit?" Crabbe asked.

"Yes and no," said Mills. "I work at night and your store hours are 10 am to 6 pm. I need the extra cash."

Crabbe nodded. "This won't affect your current job?"

Mills smiled. "I have an extra switch."

"Yes you do." Crabbe remarked.

"Excuse me?" Mills chuckled.

"I want you to describe the atmosphere, what you saw when you walked inside. Does anything here disturb you?"

Mills snorted. "The dim lighting sets the tone which suits what you are trying to sell. Your personality, you prefer night over day, making you more believable when you perform your craft, palm reading, what nots, and card tricks. Nothing disturbs or shocks me, but this crystal ball's bright light blinking on and off like it's a warning to you or something annoys me."

Crabbe nodded. "It's my danger, danger, Will Robinson."

Mills gave a dubious look.

Crabbe cleared his throat. "It's a joke I sometimes say paying homage to a classic back in the day science fiction TV series... anyway you don't mind the setting?"

"I'll be right at home."

"I'm sure you will."

Mills frowned. "Excuse me?"

Crabbe got up heading to the kitchen. He came back to the table carrying a plastic tub of Atomic FireBalls.

Mills bewildered, studied the container.

"I don't have a sweet tooth." Mills commented.

"Neither do I, but you're almost home and I improvised on the hiring process." Crabbe replied.

"You do this for all your employees?" "You'd be my first hire."

"I feel honored."

"So you should." said Crabbe, reaching inside the tub grabbing a handful. "I want you to do the same, putting as many in your mouth to see if you can take the heat."

"And if I can't?"

"I hope you're right about being a fast learner."

Crabbe peeled the plastic off, counted a handful of fireballs piling them inside his mouth. Once the saliva went to work, he cringed then settled as his demon power adapted to the heat. Mills did the same taking as many pieces as Crabbe unwrapping the plastic covering.

Holding the naked candy of heat, she swallowed hard before forcing them inside her mouth. Unlike Crabbe, no discomfort, just puffy cheeks.

Crabbe crunched, swallowed and smiled. He looked at his new employee.

"Welcome aboard Mercy."

Almost there. Stout was about pulling free when one of the thoughtforms came back just in the nick-of-time. Stout shook his head. He hated being on lockdown inside a decaying body. Stout was relieved he was dead, as he couldn't smell the stench of decay.

He did however find his plan for escape would be easier at night. The two bursts of energy seemed to begin weakening and once that happened they'd go one by one to find a row of street lights playing vampire, draining them for what it's worth.

Stout found an alley for him and his dead host to call home. Stout navigated to a part of the city almost forgotten, dirty, dumpsters overflowing with garbage you smelled a mile away. Abandoned businesses, populated by lowlifes and drifters. When patrons or other nomads trekked their way, they all made a detour because of the odor.

The stink of decay from the body of a deceased man sitting with his head between his knees, Stout suspected they saw a bum in need of a shower. He picked this part of the municipality because there were no street lights. Once his captors powered down, they'd have a hell of a time finding a source of light to charge up, allowing him to fly the coop.

"How long did you know?" Mercy asked.

"As soon as you walked in, we knew," said Crabbe. He designed his wards and the serpent eye pentacle to repel dangerous demons, allowing the good ones safe passage through Parts Unknown and inside his establishment.

Mercy squinted. "We?"

Crabbe tilted his head to his right toward the glowing crystal ball.

"That glowing light bulb?" Mercy questioned. "What about it?"

Crabbe inhaled. "Morocco meet Mercy, Mercy meet Morocco."

"Your servitor?" Mercy remarked. "The one Ashes mentioned?"

"My friend, if she knows Ashes then you can't trust her," said Morocco.

"If that was the case she wouldn't be inside here with us." Crabbe stated. "How did you hear about the job opening and decide to apply?"

Mercy shrugged. "You advertised and I needed the money."

"We take what we do here very seriously." Morocco stated.

"I'm sorry," Mercy pursed her lips. "How many bosses will I have?"

"You will answer to me." said Crabbe.

"My friend--! " Morocco exclaimed.

"If I hear that one more time, I'm going to slam that crystal ball to the ground." Mercy warned.

"I will give you a broom and dustpan to clean up the broken glass." Crabbe replied. "He's a spirit."

"I didn't say I wanted to kill him since he's already dead. But to hear my friend..." Mercy sighed.

"Mercy, wait outside," said Crabbe.

Mercy pushed away from the table, rose then made her way from whence she came.

"Are you sure ab--" Morocco began to say.

Crabbe held up his hand asking for a moment till he heard the door close. He stood up. "We'll talk later." Crabbe replied leaving his servitor.

Mercy sat on the hood of her vintage 1965 black Mustang. Crabbe stood in front of her. "When can you start?"

Mercy's eyes lit up. "Tomorrow?"

"Terrific," said Crabbe, rubbing his sideburns.

"Still having some doubts about hiring me?"

"No. You're going to be more valuable than you know, but I am curious why you are stepping outside of the box."

Mercy shrugged. "This job would be a cigarette patch for me."

"You didn't love and leave any more guys for the paramedics did you?"

"That's why I wanted this job," said Mercy. "To help me understand what's important, to keep you from sending my ass back to Hades."

Crabbe snorted. "You're not bad or you wouldn't have made it through my door."

"I'm here now."

Crabbe nodded. "Demons with ill intentions against me come here at night and get caught by my wards, so I can handle them without being seen by the human eye. You came in peace."

"How am I any different?" Mercy asked.

"Yours is for pleasure and the men you engage can say no. I know you don't compel them, yet they don't know who you are and if you take it down a notch, you won't leave them in need of medical help. You're not bad so no worries."

"So I will just be your clerk?"

"You'll play a bigger role than that and it may get dangerous. You okay with that?"

"Is that why you hired me?"

"You won't get rattled and you know who I am and what I do, making it a plus to have you around." Crabbe retorted. "Speaking of, how will that affect your other job?"

"Like I said, this is my day job and the bar at night. I heard some of my human customers talking about this job on the internet. When I heard them say Parts Unknown, I knew it was you."

"Human customers? Thought you tend at the demon watering hole?"

Mercy snorted. "Volunteer. No pay and what I learned being topside is money talks."

"Your dress code and human name is what you brought with you today, so you would have to keep it that way."

"Not a problem." She smiled. "See you tomorrow at 10 am."

Mercy hopped off the hood getting inside the driver's side revving the engine and racing down the street out of sight.

Crabbe shook his head knowing he'd have to have a talk with her about driving. He spotted Bob coming out of his dealership. Crabbe raced back inside his home-business to avoid a nosy conversation. He settled back down waiting for Morocco to throw him to the wolves.

"Got a bad feeling about this." said Morocco

"When was the last time you ate something?" Crabbe joked.

"She's a demon."

Crabbe shrugged. "What gave her away?

"How she wolfed down a mouthful of fireballs without a frown."

Crabbe laughed.

"Be coy about it all you want, but don't say I didn't tell you so."

"Are you forgetting who I am?"

"Are you forgetting why you consume holy water and meditate for calmness?" Morocco fired back.

Mercy's appearance to their humble casa was not so she could infiltrate and win over their confidence, so she could inform the demon hordes on how to get under his skin.

Crabbe would have done to her what he has done to every demon trying to collect the bounty Satan put on his head. He must not abuse his powers in fear of sprouting horns and a tail.

"I know you're trying to help save the world." Crabbe said to him.

"I don't like being cooped up, my friend…"

Crabbe straightened, closing his eyes like in a mediation phase. He opened them blinking, then drew a deep breath. "I'm expecting a visitor."

"Pray tell," the servitor replied.

"You won't be here, giving you a chance to bond with Mercy."

"You think I need love?"

"She doesn't do ghosts unless you have a technique and you can keep it to yourself." Crabbe remarked.

"I don't do demons or anything anymore, but you said I'd be happy?"

"You, Mister Kit, and Mercy are going out into the field. I need a one-on-one with my visitor."

"Why must Mercy tag along?"

"She won't get rattled. She won't need therapy. You'll see why she's a valued employee."

"I'll take your word, my friend." said Morocco.

Crabbe was surprised he didn't get any argument after telling his servitor he'd be out and about putting his talents to use. The end was near and he looked forward to meeting his guest.

"My thoughtforms need your help," said Crabbe.

Crabbe felt his servitor's spirit rise from the luminous glow of his crystal ball. "Stout discovered his captors' weakness."

"That means trouble." Morocco said.

Crabbe left the room coming back with the serpent eye pentacle necklace.

Mr. Kit stepped out of the dark, circling his master's feet before settling down.

"The gang is almost all here," said Crabbe.

"If Frick and Frack are in trouble then there's no time to waste." Morocco stated.

"They're tougher than you think." Crabbe snorted. "Mercy will be here tomorrow. A big day..."

Crabbe drifted off into his own thoughts.

"Okay, sleep now friend. Patience after all is a virtue." Morocco murmured.

CHAPTER 35

"So you want me to drive your truck to this location?" Mercy asked in her human form.

"Make use of your Google Maps on your phone--"

"I know where it is." Mercy interrupted. "I know where both places are. I'm familiar with the hiding place of your evil spirit and the devil's tramping ground."

"If you're uncomfortable." Crabbe stated.

Mercy snorted. "There's a reason you hired me and if I can be a thorn in his side then I'm all in."

"You were right, my friend," said Morocco. "About what?" Mercy questioned.

"He's warming up to you." Crabbe replied.

"On this road trip is he going to be saying my friend?" Mercy asked.

"We're not friends." Morocco replied.

"Play nice," said Crabbe. "This is important."

"I won't disappoint." Mercy commented. "Working for a bonus." Crabbe retorted.

Mercy smiled. "I knew I was going to like this job."

"Park your car around back." Crabbe threw her the keys to his S-10. "You'll thank me later I'm sure. It has a full tank. Don't pick up the cargo till I contact you."

"We'll be at my place." said Mercy stroking Mr. Kit's neck. "Is your cat house broken?"

"He's well behaved. You and Morocco be cool." Crabbe snorted. "Better get going. I don't want my guest to see you."

The serpent pentacle around the feline's neck glowed. "I can breathe again," said Morocco.

"Contain Stout, Morocco." Crabbe remarked. "On my word, my friend." Morocco replied.

"Any chance he'll be there?" Mercy asked. "Getting cold feet?" Crabbe questioned.

Mercy smirked. "Fear is the devil's greatest illusion." Crabbe nodded.

The trio left through the back door.

Mister Kit got comfortable circling on top of the sofa, finding his spot, curling his body into a ball and resting his eyes. He purred, interrupting in a calm meditating rhythm with the pentacle necklace lying flat and glowing.

Mercy entered her comfort room in her demon form enjoying a fag, puffing to the couch easing into her sweet spot. She nursed a Strawberry Daiquiri.

"How long have you been his servitor?" she asked.

The serpent eye inside the pentacle luminated. "I came upon him one night when he was engaged in one of his bounty collector's fights. Unaware of his culture, I possessed an ogre making him attack his companion and we've been together ever since."

Mercy inhaled her cube allowing the smoke to drag out of her nostrils. "That could've happened yesterday."

"Five years to be exact."

"And dark and handsome here?" She stroked Kit's noggin with her pinky.

"History of those two is still a mystery. I met my feline friend when I tagged along to Crabbe's abode."

Mercy shrugged. "So you don't tell each other everything, despite your time together."

"How long you been above surface?"

Mercy gulped her drink, swallowing hard. "Long enough to know I'm never going back."

"Could have risen above yesterday." Morocco retorted.

Mercy puffed a circle. "My house, my rules."

The pentacle blinked. "Fair enough, my friend."

Mercy glared. Her cell zip sound caught her ear. She picked it up. "Show time."

Hiram got the instructions given. He followed the row of white candles like bread crumbs, Hansel and Gretel style, going to see the wicked witch. He preferred to meet the wizard, and yet there was no yellow brick road. The candles burned bright, supplying light inside confines, setting the tone for an eerie conjunction.

The scenery didn't rattle Hiram. His nerves were hard and shadows from moonlight, footsteps from behind, glimpses of figures from peripheral gone, once squared up for the naked eyes, didn't rattle him. Hiram figured conjuring and bedding a demon made him fearless. His conscience telling him his monstrosity had to go and this man could help.

An abundant mahogany round table with two chairs and one occupied by a man dressed to go back to the 1970's, sporting a neat shrubbery Afro and sideburns ending at the corners of his mouth.

"Have a seat we have much to discuss," said Crabbe.

A nail file from a nail clipper can be used to loosen and tighten a bolt, when you don't have a flat head or Phillips screwdriver. One of the few pleasant childhood memories he had, connecting the wiring of his video game console. He was too impatient to wait on his dad to do it for him.

The comparison though baffling, but that's how Stout felt when the heavenly shades of night descended. His captors were the bolts and distancing them from light, his nail clipper file turning left to loosen their grip on him. The thoughtforms resembled light bulbs flickering, grasping for their last breath.

He saw his opportunity to escape a body he'd long been trapped in. Stout was relieved to be dead, not being one of the living experiencing the smell of decaying flesh, containing rotting organs. He no longer felt his restraints, and so was smiling with his head phasing out into the night air.

Did he breathe? Did he need to breathe now he was deceased? Either way, it felt good leaving his host body that had become his prison. Chaperons asleep or dead, not his burden. Stout's quest for freedom hit a snag. He felt a presence behind him

"Not so fast." said Morocco.

"You sent five men on their way. The fateful five you served up to your demon. Five men I sent back to you with thorns, bruises, deflated egos, but at least alive."

"I am overwhelmed with guilt and I need your help," said Hiram.

"With an experiment gone bad." Crabbe remarked. "What did you hope those men would do to me?"

Hiram shrugged. "Put a scare in you to leave the Longs alone."

"And if they'd done worse?"

"Well we wouldn't be here talking and the Longs would still be in business." Hiram replied.

"And you want me to help you?"

"Yes."

"They're angry with you."

Hiram frowned. "The Longs?"

Crabbe gave a Cheshire Cat grin. "He is and she's not. The spirits of the fateful five and don't look confused." He gestured to his surroundings. "You're in my world now."

"I don't blame them," said Hiram. "Is there any way I can bring them peace?"

Crabbe smirked. "They want you dead." "Then they'll be able to cross over?"

"Your victims will move on finding peace, and you will no longer do this." Crabbe stated. "You sacrificed them to save a little girl."

"I know it was wrong."

Crabbe nodded. "You were right to protect her, but wrong how you went about it."

Hiram observed the room. "Are you going to provide a seance summoning their spirits to confront me?"

Crabbe shook his head. "You didn't sacrifice everyday did you?"

Hiram shook his head indicating he didn't.

"So when you needed to buy time how did you keep her.... damn!" Crabbe roared with laughter, as the realization hit him.

"Nothing to be proud of." murmured Hiram.

"Pleasure for her and torture for you." Crabbe snickered.

Hiram wasn't a trailblazer for humans and demons getting together to become one. Some humans didn't know because of their lover being in disguise and some knew, giving a whole new meaning to unconditional love. Hiram conjured his and whether or not he was aware of demons escaping hell, Crabbe did not know, but preferred keeping him in the dark.

He thought it best for the weary soul before him to think summoning a ghoul was the only way for them to bolt up from below.

"I can and will help because it's what I do when something supernatural harms humans. Though you helped and that's not good." said Crabbe.

"I know there's a place in hell reserved for me." Hiram remarked. "I'm curious though..."

Crabbe smiled. "Unless you're an escape artist. Some have been able to avoid their fire and brimstone fate by the skin of their teeth."

"Baptism?" Hiram asked. "Wash all their sins away."

"You'd bring the water to boil." Crabbe replied. "Also, I'm not qualified to decide. I don't know how it works, but you'd have to do something miraculous and you have a lot of work to do."

"I disbanded the club."

"Again I'm not the one you need to impress."

"Can you help me?" pleaded Hiram.

"If you don't have faith in me, I can suggest the Jungle Brothers," said Crabbe.

"Like you, they're on Google along with others, who I thought tried too hard at using colorful names."

Crabbe nodded. "Attention grabbers till you read the resume."

Hiram snorted. "So you're legit?"

"To keep you from insulting me. You're an amateur. You conjured something and don't know how to send it back.

You're afraid it might eat your ass so you got desperate, googling names of any witch, mystic, voodoo kings and queens who say a tarot card can turn your life around."

"I mentioned the Jungle Brothers because their ad almost convinced you to give them a shot. They learned from their grandmother." Crabbe shrugged. "Which one, I don't know. They help people and like you, I like their name Jungle Brothers. Sounds like the real deal. Frank and Myrrh two years apart and six younger siblings, but they are the only two dabbling in the art, because that granny of theirs told them they were the only two having the 'it' factor."

"Are you sending them business?" Hiram asked.

Crabbe held up a finger. "Let me finish... I have history with them and nothing sinister, but I'm as good as advertised. The best decision you've made in a while."

Hiram took a deep breath. He didn't nod, though Crabbe was right about him choosing his services over the others.

"Okay," said Hiram. "How much?"

"I don't want to scare you off." Crabbe smirked. "You'll get my bill and understand why I charged you."

Hiram pursed his lips, and nodded. "Paying for my sins."

"Not to me, but you will."

"Fair enough." Hiram cleared his throat. "How are we going to handle my problem?"

"Got any honey?" Crabbe asked.

"Goes great with herbal tea." Hiram replied.

"Take that as a yes." Crabbe murmured. "You have your own urine?"

Hiram gave him a dubious look. "Even when I don't need it."

"Ha. Ha. You are funny." said Crabbe. "Trust me you're going to need it."

The mage reached under the table, he then placed a plastic zip bag which sounded heavy hitting the table, a plastic container of water, and a long neck empty black bottle with a cork.

Hiram frowned. "Some kind of paranormal kit and what's the silver stuff in plastic?"

Crabbe smiled. "A better mousetrap. Iron sand and holy water. Pour into the bottle with your urine and not here." He rotated the bottle. "Bury the bottle up to the neck outside of your back door. Smear honey around the top."

"Sounds easy enough," said Hiram.

"Now the good part," Crabbe snorted. " You've got your lover inside a circle... let her out."

Hiram's eyes nearly left their sockets. "What!? Say what?!"

"Run like hell and make sure she follows you out the back door."

"She'll tear me limb from limb."

"Not if you run fast enough," said Crabbe. "What will happen if I make it outside?" "Watch from a safe distance."

"And if this works?" Hiram asked.

"Cork up the bottle." Crabbe gave him a large sticky note with instructions. "Put the address in your phone. Meet me at this spot."

Hiram looked the paper over. "And what spot is that?"

Crabbe smiling at him replied, "The Devil's Tramping Ground."

CHAPTER 36

Mercy swallowed hard. She felt too close to home, sitting off on the side of the road, near what looked like trees waiting, hoping to die. She thought why not, with this being Lucifer's vacationing site. So many names she could think of for the ruler of hell. Satan, Lucifer Morningstar and Beelzebub were his most popular ones.

Diablo is his Latin name, and some were too complimentary; Old Nick wherever that came from, Mephisto, Mephist, and Azazel. Then there were cute names; Rascal, Tease, Archfiend, Amaimon, and Apollyon, as well as suitable names not so flattering; Scoundrel, Tormenter, Wicked, Pesterer.

She'd witnessed damned souls getting tortured over and over, regretting what got them sent there to the delight of their tormentor, ordering his minions to make their eternity miserable. He did the same to demons who failed in their quest to carry out their assignments ignoring the fact his ghouls failed majority of the time, going up against a soul with a strong faith and protected by its Guardian.

Mercy took a deep breath. She'd ask Crabbe for a bonus, because she didn't sign up for this. Sitting here close to the tramping ground brought back unpleasant memories and the reason she joined other demons escaping the bowels of hell. Mercy shook her head, mulling about the fools going after a bounty that's a game to the prince of darkness, with a hollow promise. Fools.

Mercy got a chill, as the thought of running into the Devil while waiting occurred to her. He'd surely cast her back to the abyss. There's a saying and she hoped it wouldn't come true for her sake; YOU LEARN DEMONS HAVE NIGHTMARES TOO. Purgatory though her place of birth, but she'd never consider it home. They say you can never go home again when you leave, and why would she want to?

Mercy found comfort resting in her lap.

Mister Kit was sound asleep, purring to the rhythm of her fingers stroking his velvet midnight fur. Crabbe said his feline was special and he felt like a security blanket on a night that was giving her the chills while her heightened senses fought off the odor of decay.

Morocco kept the target company inside a stench infested corpse, begging for a resting place. The stiff body was stretched out in the back of the S-10, however, housing two spirits and thought forms won her sympathy.

Mercy couldn't imagine being dead, yet a puppet with rigid movements, thanks to an unwanted guest. She wished for the cadaver to have closure soon.

A tap on her window startled her. Mercy exhaled.

"About damn time." She said.

"Sorry," said Crabbe. "Had to tie up some loose ends."

"This place gives me the creeps if you can believe that."

Crabbe nodded. "Won't be long, we're waiting for two more players." He looked at her lap. "Kit will keep you company."

Crabbe moved to the back of the truck. Mercy wound up the window. He opened a small box containing two rose quartz crystals. Frick and Frank wasted no time returning home and once Crabbe got a whiff of the deceased he didn't blame them.

"Okay Morocco, follow me." Crabbe instructed. "My pleasure my friend." Morocco replied.

Crabbe and his company walked deep into the woods stopping at a large hard bare clearing where plant life feared to grow except on the outer edge. Crabbe brought a water cooler bottle of rock salt and a box of chalk. He smiled, drawing his pentacle on the tramping ground.

Hiram took deep measured breaths, trying to gather his nerves, walking down the stairs of his basement. He felt like he was taking a journey. The lights were turned on to keep his mistress from the underworld under control. Hiram figured if she didn't fare well in natural light, then artificial light might contain her till he completed his task. She growled once he stepped on the pentacle circle. Erase it and she'd be free to pursue him.

He shook his head at the thought of committing suicide. Hiram swallowed hard. He glanced at the stairwell knowing he'd have to kick it in gear to escape her clutches. Okay he thought, rub out the circle then sprint like crazy.

His demon lover was built wide and thick, He hoped her physique would make her lethargic once she gave chase. Hiram got angry and murmured to himself. "Fuck it, let's get this over with." He noticed her trying to focus under the brightness of the lights. Hiram took out his cell, pressing the flashlight icon, adding more light point blank in the demon's face. She shut her eyes, shielding them with her tree trunk like forearms, staggering backwards falling on her butt.

Hiram took a moment to consider why he didn't do that before. It could've prevented those disgusting sexual encounters. He shook off the thought then stamped his foot on the circle scraping it toward him, breaking it.

The house trembled and the demon sprang to her feet. Hiram turned darting towards the staircase racing up the stairs.

He reached the top and raced out the backdoor not looking back. Hiram ended up behind a Pecan tree that never gave him a harvest near his cedar wood fence. He put his hands on top of the fence in case the plan failed. The heavy-legged demon made good time dashing towards him.

She jumped off the steps, getting caught in mid-flight. A three second hang time along with a befuddled expression and she got sucked down inside the small hole like a vacuum.

Hiram wasted no time rushing, fumbling around for the cork in his jacket pocket. He got it out then dived toward the bottle, knocking the wind out of himself as he landed hard on his stomach, but corked the bottle.

He dug it out of the ground. Hiram couldn't help putting the bottle to his eye. He smirked, upon seeing the demon knee deep in his urine and fear on her face. The spell worked.

Crabbe stood beside the dead Murray inside the pentacle circle on the devil's tramping ground. "How's it going in there?" Crabbe asked.

"Haven't had this much fun in ages." Morocco replied.

"Benevolence, Morocco. He's going to need it."

The servitor needed to let off some steam. Crabbe didn't bother finding out what he was doing to Stout. He gave the evil spirit a long leash and he hung himself to a worse fate than death. Yeah, Stout had options before he went on his senseless revenge crusade, motivated by hurt feelings and disrespect from his crew who didn't attend his funeral. The phrase 'WOULD YOU GO TO SOMEONE'S FUNERAL WHO DIDN'T

GO TO YOURS?' came to Crabbe's mind.

A mind boggling question for those alive. Stout was dead, and unable to attend the funerals of his former crew being stuck inside one of them and once vacated, he will not be present at Murray's funeral. Crabbe released a deep breath.

"Growing impatient, friend? Morocco asked.

Crabbe smirked. Morocco must have Stout under control for him to stir up a conversation. "Almost time to go to work."

"Play time's coming to an end, eh?" Morocco questioned. "Be ready to escort him to his..."

"It's okay, he's sleeping."

Crabbe frowned. "You guys don't get enough rest when you're dead?"

"Remind me a year from now to laugh, my friend." said Morocco.

Crabbe spotted headlights through the thick dead forest. "Do what you got to do and boogie on down." murmured Crabbe.

"What?" Moe asked, not hearing him

"He's here."

Hiram pulled up next to the Quasar blue Geo Metro sandwiching it between the white S-10. He killed the engine, grabbing the bottle and stepping out of his jalopy. He saw a young woman eyeing him along with an emerald eyed black cat acting as her protector.

The wayward man went on with his business, using his cell phone to guide him through the labyrinth of the dead forest, with branches looking like arms wanting to grab him. Hiram felt confident nothing would happen since he carried important cargo.

He looked toward the sky and even the moon feared showing up at the Devil's tramping ground. Hiram, not quite at his destination, swore under his breath that he'd seen enough and would never come back. Hiram breathed a sigh of relief when he saw Crabbe standing inside the concrete circle. He swallowed hard seeing him beside a tall stiff corpse reeking of the stench of death.

"Glad you could make it." said Crabbe.

Hiram handed him the bottle. "Signed, sealed, and delivered."

Crabbe held the bottle up high. He looked at Hiram. "You might want to find a safe distance or do you want to give her a goodbye kiss?"

Hiram held up his hands, backing out of the circle. "Is he here?" questioned Hiram, asking of Lucifer.

"You in a hurry?" Crabbe responded.

"Forget I asked." Hiram replied. He found his safe spot, and waited to see the fireworks.

Crabbe smashed the bottle on the hard surface and the demon returned to her natural abomination size. Hiram thought she would attack Crabbe, instead her body trembled and she slumped in Crabbe's presence. He took out a star shaped object pressing it on her forehead. She grimaced in pain.

"Morocco." said Crabbe. "Wake up our friend and show him his new home."

"My pleasure, amigo." Morocco replied.

Murray's corpse gave the demon a bear hug from behind while keeping her attention on Crabbe. Her body straightened and eyes bulged from a burst of penetrating light. Hiram felt pity for the incubus. She was his lover.

Morocco released the succulent who dropped to both knees. The servitor escorted the walking dead and stood next to Hiram, watching a train wreck but couldn't look away.

"What's happening?" Stout asked. "What are you doing to me? Why am I in this body?"

Crabbe snorted. "I give you a roommate and this is the thanks I get?"

"This isn't funny," said Stout.

"Someday the two of you will look back on this night and laugh about it.....or not" Crabbe remarked.

"Okay... you can send me on those train rides or something, but not this," said Stout.

"Yeah, the Horror and Doom Express sounds good right about now, but too late. You should have paid visits and let karma kick in, instead of you taking matters in your own hands which you didn't need to do.

"It's not like I'm going to heaven anyway so what's the difference?" Stout questioned.

"Train rides can bore and that's why many people fly." Crabbe replied. "You won't be alone where I'm sending you."

"But this thing...I can't...no...please." Stout cried.

"She feels the same way about you, but give it time and the two of you will learn to accept each other." Crabbe remarked.

"You say there are more hells?" Stout questioned. "I only know of Hell and purgatory. Can you at least share?"

Crabbe snorted. "You ever heard of Dante's Inferno?"

"Can't say that I have." said Stout.

"Roman comedy, though there is nothing funny about Hell as your new host can testify. If you can see her face, she is not happy." Crabbe replied.

"I still don't understand," said Stout.

"A Roman poem," said Crabbe. "Anyway there are nine circles"

"Limbo – Pagans and unbaptized wander the caves of Limbo in loneliness desperate to meet God. You two can forget it."

"Circle two is Lust. You two may find it with each other just give it time. Anyway, they blow the soul endlessly and spiraling in winds of a violent storm. Not for you guys."

"Number three is Gluttony, a cold nature suffering in the coldness of ceaseless icy rain."

"Four is Greed and you're not going there either. Souls trying to claw their way to escape the pit get swept back into it."

Crabbe exhaled. "Five, Anger is another. An endless battle of wailing souls taking place on a murky swamp."

"Number six, Heresy is a home for the two of you guarded by demons to prevent you from escaping, but she might have relatives, so..."

"I'm going to skip seven to give you eight and nine."

"Why skip seven?" Stout asked.

"Fraud." Crabbe ignored Stout, continuing. "The eight circle where your new host could end up in a pit of darkness, with endless beatings and torture from a horde of demons."

Crabbe heard Hiram swallow.

"Treachery is where Satan is supposed to be waist high in a block of ice in the center on display, as a trophy for treachery."

Crabbe wiped his brow. He knew that to be false since Satan was topside, so he was being mischievous.

"Drum rolls please." He made the sound of drums with his mouth. "Violence will be a fitting home for you and your demon host. You two possessed a thirst for violence, so you will be condemned to drown in a lake of boiling blood. A fitting fate considering the amount of blood spilled between the both of you."

Stout and the demon howled for clemency, but the magician granted none.

Crabbe held his palm toward the sky holding a flaming ball chanting "I CAST THIS SPELL INTO THE NIGHT. TO BIND MY ENEMIES AND LIMIT THEIR FIGHT BY EARTH, BY WIND, BY WATER, AND BY FIRE, I WISH TO STOP THEIR EVIL DEEDS

THE EVIL WORDS AND ACTIONS THEY SPREAD SHALL ONLY CAUSE THEM TO FEEL GREAT DREAD TO LEAD THIS FIGHT AGAINST THEIR DEEDS,

AS I WILL,

SO MAY IT BE."

The pentacle circle inside the devil's tramping ground trembled and started to crack. Like a pitcher on the mound, Crabbe threw a fast fireball at the demon's feet. It exploded and the concrete surface where plants fear to grow opened up, swallowing the doomed spirit and ghoul inside a mouth of flames. The hole closed as fast as it opened without a trace of the pentacle circle. Crabbe walked up to the dead Murray.

"Okay big man, let's put you to rest," said Crabbe. "What about me?" A shivering Hiram asked. "Go on about your business." Crabbe replied.

Hiram staggered, following close behind Crabbe and the corpse. He muttered to himself about finding a church and getting baptized.

Murray was laid flat in the back of the S-10 with the help of Morocco.

"What are we going to do with him?" Moe asked Crabbe.

Mercy and Kit were all ears hanging their heads out the window.

"Follow me," said Crabbe, cranking up the Metro.

The decayed body of Murray was placed in the cemetery.

Crabbe texted Silva telling her about Murray lying in the boneyard.

"Is that wise?" Morocco asked, glad to be inside the pentacle necklace wrapped around Kit's neck.

"She'll know what to do." Crabbe replied.

A small white church outside the city was giving a baptism ceremony. Hiram, dressed in white, had his sister and nieces sitting on the front row to witness his baptism. The water didn't boil. He celebrated his revival with Lisa and the girls, spending the night at her house under the watchful eyes of the monsters in the closet and under the bed. Hilda and Elmo were thrilled having three little girls under their imaginary care.

Crabbe switched off his flat screen after watching the news, featuring Silva interviewed by a reporter playing spin doctor about how they found Murray, the last member of the Sal Dana gang. The spellcaster sat down sipping his coffee reading the file Father Leary gave him.

"Are you at peace for a job well done?" Morocco asked from one of his glowing crystal balls.

Crabbe nodded. The spirits who became victims of the demon and Stout chose their path. Others inclined to roam the earth pondering what could have been, while others crossed over, accepting their fate, realizing they were not the first and won't be the last to suffer an unfortunate end to their life they couldn't explain.

"Yes," he answered smiling to himself, "and now I have to do some house cleaning."

Sitting in a recliner next to an open window, basking in the light given by the moon. It was midnight when the floorboards creaked under heavy feet. Its knuckles dragged on the floor, threadlike hairs hung over its ogling urine colored eyes, a grin from its toothless mouth, drool plopping on the floor.

"Ah, another one to play with," the demon said. "Are you going to run from me then tumble down the stairs?"

"Not a chance." said Crabbe, swiveling around, facing and stopping the goblin in its tracks. It stood over six feet even though hunched over. Its eyes went wide in horror, after recognizing the face behind the voice. A demon's worst nightmare. Their own version of the Boogeyman.

Crabbe rose, walking up to the monstrosity pointing his cane, showing off its glowing pentacle.

Crabbe flashed a grin. "I'm not surprised you know who I am and that's a good thing. You don't have the talent to metamorphose your appearance, so you lurk in the night standing over helpless sleeping humans, only to dash out of sight when they awake, giving them a restless night, knowing something was standing over them and chasing children just for fun." Crabbe shook his head at the milky colored troll wearing a veil of fear.

"Fun time's over and before we play the last game, yes I know you know who I am, but allow me to introduce myself because I'm cool like that."

The magician took a bow. "Crabbe H. Appleton, at your service."

International Writers Inspiring change
MOST INSPIRING AUTHOR AWARD
2017
Wilson Jackson
Category: Thriller/Horror
Things that go Bump in the Night - here
there be Monsters

"Fiction is the truth inside the lie." - Stephen King

Milton Keynes UK
Ingram Content Group UK Ltd.
UKHW042111131124
451149UK00006B/786

9 798894 790602